INTREPID JOURNEY

Book One: An Untamed Frontier

LILLY ROBBINS BROCK

Dedication

In Loving Memory of My Grandmother

A Bennett Family Saga

INTREPID JOURNEY

Book One: An Untamed Frontier

River Cliff Publishing

Copyright © 2015 Lilly Brock

All characters in this book and many of the locations are fictional, but the story is inspired by actual historical events. The author and publisher do not assume and hereby disclaim any liability to any party for any loss, damage, or disruption caused by errors or omissions, whether such errors or omissions result from negligence, accident, or any other cause.

Official Website: http://www.lillyrobbinsbrock.com

Table of Contents

About the Story

Although this is a work of fiction, many of the events are based on fact.

The Introduction is part truth and part fiction. The grandmother and the two granddaughters represent my grandmother, my sister, June, and myself. The recollections are real. The quilt is real. I still have the quilt, still unfinished. People have offered to finish it for me, but somehow, I need it to remain frozen in time. The fiction begins with the trunk and the story beyond.

The theme of this book was inspired by a journal, which I came upon during my research. It was written by a pioneer woman in 1855 about her and her family's journey to Washington Territory. During that time, the route most people took to travel West was the well-known Oregon Trail. This family, however, took a different course. They left New York City on a paddlewheel steamship to travel via the South American route toward their final destination—Washington Territory.

I had never heard of such a journey and learned through inquiry that many others had not as well. After delving into the history about this route, I knew I had to write a story surrounding it. Thus, the saga of my imaginary family—the Bennetts.

Through many hours and avenues of historical research, actual events and places in real time are brought to life throughout this book. You will find my characters taking part in the devastating fire in December of 1835 in New York City, traveling on a nineteenth-century paddlewheel steamship crossing two oceans, then finally becoming involved in the Indian War of 1855 in Washington Territory.

I invite you to take a step back in time and join the Bennett family on their journey.

Lilly

Prologue

*I*t had been awhile since I opened my trunk, but I was in a nostalgic mood. The contents were layered in the order of the years gone by. When I came upon my unfinished quilt, it triggered a flood of memories about my grandmother, and the moment she surprised me with the quilt.

It was 1914. I was nine. My father worried about grandmother being left alone, so he rotated my sister, Ruth, and me to stay with her on the weekends. Ruth was nearly eight years old. We were very close, and people often mistook us for twins.

I can still visualize the rose-covered cottage sitting at the end of the blackberry-bordered lane. The yard was carpeted with a plethora of flowers with yellow and black monarch butterflies flitting from flower to flower. The lilac bush was my favorite, and when it bloomed in the spring, its perfume permeated the air. It attracted the resident honeybees from which I felt a certain comfort as I listened to their soft humming while they labored to gather their nectar.

Upon entering grandmother's house, I was greeted with the melodic voice of her golden canary singing its repertoire of songs, and there were sweet-scented flowers from her garden arranged in a Mason jar she had placed in the center of the table next to the lace-curtained window. When the window was open, the curtains caught the breeze and billowed like sails on a boat.

Breakfast was always special. I remember the sizzling bacon and eggs she fried in her seasoned black skillet, and the French toast smothered with butter and rich strawberry preserves. The aroma filled the kitchen and pulled me in like a magnet.

One day, she went to her trunk that resided at the foot of her iron bed. The trunk was always a curiosity to me. It was a steamer trunk made of oak with a dome lid. It was fitted with wood straps and leather handles, and embellished with hammered nailheads. On the front of the trunk were two black filigree metal latches along with a sturdy brass lock in the center. As she lifted the lid, the hinges creaked and groaned as though being awakened from a deep sleep, and a musty fragrance from precious remnants of the past wafted into the atmosphere. I watched with a sense of unchecked anticipation. What secrets did her trunk hold?

With gentle hands, grandmother lifted out what looked like the beginning of a beautiful quilt, but it wasn't an ordinary quilt. Instead of being made of the customary gingham and cotton prints, it was made of velvet, satin, and silk with detailed embroidery stitches. Grandmother had worked on the quilt secretly as a gift for me, and decided the time had come to teach me how to work on it with her. I could not know at that time we would never finish our quilt together. Years later, I would gaze upon our unfinished quilt and smile at the contrast of the stitches of an inexperienced nine-year-old girl and those of my grandmother's skilled hands.

The image of my grandmother will forever be burned in my memory. It seemed she was never without her cotton flower-printed apron, and she wore her long silver hair in braids. We spent many hours together—she in her rocking chair and me on the settee next to her.

On one of my visits, grandmother said, "Julia, I'm feeling a little tired today. Would you go to my trunk and bring out our quilt?" Oh, I was thrilled at the prospect of snatching a glimpse at the contents of the trunk. I controlled my excitement as I lifted the creaky lid and embraced once again the musty fragrance escaping into the room. When I retrieved our quilt, I noticed a handsome wool plaid cap and a leather-bound journal lying side by side. I wanted to open the journal. Would I be intruding? She did tell me to open the trunk, and she must have known I would see it. I carefully lifted it out and stroked the soft leather cover. When I opened it, I discovered an envelope tucked inside. The envelope held a lock of soft silken hair that was wrapped in tissue and tied with a ribbon. I caressed it, and it seemed sacred, so I put it back the same way I found it. Then I laid the journal into its resting place and closed the trunk lid. I handed grandmother the quilt and the embroidery needles and threads—a skein of thread and a needle for her, and the same for me. While we worked on our project together, I couldn't contain my curiosity any longer.

"Grandmother, whose cap is in the trunk? And tell me about the journal and the lock of hair."

She laid her needle and thread down onto her lap for a moment, and gazed out the window. Her faded blue eyes welled with tears. Suddenly, I felt a surge of guilt. I had intruded, and now I caused my sweet grandmother pain. She broke her gaze, composed herself, and began stitching again. When she saw the look of guilt on my face, she reassured me in her own way, "Darling, you're doing a beautiful job on that feather stitch." She looked toward the trunk and back at me and sighed. "The cap belonged to your grandfather. I will never forget the day I first saw him wearing it. While we work on our quilt, I'll tell you about the cap and my journal with the lock of hair."

"My father, Thomas Bennett, and his two brothers emigrated from England to begin a new life in America where he met my mother, Jane McKenzie, in 1834 …"

Chapter 1

March 1834

Weymouth, Dorset, England

*T*homas and Robert Bennett dreaded the impending conversation they were about to have with their parents. It was a typical gray day in March in the seaport town of Weymouth. At the appointed hour, the brothers approached the timber-framed thatch cottage, which had been the only home they had known.

Inside, Jonathan Bennett paced the creaky wood floor in the parlor as he awaited his sons' arrival. Agnes busied herself in the cozy warm kitchen preparing tea for her adored sons.

From the moment Thomas and Robert entered the cottage, it was obvious by the look on their father's face, he knew what they were about to say. He looked at them with a stern expression and grumbled, "Well, out with it, lads."

Agnes interrupted. She knew too, but wanted to delay hearing the words. "Jonathan, give the poor boys a chance to get in the door, would you? Come, let's all have tea. I have the table set in the kitchen where we can be warm."

In silence, the family gathered around the table. Agnes had always been the peace keeper between Jonathan and his three sons. "Now, I don't want to hear any harsh words from any of you," she said. "We're going to enjoy tea together."

Afterward, they adjourned back to the parlor.

Thomas began, "Well, I might as well say it straight out. Father and Mother, Robert and I are leaving England. We're sailing to the New World."

"When?" cried out Agnes.

"In three days," said Robert. "Philip plans to see you both before the sailing."

Jonathan shook his head in disappointment. "I've been expecting this. I always assumed the two of you would have joined me at my tannery. It looked like you were planning to do just that. You, Thomas, a skilled shoemaker, and you, Robert, an apprentice to a furrier. I see now, neither of you had any intention of working with me."

"I'm sorry Father," replied Thomas.

Jonathan continued with his rant, "First Philip took off, and now you two. I had always hoped to have my three sons by my side. Of course, I knew early on, we would lose Philip to the sea. I couldn't pull him away from the wharf. He spent all day gazing at the sailors working on the ships coming in and out of the harbor. It took a long time for me to forgive him for leaving without my permission or *even* a word to us. He was only twelve, for God's sake. Always trouble. I could never control him. If it wasn't for your mother, I might never have forgiven him."

Agnes couldn't remain quiet. "But Jonathan, at least he made something of himself. Yes, it hurt at first, but he worked his way up from ship boy to becoming a fine captain. The captain liked Philip and took him on as his protege. He saw the good in our boy, Jonathan. It took Philip nearly ten years to work his way through the ranks. Then he passed the examination, and now he's a captain. I'm proud of our boy, and at least we *do* see him from time to time."

Jonathan was still upset, and he pounded his fist on the table. "Yes, and what does he do? He sails into port and talks his brothers into leaving us too!"

With tears welling in her eyes, Agnes looked at her two sons standing before her, "Will we ever see you again?" She began to cry. Robert put his arms around her and held her close.

Thomas softly rested his hand on his father's shoulder. "It was only a matter of time before we left, Father. Every time we hear from Philip, he tells us about the opportunities in America. He offered us passage on the next sailing to the port of New York City. We can't turn this opportunity down."

Jonathan turned to Robert, "And you, Robert. What about your young lady? Is *she* going with you?"

Robert frowned, "No, Father. It isn't working out." He stared out the window. "In fact, it was doomed from the beginning."

Jonathan softened, "I'm sorry, Robert. And I can see I'm not going to change either of your minds." He looked at both sons. "I won't allow you to leave without our blessing. But I expect your brother to bring you both back to us from time to time."

Agnes cried out, "It has to be that way. I couldn't bear not seeing you again."

Thomas said, "It shall be so, Mum."

"Yes," said Robert, clasping her hands in both of his.

Chapter 2

June 1835
Delhi, New York

*I*t was a sunny day in June in the candlelit parlor of the McKenzie home in Delhi. Thomas Bennett and Jane McKenzie were about to exchange marriage vows.

The perfume of white roses and purple lilacs permeated the chamber and mingled with the warm scent of melting wax from the glowing candles. The profusion of candles cast a soft amber glow, dancing off the ivory satin streamers spiraling the room.

An intimate group of family and friends had gathered to witness and celebrate this union. The pleasant hum of their voices depicted a happy mood as they exchanged greetings and chatted about the latest events in their lives.

A pianist sat at the *cottage piano,* and a violinist stood nearby, both playing soft, harmonious music as they waited for their cue to play Jane's chosen wedding march.

Thomas stood in position near the windows at the front of the room along with his brother, Robert, his best man. Feeling anxious, Thomas tugged at his neck scarf. He was about to marry the love of his life and he could barely control his nerves.

When he thought he couldn't wait another moment, the music changed, and the wedding procession began. Everyone became silent and turned their attention to the back of the room, awaiting the bride's entrance. Jane's sister, Abigail, the maid of honor, was the first to appear. Two of Jane's girlfriends from school, now young ladies, followed. Then Thomas heard the music shift again. The wedding march began. His heart pounded. When Jane and her father, Edmund McKenzie, appeared, everyone stood and watched the beautiful bride and her father walk down the rose-petal-strewn aisle.

Thomas gasped and reveled at the beauty of this woman he was about to marry. She had always been beautiful to him, but today she was breathtaking. As she walked down the aisle, rays of sunlight shot glints of gold onto her chestnut brown hair. Her long hair was parted in the center with elaborate curls framing her face, and a braided topknot rested on the crown. The thin lace veil, held in place with shell pins, screened her dark brown eyes. She wore an ivory silk dress cut low off the shoulders, baring her neck and décolletage. Short billowy sleeves graduated from the shoulder line, and a sculpted bodice hugged her narrow waist, further accentuated with an ivory satin bowed sash. The full skirt dropped from the waist and was embellished with a row of satin roses. Her matching square-toed shoes peeked out from under her dress. Her husband-to-be was an expert shoemaker and had made the shoes as a wedding gift to her.

As Jane glided toward Thomas, he smiled, and their eyes locked. His grey-blue eyes looked straight into her soul. She thought about everything she admired about this handsome man who was about to become her husband. She had come to know him as a man of integrity and strength. He was charismatic; yet, there were times he seemed boyish, especially when a stray lock of his dark blonde hair fell onto his forehead. In contrast to the errant lock, his sandy-colored mustache, beard, and sideburns were always meticulously trimmed.

Seeing Thomas in this formal attire was a new experience for Jane. He wore a cream-colored linen shirt styled with a high standup collar, a ruffled jabot, and cuffs. A silk black neck cloth wrapped around the collar ending in a tailored bow at the front. His ensemble included a dark blue cut velvet vest, a black broadcloth tailcoat accented with a white rosebud on the lapel, and ivory cotton twill trousers. And finally, a pair of black flat square-toed leather shoes, made by Thomas, finished the outfit.

Jane stepped forward to Thomas's side, and her father nodded his head to the groom and stepped back. She handed her bouquet of white roses to her sister. Just as the ceremony was about to begin, Thomas leaned toward Jane and whispered, "You, my love, are a vision to behold."

While Mr. McKenzie watched them exchange their vows, his thoughts were not of happiness, but of apprehension. He had hesitated to give his blessing to the couple, but when Jane cried incessantly, he couldn't bear to see her so unhappy and finally gave in. Mrs. McKenzie had already chimed in to side with Jane and reminded Edmund that they, too, married for love, despite their humble circumstances. He wanted his daughter to have more than what they had when they married. What kind of life would she have with this man of limited monetary worth? He knew for certain she would have been financially secure if only she would have agreed to accept the wealthy Mr. Stanton's proposal of marriage. Was it so wrong to want a secure future for his daughter?

***

After the ceremony, during the celebratory feast, Robert stood and raised his glass to the bride and groom, "And now, ladies and gentlemen, may I have the honor of asking each of you to stand and raise your glass to my brother, Thomas, and his beautiful bride. Jane and Thomas, may you both live long, and never want or need for as long as you live."

The jubilant guests joined in clinking their glasses and shouted, "To Jane and Thomas!"

Thomas smiled at his brother and stood, raising his glass. "Thank you, Robert, you're not only my brother, but my best friend, and now today, my best man. Indeed, I'm a lucky man to be wedded to this beautiful woman."

He looked directly at Jane and met her eyes while he raised his glass, "Please join me in a toast to my bride. Cheers!" She smiled with tears welling in her eyes.

Then Thomas turned and faced his future family, and the guests. "I extend my gratitude and appreciation to you, Mr. and Mrs. McKenzie, for hosting our ceremony here in your home. Thank you, also, to Jane's sister, Abigail, and her husband Charles, and all of you who have gathered here to share our happiness. I only wish our brother, Philip, was here, but alas, he's on the high seas. Cheers."

During the celebration, Thomas reflected on the day he met Jane and the moment he fell in love with her. It was in New York City. She was shopping, and he was on his lunch break from his job at the local tannery when they collided. Thomas was reading a newspaper while walking and only lifted his eyes periodically to check his path ahead. Jane was carrying an armful of packages piled so high, she didn't see him until the moment of impact. The packages flew into the air, tumbling down around their feet. In unison, they proclaimed their apologies as they bent down to gather her packages.

Jane's creamy white face flushed to a crimson glow. "I was so careless," she said, "Please pardon me, sir, for being such an inconvenience."

Thomas was mesmerized, and grinned as his eyes found hers, "I find this to be a very pleasant inconvenience, miss." He had picked up most of her packages. "Please, allow me to carry your packages and escort you to your destination." Then he offered her his arm.

Jane hesitated for a moment. *Would this be proper? It is a short distance.* She and her sister had come to the city together but broke protocol and separated, agreeing to rendezvous at the carriage in an hour's time.

"Thank you, kind sir," and she took his arm. "My carriage is just down the block. My sister should be waiting for me."

Thomas knew he couldn't lose this captivating woman, and he had one block to convince her to see him again. *Here I am a year later, and Jane is my bride.* He smiled as he relived his victory during that providential walk down the block.

Now, on this wedding day, Thomas had the answer to the question he had asked himself during his voyage across the vast Atlantic Ocean to New York City. Leaning on the ship's railing leaving his homeland behind, he had pondered his future and his role in marriage. *Will I marry, and if I do, will the marriage be one of convenience or for love?* He still had one question remaining to answer. *Will I prosper?*

Chapter 3

September 1835

New York City, New York

The summer passed quickly, and Thomas and Jane had still not taken a honeymoon. Jane had moved into Thomas's tight quarters, and they spent his time off searching for a larger place to live. After looking for several days, they had not yet found a suitable place to rent. Jane wondered if they ever would. It was obvious to Thomas that Jane was discouraged and felt neglected. With his rigid schedule, the couple had shared very few intimate moments. *My bride doesn't smile anymore. I've neglected her long enough.*

The following week, Thomas came home with a wide grin on his face. Jane had missed that grin. "Thomas, you look like you have good news. Are you going to share it with me?"

"Jane, we're finally going to spend some special time together. We're going on our honeymoon!"

Jane was ecstatic and ran to him wrapping her arms around his neck. "Oh, Thomas, I've been waiting for this. Where will we go?"

"I have it all planned. Mr. Simpson agreed to give me some time off on the condition I work overtime to make up for the days off. That's why I've been coming home so late. I wanted to surprise you. We're leaving tomorrow morning."

"Thomas, I'm so excited, but I confess I feel guilty for being so unpleasant to you because of your late hours. You never said a cross word to me in return. Will you forgive me?"

"There's nothing to forgive, my darling. I know it's not been the life you may have visualized or could have had. Do you regret your decision to marry me?"

Jane clasped his hands in hers and gazed into his eyes. "Thomas, it's true I could have married the wealthy Mr. Stanton. Marrying him would surely have put my parents' minds at ease, but, darling, you stole my heart, and instead, I married you for love."

He had indeed married for love.

* * *

Thomas had booked a hotel within walking distance of Niagara Falls. It was a beautiful hotel, and they enjoyed a romantic candlelit dinner in the dining hall. The next morning, they walked to a viewpoint where they could see and hear the thunderous waters of the mighty falls. They lingered in the surrounding area for the remainder of the day.

Jane was in awe of the tumbling water, and remarked, "Thomas, I've never seen anything so beautiful!"

Thomas drew Jane into his arms, and answered, "I have—you, my beautiful bride."

They shared a lingering kiss while the mist from the falls enveloped them.

Jane was chilled, so Thomas wrapped his arms around her. She sighed and cuddled into him. "Thomas, this was such a wonderful place to come for a honeymoon. It's been perfect. I'll always remember our time here together."

Thomas extended his arm to her, "It's getting late. Shall we go back to the hotel and create another memory, Mrs. Bennett?"

"I'd be delighted, kind sir, especially if it's anything like last night."

***

Upon returning from their romantic interlude, the newlyweds resumed their search for larger living quarters. Finally, several days later, they found their temporary home in a rooming house situated in the center of the city. The abode wasn't as large as Jane had hoped, but she refrained from sharing her disappointment. She wasn't accustomed to living in a rooming house. It was a stark contrast to her spacious childhood home in the countryside of Delhi. In the city, a large percentage of the population either lived in rooming houses or rented out rooms. Some quarters were decent, but many were not. Thomas was pleased with this choice since there was a space available for Robert to rent as well. Jane was not so pleased but remained silent.

Since there wasn't a place for boarders to cook in the rooming house, the rent included three meals a day. At the set hour, the tenants gathered together in the dining room for their meals. It was at mealtime when the different personalities collided into one space. There was deception, backstabbing, gossip, and the occasional drunk who staggered to the table. Jane could always tell when the drunk entered the room by the stench of alcohol that clung to him. Then there was the intrigue of flirtations. Jane was quite aware of the buxom unmarried red-headed woman by the name of Anita who couldn't keep her eyes off Thomas during the dinner hour. Jane was sure Thomas was oblivious to Anita's attention.

The walls were paper-thin. Jane knew about the married woman having an affair with the traveling salesman while her husband was away at work. Everyone knew except the husband, and it gave the gossipers plenty to whisper about. Jane witnessed an abundance of deception, and felt she couldn't trust anyone. There was the couple that constantly fought about the husband coming home drunk every night causing the baby to scream as it reacted to the tension and noise. Jane was even afraid to leave their apartment. She had heard there was a thief loose in the place, but she had no choice when it came time to do their laundry. The laundry area was located in the basement, which was dark, gloomy, and damp. She dreaded laundry day.

Jane was miserable and lonely. Thomas had resumed working overtime to earn extra money, and came home late into the night. She tried not to blame him, and promised herself she wouldn't complain. She knew he was doing his best. But she was frustrated, and wondered, how long could she hold out in this place?

Thomas was dealing with his own frustration. The red-headed woman had become a problem. She was obsessed with him. It began one evening when he came home from work after dark. Anita stood in the shadows on the rooming house porch waiting for him. He didn't see her as he climbed the steps until she thrust herself toward him.

She pressed her body to his and surprised him with a passionate kiss. Then she ran her hand on his upper thigh up to his groin. In the midst of this, Thomas thought he heard someone at the bottom of the step. *Was someone there to see this scandalous display? Jane can't know about this.*

He pushed her away. "Haven't you noticed I'm happily married, madam?"

She grabbed his arm and put his hand on her breast, "Are you sure you're happy? She looks awfully tame to me. I can make you forget her."

Thomas glared at her and pulled his hand away "Stay away from me, Anita. Understand?"

Anita continued to wait on the porch every night for Thomas hoping to change his mind. Then one night she reminded him of the kiss.

"Do you remember our first kiss, Thomas? We weren't alone you know. I know who saw us, and he'll be more than willing to do whatever I ask. What if that little Jane of yours were to hear about our kiss? I know she's seen me looking at you."

"You accosted me! I in no way kissed you back!"

"My witness doesn't know that. It would be my word against yours, lover."

"What do you want from me, Anita?"

"I want you to bed me." She snickered and wet her lips with her tongue. "I've already felt what you have to offer."

Thomas's stomach felt like it had turned upside down, his mouth was dry, and his heart pounded faster than he thought was possible. He felt like a trapped animal that had been backed into a corner. *What am I going to do? Jane would be devastated. Maybe I can stall this annoying woman.*

"This is a big decision for me, Anita. You're going to have to give me time to think about it."

"Very well, lover. But I won't wait long." She reached up to brush back the lock of hair that had fallen onto his forehead. Thomas backed away in disgust. He glared at her. *Jane is the only woman allowed to do that.* He quickly made his exit.

Thomas yearned for Robert's counsel. As he hurried up the stairs, he debated his quandary. *Should I say anything to Robert about my predicament? Maybe I won't have to if we find a new place to rent right away. If we could only find a place before I have to deal with that nuisance Anita again.*

***

October 1835

New York City

Thomas and Robert had grand plans for their *American Dream*. New York City had recovered from the cholera epidemic of 1832, and was in the middle of an economic boom. It was considered the premier American city.

They had both been working hard to earn and save enough money to rent shop space for their businesses. The brothers had also done a little detective work to learn where their employers bought their leather and fur skins. They discovered the distributors' warehouses were located in the financial and merchant district. Now, they knew the approximate locale for their business site.

Finally, the day arrived to begin their search. They had both gambled and cut their full-time jobs down to part-time so they could concentrate on their business venture. Day after day they scoured the streets of New York City on foot. The brothers were tired, discouraged, and worried about running out of money. They had searched the entire mercantile district and found nothing available. Neither of their employers was happy about them cutting their hours, and if the Bennett brothers weren't so skilled, the employers probably would have let them go.

Finally one day, Robert cried out, "Thomas, hurry! Our search is over!" Robert had turned the corner onto Broad Street. It bustled with cabs and private carriages.

Thomas caught up with Robert who was pointing at a building across the street. He followed Robert's line of sight and fixed his eyes on a four-story red brick building. The first story consisted of two spaces side by side, and each was framed with wooden pillars making the space its own. Across the top of the single story, suspended awnings shaded the sidewalk while offering protection from rain. Living quarters were located on the upper levels. Dodging the busy traffic, the brothers crossed the street to take a closer look and inquire about the space.

"Robert, I can see it! Our sign *Bennett Bros.* spanning across our two spaces, and there's enough room for our trade signs *Shoemaker* and *Furrier* over our doors."

Robert nodded. "Yes, this is the perfect location. Broadway is nearby, and the mercantile district is next door. Just look at the activity!"

"And having access to the Canal should be a great boon for us," said Thomas.

Thomas and Robert were aware of the importance of the Erie Canal to the city. Since its completion in 1825, New York City was energized and had become one of the busiest ports in America. The canal opened up commerce to middle America. Not only would the Bennett brothers be able to sell to the people of New York City, but to the people beyond. Success and wealth would be guaranteed. They anticipated a prosperous future.

Robert smiled at his brother, "Are we ready to commit and give notice to our employers?"

"I'm ready. I hope the building owner is willing to negotiate. We have to make this work." It wasn't a day too soon for Thomas.

* * *

Thomas was anxious to share his good news with Jane. "Robert, Jane will be so happy to leave the rooming house. She hasn't complained, but I know she's unhappy. She doesn't smile anymore. She dreads mealtime with so many strangers sitting at the dinner table every day. There is little for her to do in such small quarters."

"You two aren't having trouble, are you, Thomas?"

"I don't think so, yet, but I wonder if she regrets not marrying the wealthy Mr. Stanton. She would have been living in a country manor in upper New York, being waited on, hand and foot."

"I see how you two look at each other, and it's true love, Thomas."

"Well, at least now we won't have to be put to the test." Thomas looked away for a moment and thought, *It could have been more of a test than anyone would have realized.* "Let's hurry back so I can give her the news."

Jane listened for Thomas's arrival. She couldn't wait for him to come home. She had news. Then she heard the sound of hurried footsteps. Despite his tired feet, Thomas sprinted up the stairs to share his news with Jane. When he opened the door, she flew into his arms. He noticed she seemed happier than usual. *She must have had a good day.*

Thomas lifted her up and twirled her around. He exclaimed, "Jane, I have the most wonderful news. We found it. We're moving as soon as we can pack."

Jane was set to tell Thomas they were expecting a child but decided to wait until they settled into their new home. He had enough to think about. Besides, it had only been a little over a month since her last flow. Better to wait at least another month to know for sure. Then she thought about Thomas's birthday, which was December 7th. *I'll tell him on his birthday. It'll be the perfect gift.* She was pleased with her decision.

* * *

"So, Mrs. Bennett, what do you think of our new home?"

Jane was excited with what she saw. The area was comfortable and spacious. There was a small parlor, a large central living space, a library, one bedroom, a kitchen with a coal stove, a small dining area nearby, and indoor plumbing. A stairway led down to the business space. Thomas wouldn't be far away.

"I love it, Thomas." Then she walked directly to the bedroom to think about where she would place the crib. She put her hands upon the life inside her, and whispered, "This is where you shall sleep, my precious babe. Soon, we'll share our secret."

Having quit their jobs, Thomas and Robert were quick to set up their shops and proudly hung their open sign. Jane was finally happy and content, especially since she no longer had to share a bathroom with strangers. Soon, she joined a sewing group and made new friends. Thomas was delighted to hear her singing as she went about her activities. He felt a sense of relief to have come through for his wife, and to have escaped Anita's clutches. Fortunately, neither Jane nor Robert found out about his *situation*. Since he and Jane had very few belongings, they were able to make a fast and unnoticed getaway. Even so, Thomas was always on the lookout for a woman with red hair.

The Bennett brothers' businesses were off to a good start. They had developed a good rapport with a particular distributor and were proud to have their first order of leather and fur stored in the distributor's warehouse. The purchase took every cent they had, but they expected an immediate return on their investment.

Life was good. They were on their way toward fulfilling their dream.

* * *

December 1835

New York City

The month of December began with unusually frigid weather. Thomas faithfully kept an ample supply of coal on hand for the kitchen stove. During the day, Jane kept the fire burning, periodically adding coal as needed. The kitchen was the warmest place in the house, and she found herself spending much of her time there. When the temperature started dropping, Thomas moved her special chair next to the stove.

It was in that chair she put the final embroidery touches on her gift to Thomas. During the past couple of months, she had been making a quilt for their babe during the sewing circle meetings. She had shared her news with her friends, and in response, they happily brought her pieces of yellow, pink, and blue fabrics for her quilt. Jane knew for sure she was with child. She felt nauseous every day, and frequently couldn't keep her food down. Thomas hadn't noticed yet since he worked so many hours.

It was December 7th. Jane hummed as she prepared Thomas's birthday dinner. Normally, she would have savored the mingling aromas while preparing the meal, but she felt so sick. Previously, before Thomas had come into the dining area, she brought in a package wrapped in cotton muslin and placed it where he sat at the table. She planned to present it to him just before dinner, and before Robert's arrival.

She was sitting at the table when Thomas walked in. "Happy birthday, my darling." As she stood up to give him a birthday kiss, she wobbled slightly with dizziness.

Thomas caught her. "Jane, are you not feeling well?"

Jane looked toward Thomas's package and said, "Maybe you should open the package before I answer."

Her eyes sparkled, enjoying Thomas's quizzical expression. "Open it, my darling."

First, being the gentleman that he was, he helped her sit again, then with great curiosity, opened his package. He gazed at the pastel-colored quilt. "Jane, what does this mean?"

"Can you not guess, Thomas? It's a quilt for our babe. By springtime, we will be three instead of two. I believe I'm about three months along. I've been very ill. Food makes me nauseous. If Robert weren't coming, you might have been eating your birthday dinner alone. It was all I could do to prepare it."

Thomas leaned over and kissed her affectionately. "You've made me so happy, Jane. I couldn't think of a better birthday gift. Robert will be ecstatic to learn he's about to become an uncle."

Jane heard footsteps in the hall, and then a knock on the door.

"Oh, there he is now," said Thomas as he went to answer the door. Robert had barely entered the room before Thomas blurted out their news.

Robert exclaimed, "You mean I'm going to be an uncle? I'm happy for you both. Thomas, fill the wine glasses. Let us make a toast to Jane!"

Chapter 4

December 1835

New York City

*D*ecember 16th was one of the coldest nights yet. The temperature stood below zero. Both the East River and Hudson River were frozen solid. Jane and Thomas had huddled near the stove since supper and were getting ready to retire. It was nearly 9:00 p.m. Then, oddly, they heard the dishes in the cupboard rattle.

Jane gazed at the cupboard. "What in heaven's name was that?"

Thomas shrugged his shoulders, "Maybe it was a small earthquake?"

They waited. Nothing happened.

"Everything seems fine," said Thomas with a sigh of relief. "Let us get ready for bed."

"I think we're going to need the bed warmer tonight," said Jane. "While you prepare it, I'll add some more quilts to our bed."

"At your service, my love. I'll bring it in when it's ready."

Thomas reached for the brass bed warmer hanging on the wall and filled it with hot coals. The bed warmer was ornate with an intricately pierced pattern, which allowed the coals to smolder. It was one of Jane's most special possessions, having been passed down to her by her mother. It had been handed down in her family from generation to generation. When the warmer was ready, Jane slid it up and down the sheets.

"This is all very well and good," said Thomas, "but I insist we keep each other warm with some cuddling."

Jane laughed. "Thomas Bennett, is cuddling all you have in mind?"

Thomas grinned. Suddenly, he smelled smoke. "Jane, is the warmer burning the bedding? I smell smoke."

Jane checked. "Nothing burning, Thomas, but I do smell smoke."

Thomas dashed to the kitchen to make sure nothing had caught on fire. No fire, all was well. Then he heard fire bells clanging a short distance away. He ran downstairs and looked outside. He couldn't believe his eyes. The night sky was lit with angry crimson flames.

Firemen had rushed to the scene. Citizens were pitching in to help the undermanned fire department. Thomas ran upstairs to tell Jane and Robert. Robert was already running down his set of stairs.

"Jane, the city is on fire! I must go help. So far, it looks like our building won't be affected as long as the wind doesn't shift and blow the fire in this direction. Keep an eye out. If you see it coming this way, bundle up and get out of the building. Find refuge somewhere."

Thomas added on several more layers of clothing and rushed off to join the fight with Robert. By the time Thomas and Robert had arrived, nearly fifty buildings were in flames, including the warehouse holding their inventory. They learned from a fireman that an explosion had been reported around 9:00 p.m. near Exchange Street.

Gail force winds fanned the flames, spreading the fire from building to building. The arctic outbreak made it nearly impossible to fight the fire. The temperature had dropped to seventeen degrees below zero. The firemen even poured whiskey in their boots to prevent their toes from icing up. Every cistern and well was frozen. The firemen and volunteers, including Thomas and Robert, cut holes in the frozen East River to get water into the fire hoses, but it was so cold, the water froze in many of the hoses. The exhausted firemen, who had fought a fire the night before, were soon overwhelmed.

Some help arrived. The same train that carried the urgent news of the fire to New Jersey, returned in one hour's time with fire engines from Newark, distanced nine miles away.

The beautiful Exchange building, which sat on the far side of the district on Wall Street, hadn't escaped the fury and resembled the ruins of an ancient city. The magnificent fifteen-foot white marble statue of Hamilton, which stood in the Rotunda of the Exchange Room, fought bravely to remain standing, but finally fell. The Post Office building was also lost, but not before the valiant postmaster and clerks saved the mail from becoming a pile of ashes.

In Hanover Square, several French merchants had carried out their fine goods to a place they thought was safe, forming a pile nearly a hundred feet square. Suddenly, a strong wind blew a gust of flames over the square consuming everything in its path, reducing the valuable goods to a pile of cinders.

Thomas and Robert were surrounded by burning buildings and living walls of flames. They were cold, exhausted, and covered in soot, and were in such a frenzy, had not yet thought about their own potential loss.

Iron shutters and copper roofs on many of the newer buildings melted into molten streams. They saw fiery tongues of flames leap from rooftop to rooftop. They heard walls crashing down, surrendering to the inferno. The bay looked like a sea of blood. By midnight the entire business district was on fire. The glow could be seen from as far away as Philadelphia, eighty miles away. Finally, the brothers worked their way to Coenties Slip to check the Watkins warehouse, which contained their inventory. The building was fully engulfed in flames. The reality of their loss struck them like a bolt of lightning.

Deflated, Thomas turned to Robert. "Well, there goes every cent we had."

Robert placed his hand on Thomas's shoulder, and said, "There is some hope. Watkins is covered by insurance. If he gets paid, we'll get paid. I know him to be a trustworthy man."

Then their attention was diverted to the wind pushing the fire toward Broad Street. It had been fifteen hours since the fiery siege had begun, and it was now spreading outward. They panicked and ran toward their building. Thomas was prepared to evacuate Jane if the fire came any closer. He dashed into the building to check on his wife.

Smoke had seeped into their building, but Jane was safe. She was holding a kerchief over her nose and mouth.

"Jane, are you all right? The fire is coming in this direction. I need to get you out of this building. Robert's downstairs keeping watch. Dress in as many layers of clothing as you can."

When she saw Thomas, she barely recognized him. He was covered in black soot. One of the sleeves of his jacket was scorched. She ran to him.

"Oh, Thomas, I've been so worried. I didn't know if I'd ever see you again." Her eyes diverted to his jacket sleeve. "Your jacket! Were you burned?"

"Not badly, thanks to Robert. My sleeve caught on fire, and Robert tore off his jacket and used it to smother the flames. If I hadn't been wearing so many layers of clothing, the burn could have been worse. I must admit, it was a frightful experience looking at my arm ablaze. Now, hurry my love. Bundle up."

Suddenly, they heard several loud explosions. The dishes in the cupboard rattled again. Thomas and Jane looked at each other in horror. "Stay here, Jane, while I find out what happened." He rushed down the stairs and out of the building.

"Robert, what's happening?"

"It's a sight, Thomas. I spoke to one of the firemen. Because there's no water available, as a last resort, the Marine Corps brought gunpowder from the Navy Yard in Brooklyn to blow up some of the buildings to create a firewall. Damn genius. It looks like it's working."

"Thank the Lord. Now that it appears our building is out of danger, let's go warm up. Jane can make us a cup of hot tea. I'm sure they'll need our help in the aftermath."

* * *

By the time the fire was out, seven hundred buildings covering seventeen city blocks were destroyed, and nearly three thousand workers were left without a job. The Bennett brothers stood in the smoking rubble in disbelief. Their view from Wall Street to the East River, and then the Coenties Slip, was no longer interrupted by buildings. Those buildings were reduced to ashes. It looked like a war zone. As they trudged through the remains of the once thriving business district, they saw merchants laying out their rescued goods on each side of the pavement. There were dry goods, groceries, hardware, furniture, desks, books, and papers. On South Street, the wharves were crammed with casks, barrels, crates, and chests.

With such pandemonium, plundering became a problem. Officers and soldiers volunteered to patrol the area during the night succeeding the fire. More than ninety robbers had been caught in the act of carrying away property during the night.

The next day another two hundred robbers were arrested. By the third day, hundreds were confined in any place that could be used for detention. In an act of mercy, the wrongdoers were discharged without arrest or punishment.

* * *

On Monday, December 21ˢᵗ, officials commenced an investigation in the Grand Jury room to determine the origin and cause of the fire. After numerous testimonies were given, one, in particular, revealed the facts.

A night watchman had been making rounds in downtown Manhattan and smelled smoke at the corner of Pearl and Exchange Streets. It was coming from a five-story warehouse. He and his fellow watchmen broke down the door and discovered a fire already raging out of control. Within fifteen minutes, fifty buildings were in flames.

The examiners reported it was their opinion that a gas pipe had burst and emitted gas, which then came into contact with the still hot coal in a stove or grate. They determined no one to be at fault.

For such a massive fire, only two people were killed. Fortunately, very few people lived in the area, and the workers had gone home at 5:00 p.m.

* * *

It was Christmas day, but no one felt like celebrating. Instead of thinking about a Christmas celebration, Thomas and Robert nervously awaited news from their distributor about a payoff for their inventory. They had started out with a small order of leather and fur, and in one month's time had successfully fabricated and sold all of their products to an exporter. They made a healthy profit, and with the exporter's surety for a much larger order, the brothers felt confident they could increase their inventory. The commitment stretched their budget beyond their comfort zone, but they expected to turn a profit as fast as they could produce. They could taste their success. Now, success was in fate's hands.

Jane had insisted that the three of them would sit down to a Christmas dinner. The dinner wouldn't be as lavish as she planned since the grocer with whom she usually patronized no longer had a store. She used what she had in her pantry. Thomas moved the dining table into the kitchen so they could be closer to the stove. He couldn't seem to get warm after the night of the fire. Jane lit a candle, and she, Thomas, and Robert sat down, bowed their heads in prayer, and broke bread.

After dinner, they traded gifts. Money was tight, so they had been creative and used what was on hand. With the weather being so frigid, Jane had knitted heavy scarves for Thomas and Robert. Thomas made Jane a pair of leather gloves from left-over pieces of leather and made a belt for Robert. Robert used remnants of his fur skins to make a fur collar for Jane, and a fur hat for Thomas. As they exchanged gifts, and admired each other's ingenuity, they put their worries on hold for a short interlude, and enjoyed their time together as a family.

* * *

On Monday, December 28th, Thomas and Robert received a visitor. Arthur Watkins, the owner of the distributorship, walked into Thomas's shop. He looked serious and asked for Robert to join them. Thomas ran next door to fetch Robert. "Watkins, is here, Robert. He wants to talk to both of us. I don't have a good feeling."

"Fellas, I'm afraid I have devastating news. My insurance company has gone bankrupt. They're unable to pay me for my losses, and I'm so sorry to tell you, I won't be able to cover your loss. I've been forced into bankruptcy. If I didn't have a family to try to take care of, I'd probably shoot myself. I don't know what I'm going to do. The day before the fire, I was happy and prosperous, and today I'm bankrupt, utterly ruined." He shook hands with Thomas and Robert. "I hope you two can recover. I hated having to give you this news." He left with slumped shoulders and his head down, a defeated man.

They watched Arthur Watkins walk away down Broad Street. He silhouetted a scene of buildings reduced to black skeletal remains and piles of ashes. A prosperous metropolis gone in one night.

"What are we going to do, Robert?"

"I don't know yet, but we can't stay here. I can't bear looking at the devastation. It's the first thing I see out my front door. Have you noticed how the smell of the fire lingers? Every morning when I wake, I smell it. Who knows how long it will take before reconstruction can begin? We don't have time to wait, Thomas, we have no money."

"It's true about the money. There's only enough for one month's rent. I'd better break the news to Jane. She's been so happy, Robert. I dread seeing the disappointment in her eyes, and at the moment, I can't even tell her we have a plan. And a babe on the way! Where will we go now? Surely Jane's father will judge me as a man who can't support his wife. He was never in favor of his daughter living in this city."

Robert reassured Thomas. "Jane could surprise you. She may be stronger than you think."

Robert was correct. Jane was the one who came up with a plan. "We'll go to my parents for help, Thomas. I'm certain they'll let us stay with them until we can re-establish our lives, and I know mother will be happy to have a grandchild underfoot."

Thomas didn't like the idea of asking for help from Jane's father, but he knew she was right. He saw a new side of Jane. This wasn't the delicate and fragile woman he had vowed to care for and support. This was a strong and resilient woman.

Thomas grasped Jane's hands and looked into her eyes, "I promise you Jane, our stay with your parents won't be for long. One day, we'll have our own land, and I'll build you a house fit for a queen." Thomas, Jane, and Robert closed up the businesses, packed up their belongings, and left New York City behind.

Chapter 5

January 1836

Delhi, New York

*T*he McKenzies graciously opened their home to the Bennett trio. Thomas was uncomfortable knowing Jane's father had wanted her to marry Mr. Stanton. Now, Jane and the man she had chosen to marry were homeless. But to Thomas's surprise and relief, he learned Edmund McKenzie wasn't passing judgment.

Very soon after they moved in, Edmund pulled Thomas aside, and said, "Thomas, I'd like tae tell ye and Jane a story. Come, let's sit by the fire. Is Robert back from Delhi? He's welcome tae listen."

"No, Mr. McKenzie, he hasn't returned yet." Thomas wondered what Jane's father was up to. He could be a formidable force. He was a husky man, had a will of iron, and feared no one.

"Oh Father, I love your stories. I remember how we all used to huddle around the fire while we listened, and we were in this very room." Jane was ecstatic to be back home. Maybe her father was telling stories again like old times. She dared not let Thomas know how happy she was about their unexpected turn of events.

Edmund smiled at his daughter. It made him happy to hear how much his stories had meant to her during her childhood. Then he turned to his wife, "Brenda, mah darlin', would ye bring us a cup of tea?"

"Aye, Edmund. It'll just be a moment." Brenda left and returned with the tea, then swooshed away, busying herself in the kitchen.

She wanted to give her husband time alone with Jane and Thomas. She had sensed Thomas's apprehension about having to ask for help. She couldn't help herself, however, and stayed within earshot, not wanting to miss a single word.

Edmund continued, "Jane, ye were too young to remember when we came tae this wonderful country. Ye see we know what it feels like tae need shelter and a helping hand. We thought we'd never leave the Highlands of Scotland.

"Ah still remember the day it all changed. It was April 10, 1819. Ah stood frozen in mah tracks when Ah heard the crackle of gunfire in the distance. Then plumes of smoke shrouded the sun. Suddenly, the sky was dark. Ah knew what it meant—the Highland Clearances had begun.

"We were tenants of Sutherlandshire and each of us had received a notice tae quit at the ensuing May term. We thought we had more time, but our time had run out.

"By the orders of Lord and Lady Stafford, a man by the name of Patrick Sellar, known for wreaking death and destruction, began burning the heath and pastures surrounding Strathnaver tae prepare the land for planting grass for hundreds of flocks of sheep tae replace all of us, their tenants!

"Ah had heard horrifying stories about recent evictions. We were next. Ah had first learned about the Highland Clearances three years earlier when our friends Jamie and Catherine Stuart were in the first group of tenants in their area tae be evicted from their homes. At that time, the landlords allowed our friends tae remove their possessions and animals, and then leased them a small allotment of land on the coast. They had tae build their home at their own expense and were expected tae harvest and burn seaweed. Burning seaweed produced kelp ash, which provided a valuable commodity for the landlords. It was profitable for the landlords, but not for our friends. They endured a barely livable life. It was hard backbreaking work, and inhaling the smoke made them sick. They were desperate tae leave, and saved every shilling possible from the pittance they earned. Finally, after a year, they sold their possessions and bought tickets tae sail tae America.

"Mah eyes were opened, and Ah started tae plan our escape. Ah would move us tae the city of Glasgow. In a past life, Ah had been a master weaver. Ah figured with any luck, Ah would weave again. If not, Ah was willing tae do any kind of work necessary tae provide for Brenda, and Abigail, who was three years old, and ye, Jane. Ye were only a year old.

"Ah systematically sold any possessions we couldn't take with us. Ah told Brenda we could only keep what the cart could hold."

Edmund smiled when he remembered how Brenda stopped him from selling her spinning wheel.

"Jane, do ye see that spinning wheel sitting over there in the corner? Yer mum wasn't about tae let me sell it. She put her hands on her hips and said, 'Mr. McKenzie, ye shan't be selling mah spinning wheel. Where Ah go, it goes.'"

Edmund continued. "Aye, she surprised me. We hadn't been married very long. She was always so quiet and agreeable. Ah was actually glad tae see her spunk. We had so much uncertainty in our life, Ah had worried how she would handle what the future held for us. Ah was right proud of her.

"On that day in April while Ah watched the pastures burn in the distance, Ah thought about the cattle Ah had owned. Ah had sold the cattle during a lull time of the clearances. At first, Ah was hesitant tae sell mah herd so soon, but it was the right time tae get the best price. As Ah looked at those burning pastures, Ah knew Ah made the right decision. If Ah still had mah cattle, with no pastures for grazing, how would Ah feed em? The poor beasts would have starved tae death. With the smoke getting stronger, Ah dropped my garden hoe and ran tae our cottage.

"Brenda was surprised tae see me so early for dinner. Ah said, 'It's time, Brenda,' and Ah walked straight tae our bed and slid it aside. Ah loosened the floor plank, yanked it up, and grabbed our tin money box sitting in the hole below. It was a relief tae see our money box filled tae the brim. Ah emptied the contents onto the floor, which was every shilling we had saved, mah gold watch, and a letter. Ah counted our pile of coins. We had enough tae leave, but only because ah sold our cattle and possessions.

"Brenda picked up the letter. It was still crumpled and damp from its long voyage across the sea. It was dated January of that year. The letter meant everything tae her. She said it contained words of hope. Back then Brenda didn't read and write, so she asked me tae read it. She needed tae hear the words again. We saved the letter, and Ah've brought it out tae show you."

Edmund handed the letter to Jane. "Take a moment and read it, mah lassie." She opened it and shared it with Thomas. While they read the letter, Edmund gave them some time alone and went to the kitchen to have Brenda refresh his tea.

Delhi, New York

January 10th 1819

Dearest Edmund and Brenda,

Ye must come to America. It's indeed the land of opportunity. We own our land and have built a fine house. We offer ye shelter with us until ye're settled. There are many Scots here. We pray ye'll come join us.

Yers in friendship,

Jamie and Catherine Stuart

Edmund returned, and Jane handed him back the letter. She commented, "I remember them over the years. They were always so kind to us, but I never realized how important they were to us. I must visit them once we've settled. I'll be seeing them in a new light."

"Aye, they were honored tae be at yer wedding. They've always been fond of ye, Jane. They'll welcome yer visit. Now, would ye like me tae continue with mah story?" Jane and Thomas nodded.

"Two weeks later, Ah hitched our Bonnie tae the cart and loaded it with our few selected possessions, including Brenda's precious brass bedwarmer, which now belongs to ye, Jane. Brenda had stacked blankets behind the seat tae make a comfy bed for Abigail and ye, Jane. After ye were both tucked into the makeshift bed, we were ready tae travel. First tae Glasgow, then on tae America.

"As we left, we looked back at our little thatch-roofed cottage for the last time. Soon tae become a pile of ashes.

"After a weary trek, we arrived tae Glasgow safely. Ah found mah job as a weaver, and Brenda took on sewing work. Life wasn't easy in the city, but we were thankful tae be safe with a roof over our head.

"One day in late May, we heard a frightening report about the fate of our neighbors in Strathnaver.

"In mid-May, Patrick Sellar and his men began burning Strathnaver. Without warning, Sellar swooped upon the Strathner residents tae burn their homes. They weren't given time tae remove their belongings nor any invalid people still in the house. Two people died in the fires. The outcasts were left with only the clothes on their backs, and no place tae go for shelter. Some died from exposure. Two hundred people lost their homes.

"We had barely left in time. After saving our earnings and living frugally, the day came when we could finally purchase the tickets for our voyage tae America, and we set sail in the early spring of 1820."

"Father, what happened when you arrived here?"

At that moment Brenda returned to offer more tea. "Would ye like some more tea, mah darlins?"

"Aye," said Edmund, "then come sit with us."

Brenda served more tea and happily joined the circle.

Edmund's mind drifted back to that late spring of 1820.

"We arrived in Delhi six weeks after leaving Liverpool and found our friends, Jamie and Catherine Stuart. And true tae their word. As promised, they offered their home as a refuge to us.

"Like our friends, we settled in this Scottish community of Delhi. The land reminded us of our homeland. It was a picturesque scene of velvety green hills and valleys. The Delaware River runs through the center of town providing broad lowlands of fertile soil, and the flowing water brings a feeling of tranquility and security to the community.

"When Brenda and Ah moved into our friends' home, we came tae know and love the Scottish community, which in turn embraced us. Ah found a job, and Brenda took on sewing tasks. We worked and saved our money until we had enough tae buy our land.

"We chose a parcel with abundant timber and rolling hills with lush meadows dotting the riverbank. We were anxious tae select a location tae build our house, so one day, Ah said, 'Brenda, it's a sunny day. It's time we explore our land and find the perfect spot fer our home.' Catherine offered to look after ye and Abigail, so off we went.

"When we set foot on our land, a breeze swept the sweet scent of grasses and wildflowers into our path. We inhaled the moist air. We listened tae the rushing water of the Delaware River, and watched the sun turn the ripples into sparkling ribbons. Ah spread a blanket on the ground under a canopy of trees, and we relaxed a moment tae savor our experience. The breeze lingered, brushing over us, and rustled the leaves in the surrounding trees. Ah already had an idea where the house should sit. Gazing upward, Ah stood, and grabbed Brenda's hand." He looked at Brenda, "Remember, darlin'?"

Brenda smiled and nodded, "Aye, Ah do, Edmund. It was a special moment, indeed."

"Ah pointed tae a hill covered with trees and underbrush. Ah said, 'Brenda, walk with me tae the top of that hill.'

"The hill was a gradual incline, and soon we were at the top. A large flat area provided an ideal site tae build our house.

"Ah said tae Brenda, 'This is where our house shall be. Look at the view of the river, and we can see fer miles.'"

Brenda interjected, "And Ah said, 'It's so hard tae believe we have our own land. No landlord demanding rent or evicting us.'"

"Then Ah thrust mah arms into the air, and said, 'Ah feel like a king on a throne. Ah want tae shout!'

"Tell them what ye said, Brenda."

She replied, "Ah said, 'Ye'r free tae shout, Edmund, so shout!'"

"And so Ah shouted, and we could hear mah echo bounce through the hills. Tae us, it was an echo of freedom."

Jane was stunned and captivated by their story. She had never realized how much her parents had struggled. She had the good fortune of starting life out in Delhi. Now, she was more forgiving and understanding of her father's obsession for her to marry Mr. Stanton. He was prejudiced by his past. Her father simply wanted the best for her.

She ran over to Edmund and hugged him. "Oh, Father, why have you never told me about why we left Scotland? Does Abigail know?"

"Naw, we haven't told her, but Ah suppose we should. Ah chose tae tell it now because Ah wanted tae sooth yer pain about leaving New York and yer discomfort of asking for our help."

Thomas was in awe of Edmund's story. He felt humbled and realized he had misjudged Jane's father. Sitting before him was a man of great courage and fortitude who refused to allow adversity to control his destiny.

Thomas was nearly speechless but had to say something. "Mr. Mckenzie, I had no idea what you all went through. You have my deepest respect. Looking at your comfortable home, your timber-laden land and your cattle ranch, one would never guess the adversity you overcame."

Now he understood Edmund's great love and obsession for his cattle and the land. But, while Thomas now saw Edmund in a different light, hearing the McKenzie story made him even hungrier and more determined to become his own man.

"Thank ye, Thomas. Yer words mean a lot tae me." Then the husky Scottish highlander embraced Thomas while giving him a hearty two-handed pat on the back.

***

Forthwith, Jane, Thomas, and Robert settled well into the McKenzie home and community. The people of Delhi welcomed the newcomers warmly just as they had done for the McKenzies so many years ago.

While exploring the village, the Bennett brothers saw promise and felt confident they could successfully set up their business in Delhi. As they toured Delhi, Robert said, "We're fortunate to have another chance, Thomas." He thought back to New York City when they had walked for days looking for a building for their business, and how much their feet hurt. *No chance of my feet hurting here. It won't take more than a day to walk through this village.* Thomas replied, "And a chance to become independent again."

***

Over the years, the McKenzies' landholdings had grown, and were laden with large stands of timber. Edmund offered a parcel to Jane and Thomas so they could build a house of their own. They accepted his generous offer. Thomas was grateful, but he didn't like having to accept charity. He yearned for his day of independence. Jane was excited and happy to be living near her parents. This was where she grew up. She was home again.

One day, shortly after Edmund had gifted the land to Thomas and Jane, several Scottish men from the village arrived equipped with tools to cut down trees and build a house for the young Bennett couple. The wives, too, came with enough food for all to partake. It was a scene of neighbors helping neighbors. Before long, a fine frame house stood ready for Thomas and Jane.

Robert continued to stay with Edmund and Brenda until he could settle into the village where he and Thomas would run their businesses. He didn't plan to stay there long.

After the house was built, the McKenzies organized a banquet to thank their neighbors. Tables covered in tartan plaid cloths held an abundance of food. The scene radiated an air of festivity as they sang their Scottish songs and drank tankards of ale. The piper played his Great Highland Bagpipes, stirring fond memories of their Scottish homeland. The nearly forgotten sound drifted through the surrounding hills and valleys. Jane's mother, Brenda, said, "Oh, how wonderful it is. Ah feel like Ah'm back in Scotland!"

Chapter 6

1836

Delhi, New York

*T*homas and Robert began their quest to find a site for their businesses. Since Robert would be residing in Delhi, it was more practical that he would be the one to look for the business building.

He had found a room to rent in a friendly boarding house in the village. The house wasn't large, so there were only a handful of tenants. The landlady fancied Robert. She was a widow and was looking for a husband, and Robert was a man she could easily love. He was ruggedly handsome, well built, mannerly, and well spoken. She enjoyed cooking for him and told him he was welcome to eat in the dining room, but he would always thank her kindly and take the food to his room. He appeared lonely and kept to himself. She wondered how such a handsome gentleman could still be single.

After two days of surveying the village, Robert found an available space he and Thomas could share. Robert also discovered a competitor—a large tannery located on the outskirts of the village.

Since the day was young, Robert rented a buggy from the livery and drove to the McKenzie property to give Thomas his news.

* * *

"Thomas, I found a place for us, which we'll need to share. I've been thinking—since we'll be together in the same space, why not combine our businesses into one? We'll need to make another change, too. I discovered a large tannery that's been established in the area for years. Our business is too small to compete, but perhaps this could become an opportunity for us if we form a partnership with them. I've scheduled a meeting with the owner tomorrow morning. I have the impression he's an oldtimer."

Thomas hadn't expected such a change in their business plan, but was pleased with Robert's report.

"Brilliant, Robert, you always come up with a plan. It'll be a relief not to be responsible for the tannery side of the business. This merger will enable us to put all our efforts into fabricating our products and increase volume. I'm looking forward to our meeting tomorrow.

"So, Robert, tell me, what do you think of the village?"

"I must say there's a striking contrast between Delhi and New York City. The streets are narrower and the buildings aren't as tall, but the folk here are friendlier." He chuckled, "The carriage drivers are less likely to run over anyone, and the businessmen always tilt their hats as they pass by. There's a local newspaper called the *Delaware Gazette*, which provides current news from New York City. It's certainly a picturesque and serene village with the river flowing through the center. I think we'll like it here."

"That's all good news. Can you stay for a meal, Robert? It's easy to set an extra plate."

"No thank you. I want to make sure to get back to the village before dark and return this buggy. I'll see you in the morning?"

Thomas patted his brother's back, "Nothing could stop me. I'm anxious to get started. I'll meet you at the boarding house."

Later, after Robert returned to the boarding house, he reflected on his conversation with Thomas. *Will I be happy here? I'm alone. I've been alone since I arrived in this country. Should I have stayed in England where I once knew love? Should I have tried harder to be with her? Will I ever know that love again?* He sighed and resolved that at least he had his brothers in his life—especially Thomas. The two of them had always been close, even as children.

Their older brother, Philip, had distanced himself from the family, and that distance widened when he chose to spend his life on a ship. Maybe one day a door would open, bringing the three brothers closer together.

Then there was his and Thomas's business. He would devote himself entirely to its success. *Wouldn't I be too busy to be lonely?* As much as he tried to convince himself the business would become his mistress, it didn't prevent him from pulling out his fine pocket watch to gaze at the portrait of a woman residing on the underside of the dust cover. This ritual frequently took place at night after settling into his room.

The next morning, Thomas and Robert met with the tannery owner. The meeting went well and they struck an agreement. The newly formed Bennett Bros. Co. would purchase at wholesale any leather or fur pelts they needed to produce their products. Should the tannery company owner have a source to sell any of the Bennett Bros. Co. products, he in turn, would have the opportunity to purchase such products at wholesale.

Thomas and Robert had one challenge to work out since Thomas no longer lived near their business as he did in New York City. They would have to work out a schedule flexible enough for him to commute back and forth. Robert would be the one to open and close their business. Thomas wondered how long such an arrangement could last. Robert assured his brother he would make it work. If their company was successful, perhaps Thomas and Jane could move to the village, or Robert could buy Thomas out. After all, what else could they do?

"I do hope the community will support our business," said Thomas with a resigned sigh of acceptance.

Chapter 7

June 1836

Delhi, New York

*I*t was the month of June, and Thomas and Jane celebrated their first wedding anniversary. Jane hoped they would be celebrating the birth of their child soon. She felt as big as their new house, and it took every ounce of her energy to perform the simplest of chores. Her back ached and her feet were swollen. Jane was nervous about giving birth, but she was ready for it to be over.

Thomas offered to assist her whenever he was around, but he learned he was better off to keep his distance when she was moody and short tempered, which was most of the time. There were instances when he wondered if he was her target. *Another side of Jane?*

About a week after their wedding anniversary, Jane cried out to Thomas in the middle of the night. "Thomas, fetch my mother. I think it's starting." She moaned, "And I need the midwife!"

Thomas lunged out of bed and ran for the door. Jane cried out after him, "Thomas you forgot your trousers."

He ran back in a frenzy and finished dressing. "I'll be back soon, my love." He ran to the McKenzie house and banged on the door. Edmund opened the door. Brenda was awake and surmised there could be only one reason Thomas was banging on their door in the middle of the night. She was already dressing.

"Thomas, take our wagon and fetch Vera. Ah will go tae Jane."

Edmund ran out to the barn and hitched his horse to the wagon.

Thomas boarded, shook the reins, and drove pellmell to Vera's house. As he drove, he thanked himself for having taken a test drive to the midwife's house before the event. Not a minute would be wasted, lost in the dark of night.

Within minutes, Brenda was by Jane's side while Edmund rushed to alert Abigail, who lived nearby. Within an hour, Thomas was on his way back with the midwife.

Jane cried out, "Mother, it hurts so much. How much longer does it go on? I'm afraid. Will I die?"

Brenda held onto Jane's hand. "Jane, ye could be in labor for several hours. Ye'r strong, and Ah forbid ye tae die. Ah'm here with ye, and Ah won't leave yer side. Soon, Abigail and Vera will be here."

Several hours later, the midwife told Jane it was time to push. Jane strained and pushed.

Vera said, "I see the head!" She eased the babe out, and it cried immediately without any encouragement. "Jane, you have a strong boy." She cut the umbilical cord, tied the bellyband, and handed the babe to Abigail. "Cleanse him, to prepare him for his mother."

"I want to see him, please hold him up, Abigail," said Jane.

Vera exclaimed, "Oh my, you aren't finished, Jane. Another babe is coming. Push!"

Jane had no time to react to the unexpected announcement of a second child. She pushed hard. Within minutes, a second babe was born.

The midwife said, "You have another fine boy, Jane. You have given birth to twins!"

She prepared him the same as his brother and handed him off to Brenda. Then she said, "Be patient, Jane, while I deliver the placentas." Vera gently massaged Jane's belly, coaxing the placentas to leave her body.

Thomas pressed against the other side of the door and heard two babes crying. *Were his ears deceiving him?*

When it was the proper time, Brenda, with tear-filled eyes, opened the door and signaled for Thomas to come in. "Jane has presented ye with two strong sons."

Thomas hurried to Jane, who was holding both sons. "Oh, Jane, thank you for this gift. You have never looked more beautiful. I love you." He couldn't stop smiling as he gazed at his sons, "I have two sons!"

"Now I understand why I was so big! I thought we would be a family of three, and now we are four!"

The midwife interrupted, "I'm sorry to break up such a beautiful family moment, Thomas, but Jane needs her rest, and you need to take me back home."

Thomas obliged.

Jane said, "Thomas, on your way back, will you think about what we should name our sons? I'm so tired, my mind is numb."

A few minutes later, the room was quiet. Jane looked sleepy, so Brenda and Abigail took the twins from her arms.

Abigail's husband, Charles, arrived to offer assistance. He had made a crib as a gift for Jane and Thomas, but now they needed two cribs.

"It looks like I need to make another crib, but for the moment one of the drawers in the chest will have to do." Charles pulled out a drawer from the chest and transformed it into a temporary bed for one of the babes.

When Thomas returned, he checked on Jane to see if she was awake. She was half awake when she heard him enter the room. He had decided what the twins' names should be.

"Jane, if you're agreeable, I'd like our oldest son to take the name of Jonathan, after my father; and our younger son, to be called Jeremy, after my uncle. My uncle was like a second father to me. What do you think?"

"I like the names, Thomas."

"Brilliant. I'll post a letter to my father and uncle right away. I know they'll be thrilled and honored."

The twins were far from identical. Jonathan appeared to resemble his father. The small amount of hair on Jonathan's head was blond, and his eyes were bluish grey. Jeremy had dark curly hair and brown eyes, resembling his mother.

The quietude didn't last long. Little Jonathan and Jeremy were wide-awake and cried simultaneously. Thomas picked up Jonathan and handed him to Jane to nurse him. Then he picked up Jeremy and walked the room with him until Jane could take him as well.

Abigail, who was nearby, came into the room, and said, "My dear sister, you look exhausted. Of course Thomas won't always be able to be here. I'll be coming back to help you, and I'm going to ask some of the neighbor ladies to assist, as well. At least until you get your strength back."

Jane was already feeling overwhelmed at the thought of two babes crying for attention at the same time. She sighed as she looked at her two sons. "Oh, Abigail, thank you. I accept your generous offer. I would never have asked for your help."

Abigail bent down toward the bed and hugged her sister, and said, "I have to leave for the moment, but I'll be back. Mother is staying with you for now. We told Thomas not to worry, he'll be free to go back to work in Delhi."

Thomas thanked Abigail and her mother. It had been a hectic morning. "Robert's probably wondering what happened to me this morning. I do need to ride to Delhi to tell him he now has two nephews!"

* * *

1837

Delhi, New York

Before they knew it, a year had passed. It was 1837. Business was good for the Bennett Bros. Co. Thomas and Robert enjoyed a steady stream of customers and had begun to show a profit. Even so, they still yearned for something more in their lives, and kept a close watch on New York City, hoping to return one day.

Thomas often fought his feeling of restlessness. Couldn't he be satisfied? He had a roof over his head, the business was successful, he loved his wife and sons, and another child was on the way. Why wasn't he satisfied? He answered his own question. As long as they lived in the middle of McKenzie land, he would never be his own man. The McKenzies had been charitable, and he was thankful, but charity was a hard thing to swallow.

Thomas would soon realize they should be counting their blessings. On a sunny day in May, he and Robert had been working side by side on a large order from the tannery. Establishing a relationship with the tannery was one of the best decisions they had made. Between the repeat orders from the tannery and the regular customers who walked through their door, they had more than enough business.

When they finished the order, Robert inspected their products while Thomas gathered their tools to clean and put away.

Robert shouted out to Thomas, "We're ready to load the wagon."

"Brilliant! I'll fetch it. Be back soon."

On his way to the stable, Thomas walked past the newspaper boy on the corner selling the *Delaware Gazette.*

The boy shouted, "Read about the panic in New York City!"

Thomas stopped abruptly and turned back to buy a copy. He thanked the boy, tipping him a penny. Thomas was obsessed with New York City. Since the day he had arrived in New York Harbor, he believed New York City was where he and Robert would establish their business. In his mind, leaving the city after the fire was only temporary. The brothers never gave up on returning to make their fortune.

As Thomas unfolded the paper, he read the headline on the front page dated May 12, 1837, *PANIC IN NEW YORK CITY.*

Anxious to show the story to Robert, he quickly procured the wagon and returned to their storefront. By the time he made it back to Robert, many of the townspeople had seen the newspaper headline. Three Delhi businessmen were with Robert discussing the news.

According to the *Gazette,* the city was in chaos. First, the city had suffered from the plague, and then the fire. And now, a financial crisis. People were unemployed, and stood in breadlines. Several charitable organizations had established soup kitchens. Mobs in the city were out of control and raided warehouses to steal food. Banks had closed down, and prominent businessmen had lost everything.

One of the Delhi businessmen said, "It's the gloomiest period New York City has ever known."

Another man added, "My banker told me this crisis might last for several years. We're better off living in a small town where we can all look after each other."

Thomas and Robert exchanged knowing looks—New York City was no longer their future.

Thomas took the paper home to share the news with Jane and

the rest of the family. When they sat down to dinner that night, they bowed their heads and gave thanks that they were living in a safe environment. Then they said a prayer for the people of New York City.

* * *

As the months slid by, Thomas stopped thinking about New York City. It was true, they *were* better off than the people in New York. He couldn't imagine his family standing in a breadline. By living in the countryside, they had access to a bounty of food from their gardens and crops. From the chickens they raised, they gathered eggs, and from their Jersey cows, they had milk. They hunted for meat, and the Delaware River gave them fish.

He focused on his family and the business. The year was nearly over, and the Christmas season was upon them. He and Robert had been busy filling Christmas orders. Despite being busy, his mind was on Jane. She was due to give birth to their next child sometime during the week of Christmas. This time, he thought having a daughter would be nice.

On Christmas Eve, Jane went into labor. As before, Brenda and Abigail were by her side. Thomas rushed to fetch the midwife. Vera hadn't been there long before the babe entered the world. Thomas's wish came true, he had a daughter.

He was in love with his little girl. She had dark hair and eyes, and a pink rosebud mouth. Since she was born on Christmas Eve, they named her Mary. Thomas called her his Christmas child. The Bennett family was growing.

* * *

1839

Delhi, New York

Two years later, Jane gave birth to another daughter, Elizabeth. The baby girl had rosy cheeks, hazel eyes, and fiery red hair. Thomas teased Jane, "Are you sure you don't have a wee bit of Irish blood in you, my bonnie lass?" Jane smiled at him, and looked down at the little bundle so content in her arms.

* * *

1841

Delhi, New York

Two more years slid by, bringing in the year 1841, and another child was about to join the Bennett family. Jane had been in labor for three days. On the third day, Thomas rushed to fetch the midwife. Brenda and Abigail stayed by Jane's bedside until Vera arrived.

Brenda took Vera aside for a moment. "Something is different this time. Ah don't have a good feeling."

The midwife turned her attention back to Jane and reassured her all would be well. Finally, it was time for Jane to push. She pushed with every ounce of her remaining strength. Sweat poured down her face, and she bit her lip.

"Keep pushing, Jane," said Vera.

When Jane was unable to make any progress, the midwife realized there was a problem, and examined her.

"Don't you worry, Jane, I'll take good care of you and your babe. I have many years of birthing experience. Now, I need to tell you what I must do. Your babe is lodged on its side. I'm going to have to reach inside your body and turn it. Your body should do the rest. Are you ready, Jane?"

She nodded her head, but her eyes telegraphed uncertainty. "I feel so weak."

Brenda and Abigail stood next to Jane, one on each side of the bed, latching on to her. As Vera worked, Jane's blood pressure dropped, and she fainted. Vera could see the babe's head. Her experienced, gentle hands eased the babe out.

"It's a girl," she said. She coaxed the babe to cry and finished the after-birth preparation. Abigail stood ready to cleanse the baby girl. Jane woke to the sound of her baby crying and reached her arms out for her daughter. Abigail placed the baby girl in her arms.

Thomas had been pacing outside the door with worry. Finally, Vera told him he could come in. He rushed to Jane's bedside. She smiled, and in a whisper of a voice, said, "Another daughter."

49

Thomas had hoped for a son this time, but when he looked at his beautiful daughter, it didn't matter. She had a peaches and cream complexion, bright green eyes, and golden hair. They named their daughter Emily.

"Your daughter is a little fighter," said Vera.

Thomas looked at the midwife with concern, "What do you mean she's a fighter, Vera?"

Vera explained what happened during the delivery. Then she said, "While the two of you are here together, there's something you both need to know. Jane, I'm afraid you can no longer bear children. Because of the complications, you suffered some tissue damage. You're weak at the moment because you lost a great deal of blood. Your pulse was weak, and you lost consciousness for a few minutes. If this were to happen again, you could die." Then she looked at the family, and said, "Make sure Jane gets plenty of rest."

They all nodded.

Jane looked at Thomas, tears welling in her eyes, "I'm so sorry, Thomas."

"You have nothing to be sorry about, my love. You've already given me a beautiful family. Look what you gave me the first time you were with child, or should I say, children." He smiled, "Two boys!"

Jane returned a weak smile and fell asleep.

Chapter 8

Summer 1844

Weymouth, Dorset, England

*T*he steamship eased into Weymouth Harbor. It had been a three-week-long voyage, and for eight-year-old Jonathan and Jeremy, their first voyage. The twins had been ecstatic in anticipation of this trip.

They were in earshot when their father announced he had received a letter from their Uncle Philip. He had extended an invitation to Thomas and Robert to join him on his voyage to England to visit their parents. He had mentioned that the last time he visited their parents, he noticed they had aged considerably. While Thomas and Robert endeavored to forge their paths in America, ten years had slipped by since they had last seen their parents. It was now 1844. Where had the years gone? This was a trip not to put off.

Jonathan had dashed into the room exclaiming, "Can we go too, Father?"

Thomas thought it was an excellent idea, and agreed. The lads were old enough to travel, and how wonderful it would be for them to meet their grandparents. Unfortunately, their daughters were too young to go, so they and their mother would stay behind. If Jane needed help, her parents were nearby.

Robert had chuckled, "Thomas, Philip better be prepared to have Jonathan underfoot. I doubt my nephew will leave his side."

Thomas answered, "You're right about that!"

It had been a pleasant summer voyage. The twins seized everything the sea offered. They were amazed and excited to see the various forms of sea life, including whales and porpoises. They breathed in the marine air and gazed in awe of a limitless horizon. At night when the moon was obscured, the sky was like black velvet, giving the stars an extra brilliance, like diamonds. Jonathan proudly pointed out the constellations to his brother.

The side-wheel paddle steamer was an experience in itself. Jonathan had become Philip's shadow, savoring every moment. Jonathan's big moment came when his uncle allowed him to stand next to the large wheel and steer the ship. The wheel towered over him.

Jeremy explored the ship and conversed with the crew. One of the crew members let him put some hook and line out to fish. It was a different experience than fishing in the Delaware River.

Once the ship slipped into place against the long-extended wharf, it was Jonathan who called out, "Drop anchor!"

Then they all disembarked, ready for the reunion. The Bennett family would be together again, plus two. Thomas was excited to introduce his sons to their grandparents and to show the lads his childhood home. After their bags were unloaded, Philip hailed a cab to take them to their parents' house, just a short distance away. Philip recalled how he used to walk to the wharf so many years ago. Robert was deep in his own thoughts about the woman he had left behind. *I wonder how she's fared?*

The cab stopped in front of the house, and they all piled out. For Thomas and Robert, their childhood home and garden looked run down since they'd left. It was a telling sign. Their parents weren't as agile as they used to be.

The excited Bennetts knocked on the door. A much older-looking Jonathan Bennett answered. It was a bit of a shock for Thomas and Robert. At that moment, they knew they had made the right decision to come.

Their father stared at them for a moment, then teared up. "My boys, you're here! Mother, come, our boys are home!"

Then he looked at his grandsons for the first time. He grabbed both of them in one big bear hug. "Oh, my Lord, my grandsons.

I never thought this day would come. Which one of you is my namesake?"

Young Jonathan stepped forward. "Glad to meet you Granddad. I'm honored to have your name."

"Oh, you're a charmer, I can see that. And Jeremy, your great uncle will be here tomorrow. You know, you two are as handsome as your father and uncles."

Then they heard a scream mixed with crying. Agnes hastened into the room. She ran toward Thomas and Robert's arms. "My boys, my boys! Oh, how I've missed you." Then she turned to her grandsons. "You beautiful boys. I love you already!"

Thomas and Robert stared at their mother. Her hair had turned completely white, she was slightly bent over, and when they hugged her, they felt more bones than flesh. They hadn't thought about seeing their parents so changed.

Philip stood quietly in the background wishing he would have brought the family together much sooner. He walked over to Agnes and hugged her, "Hello, Mum."

"Thank you for making this happen, Philip," she cried.

Philip glanced over at his father who was extending his arm out to him. "Come over here Philip. I want all my boys together. You've made me right happy, my lad."

Agnes corralled her sons, "Come to the dinner table. I've prepared all your favorites."

She swung her attention to her grandsons. "My sweet laddies, tomorrow I want you to tell me what your favorite foods are, and I shall prepare them for you."

After supper, Thomas and Robert surprised their parents with gifts they had brought. Thomas had made each of them a pair of leather gloves, and Robert had made a fur collar for his mother, and a fur hat for his father. Agnes and Jonathan were thrilled with their gifts.

Jonathan's faded blue eyes brightened. "I see you haven't lost your touch, lads." He gave them a bear hug. "Thank you," he said as he donned the hat, and the gloves next.

Agnes excitedly put the collar and gloves on. "They feel so wonderful, my sons." She kissed each of them on the cheek as she thanked them.

The family stayed up late that night catching up on ten years gone by. When it was time to turn in for the night, Agnes led her grandsons to their father's old bedroom.

The next day Great Uncle Jeremy visited. He was younger than his brother Jonathan. "Well, nice to meet you, lads. I see I have fine looking nephews. And which of you is Jeremy?"

"That would be me, Uncle Jeremy. I've been anxious to meet you."

"You do my name proud, Jeremy. I'm looking forward to spending some time with you laddies while you're here."

Philip had made arrangements for them to stay for a full two weeks. The three brothers used some of the time to work on the garden and house. The exterior of the house had been completely overtaken by wisteria, lichen, and moss, and the garden was overgrown. By the time they finished, their childhood home looked the way they remembered it.

One day, Robert walked to the town center. He was curious how it looked now. It had grown. Suddenly, his attention was diverted to a lovely, attractive woman across the street. Two children were with her. She was beautifully dressed in the latest fashion and carried packages labeled with logos hailing from the exclusive stores. Her soft brown hair cascaded in ringlets down against her pale pink cheeks. It was her. The woman whose portrait resided inside his pocket watch. Her beautiful face, haunting him, endlessly. She was the woman he could never stop loving, Eleanor.

As she walked, she turned her head in his direction, and her large brown eyes appeared to be looking straight at him. He quickly stepped back into an alcove so she wouldn't see him, but had she seen him? Did she recognize him? Surely not, he had moved fast enough to deprive her of a second glance. His heart beat so fast and loud, he wondered if she might hear it. He adored her. He loved her. And now, his unanswered questions were answered. She was still married, had status and money, and children. She had all the trappings, but was she happy in this arranged marriage?

That night before turning in, Robert gazed at himself in the mirror. He wondered if she could have recognized him. He turned twenty-nine this year. It had been over ten years since he had kissed her for the last time. He was clean-shaven then. He had grown a short beard and sideburns after arriving in America. His brown hair had faded slightly, and he wore it longer now. He leaned in closer to the mirror. He hadn't noticed the wrinkle lines that had formed around his eyes. She had often remarked how much she loved his hazel eyes. She still looked the same to him. As beautiful as ever.

The two weeks went by much too quickly. It was difficult saying goodbye. The brothers promised to return much sooner, not knowing if it would really happen. Thomas and Robert thanked Philip for arranging the trip.

Thomas chuckled, "Philip, I hope Jonathan didn't drive you crazy on the way here, you still have the return trip to go yet."

"Thomas, I've enjoyed every moment with my nephews. Don't worry, while teaching Jonathan, I put him to work. Frankly, he's been very helpful. He has good instincts, which will serve him well later."

When they all boarded the ship, Thomas patted Philip on the shoulder. "This trip was good for all of us, Philip, and most importantly for me, my sons will have memories of their grandparents and great uncle."

Sadly, this would be the last time they would see their parents. Their mother died two years later of consumption, and their father, a year later, heartbroken.

Chapter 9

*W*eeks slipped into months, and months into years. It was 1853, and the Bennett family continued to live a comfortable life with the Mckenzies in Delhi. The Bennett brothers' business flourished. Thomas and Robert wondered what happened to the time. They had all but given up on their *big* plans. Thomas learned to be content. He felt blessed by his beautiful wife and children, and he had developed a bond with Jane's family. He reprimanded himself for wanting more. *Was this not enough*?

Thomas was a devoted father, and when he wasn't working with Robert at the business, he spent his spare time teaching his children. Besides teaching them everything about farm work, he instructed them in horsemanship and the use of weapons. The sisters could shoot and ride as well as their brothers.

When the children weren't in school, they did their share of the work at home. Jonathan and Jeremy were strong young lads and helped plow the fields and sow the crops.

The brothers loved and respected their father, but had a very strong bond with their mother. She was their angel. They were her first born, and she adored them. Jonathan was the older of the two by five minutes. She had given them nicknames, which to her, seemed more intimate—Jonathan as Jonny, and Jeremy as Jemmie.

As twins, they were inseparable. Although they weren't identical twins, they shared some likenesses. Both stood at six feet two inches, were possessed with good looks and charisma, but were distinctively different in every other way.

Jonathan loved living near the river and yearned for the day he would follow in his Uncle Philip's footsteps and sail the open seas to faraway lands. He learned as much as he could on his own. He studied maps illustrating the Atlantic and Pacific Coasts. He studied the stars and moon by night, and the sun during the day. He coveted the navigation map his uncle sent him, and mentally sailed around Cape Horn, the southernmost tip of South America. It wasn't uncommon for Thomas to find one of his ropes tied into nautical knots. Jonathan was more like his Uncle Philip than his father.

Jonathan was a risk taker and craved adventure. He possessed an intoxicating smile and a laugh that charmed the heart. People found themselves drawn to Jonathan's charismatic personality and good looks. Although Jonathan enjoyed the attention, he kept his inner thoughts under lock and key. He didn't offer affection easily, except to his mother.

Jeremy was a scholar. It wasn't unusual to see a stack of books on the floor near his bed. He absorbed knowledge voraciously, had an eye for detail, and was endlessly curious. He was a goal setter and planner. If an obstacle got in his way, he wasted little time analyzing the anatomy of the infraction and attacked it with zest and precision.

Jeremy was soft-spoken, had an uncanny ability to turn the table to his advantage, and could be assertive, but calm, in a tight situation. He was as handsome and magnetic as his brother, but was more open to interaction with others. He enjoyed watching people, observing their body language, and often found himself profiling them. In his spare time, he earned a wage at the Bennett Bros. Co. on a part-time basis. Thomas hoped at least Jeremy would join him in the business.

The girls milked the cows and made cheese and butter. Each morning they fed the chickens, then gathered eggs. They planted an herb garden, and not only learned how to dry the herbs but also studied with Vera about the many medicinal uses. They were renowned for their expertise, and before long, a steady flow of neighbors frequented the Bennett home asking the girls to mix potions for them. The neighbors never came empty-handed. Many times they brought bread or sourdough starter, or a freshly baked berry pie.

Like their brothers, the sisters were each their own person.

Fourteen-year-old Elizabeth was blossoming from a cute girl into a beautiful woman. Her hair and hazel eyes were her most striking features. Elizabeth's long red wavy locks changed color like a chameleon depending on the season. It ranged from a rich ginger red in the spring, to strawberry blonde in the summer, and crimson auburn in the winter. The girls at school envied her. She had always been slim and straight up and down. Her brothers had nicknamed her *beanpole*. All that was changing, however. Her body was beginning to form a few curves.

Elizabeth took pleasure in reading stories and writing poetry and was never without her diary. She was sentimental and kept everything important to her. Jane loved this trait in her daughter. She thought back to when Elizabeth was six years old, and she taught her how to press flowers between pages of books. Now, at the age of fourteen, Elizabeth still pressed flowers. There were times when she borrowed some of her sister Mary's books for the flowers. Each time Mary opened one of her books and found flowers or leaves inside it, the household could hear her scream her sister's name.

Elizabeth had kept a wooden crate in her bedroom to hold her mementos. It wasn't especially attractive but served its purpose. Then, on her fourteenth birthday, her parents surprised her with a beautiful dome-lid trunk.

She exuded refinement and was very lady-like. When Thomas taught his children how to ride horseback, he learned firsthand how much *being a lady* meant to her. She had fought the idea of riding her horse astride and insisted on riding side saddle. Thomas could never say no to his daughter and ordered her a side saddle.

Mary resembled her mother with her dark hair and eyes.

Hers was a quiet beauty, inside as well as outside. She was a compassionate person and wouldn't harm an insect.

To Thomas and Jane, she was always their Christmas child. Since her birthday was on Christmas Eve, and festivities were all about Christmas, her parents made an effort to single out her birthday as her own special day.

Mary never complained out loud, but her mother knew she didn't like her birthday being so close to Christmas.

In an effort to make her feel more important, Jane had said, "Mary, the year you were born was very special. It was the year that Victoria, at the young age of eighteen, took the throne in Britain, which began the Victorian era."

Mary was thrilled to have a connection to the Queen. She relished the love story of Queen Victoria and Prince Albert and followed any news about them. She dreamed of falling in love and having a family of her own. Her grandmother McKenzie knew Mary well and had given her a romance novel by Jane Austen called *Pride and Prejudice* for her birthday. The book transported her into a romantic world of courtship. The book never left her bedside. Very soon, Mary would embark on her own love story.

As for the youngest, Emily enjoyed school—not so much for education, but for the opportunity to socialize. She was contriving and flirtatious with the boys, and she never tired of being told she was pretty, which she already knew. Emily was striking with her brilliant green eyes, creamy complexion, and golden hair that glinted in the sun like gold coins. There was always a boy close by hoping to catch her eye.

Emily filled her closet with as many dresses as her mother would allow, and she kept a large assortment of ribbons for her hair. She was self-centered and thought she was above the menial chores at home. Jane, however, didn't encourage Emily's attitude and made sure she did her fair share of the work.

Jane recognized Emily's self-centeredness and stubborn streak, but she also believed that behind Emily's facade, there was a caring heart. Emily just didn't like to reveal it. She admired Emily's self-confidence, and secretly approved of her daughter's defiant spirit. Through the years, Thomas had commented and sometimes complained about Emily being such high maintenance, but he always weakened when he looked into her beguiling green eyes, and she called him *daddy*.

Thomas and Jane were astonished at how many different personalities they had brought into the world. And when the family congregated together in the house, there was never a lack of conversation or debate.

Chapter 10

1853

Delhi, New York

*T*he winter of 1853 brought heavy snowfall. Once a week Thomas and Robert checked in at the village general store to see if any mail had arrived. With such snowy conditions, the mail hadn't been coming in on the regular schedule, so they waited until the end of the week. Finally, on Friday at the conclusion of the workday, the brothers walked over to the store to see if there was any mail. Abe, the owner, was busy in the back room when he heard the jingle of the brass bells on the front door. He hustled to the counter out front.

Thomas tilted his hat. "How are you today, Abe? It's sure cold outside. Any mail delivery yet?" Rubbing their hands, the brothers gravitated toward the crackling fire in the potbelly stove.

"Good to see you two. Yes, the mail just came in. With all this dang snow, the mail came in late again. I'll check for you."

Thomas walked back over to the counter while he waited. Abe returned with one piece of mail.

"Just one letter for ya, Thomas."

"Thank you, Abe. While I'm here, give me two cents' worth of your taffy."

As Abe wrapped the candy, Thomas walked back over to the stove to join Robert who was vigorously warming his hands. The letter was addressed to Thomas Bennett and Robert Bennett from Captain Philip Bennett, postmarked in San Francisco.

"Robert, it's a letter from Philip! We haven't heard from him in awhile."

Thomas quickly tore open the envelope, and he and Robert read the letter together. Philip had news. He now owned a steamship, and he had a plan for a money-making venture that would include all of them. The captain who had mentored and trained Philip for ten years and paved the way for him to achieve the title of captain had passed away and bequeathed his ship to Philip.

San Francisco, California

September 1853

Brothers, there is free land available in the Puget Sound territory. The government has created an incentive known as the Oregon Donation Land Grant. All we have to do is stake the land we want, claim it, and homestead it. The area is abundant with timber. I frequent San Francisco on a regular basis, and it's bulging with growth. It's growing faster than the raw material can be supplied. The amount of timber and products that Puget Sound can offer California will make it an excellent place for us to make money. There's not much time to tarry. The land offer will expire by December of 1855.

How soon can you come?

Your brother,

Philip Bennett

As they read Philip's letter, Thomas's heart thumped so hard he could hear it. He was ready for a change. He was sure Robert felt the same way. The past seventeen years had been filled with nothing but distressing news from New York City. The population had quadrupled, and now with the subject of slavery becoming a heated issue, the social climate in the city was dangerous. They had given up on moving back to New York City and wondered if Delhi was destined to be their permanent domicile. Thomas was grateful to Jane's parents for offering them refuge, and he knew she was happy living so close to her family, but he continued to yearn to be his own man. To him, they were nothing more than squatters on McKenzie land.

Thomas folded the letter, put it in his pocket, and paid for the candy, bidding farewell to Abe.

Robert waved, "See you next week, Abe. It's sure tough to leave your nice warm stove!"

The brothers stepped out into the cold icy air and walked toward Thomas's horse.

"I'm ready, Thomas, but the decision's easy for me, I'm alone. What are you going to do? You have your family to convince. Do you think Jane will go along with the idea?"

"Robert, I know I'll never be happy if I don't take this opportunity. I let her talk me out of the Oregon Trail opportunity back in '43, but I'm more determined than ever now. I would always wonder, what if? It's not going to be easy to persuade her to go. She's happy here."

"I don't envy you, brother. You know, I heard the winters are milder in that part of the country. I wouldn't miss these winters!"

"No argument there. I'll see you tomorrow, Robert, hopefully with good news. If she agrees to leave, I'll draft a letter to Philip tonight, and we can post it with Abe tomorrow."

As Thomas rode back home, he planned and practiced in his mind how he would approach his wife.

It took the full evening for him to convince her to leave their nest. She didn't like it, but with a great deal of hesitancy, acquiesced. She knew Thomas was unhappy. She knew him well—he was a proud man, and not being independent slowly ate away at his pride.

They had heard stories about the Oregon Trail since the 1840s. The stories always piqued Thomas's interest. She recalled their argument in 1843 when Thomas had heard about the group of one thousand people planning to travel the two-thousand-mile trek to the fertile land of western Oregon.

"Why shouldn't we go? We aren't getting any younger," he had reasoned. Jane won the argument when she pointed out how young their children were, and how hard such a long journey would be on them. She had heard about all the crosses that marked the trail. Finally, after looking into the face of his little two-year-old Emily, he had conceded.

Now, the time had come. She couldn't hold him back any longer. In her eyes, Thomas wasn't the happy, energetic man she had married. She felt fortunate to have had seventeen years living near her family. It was his turn.

Thomas was proud of how well he had swayed Jane to leave. He didn't realize it wasn't his well-rehearsed monologue that persuaded her to go, but rather, his wife's insight into her husband's soul.

Thomas sat down and penned his letter to Philip.

Delhi, New York
November 1853

Philip, Robert and I welcomed your encouraging letter. Yes, we'll come. Nothing will stop us. It'll take us some time to prepare for the journey and to accumulate the funds we'll need. I believe we can be ready by late summer of next year.

Your brothers,

Thomas and Robert Bennett

Chapter 11

*O*n a beautiful spring-like morning of April 1854 in Delhi, family and friends filled the village church to witness the wedding of Mary Bennett and Benjamin Spencer. Beams of sunlight danced through the stained glass windowpanes creating colorful shafts of light. Candles were lit casting a soft amber glow. Festoons of evergreens and blossoms adorned the chapel.

The Bennett's oldest daughter, Mary, arrived in a carriage pulled by four white horses, accompanied by her parents. Thomas helped his daughter step down from the carriage. She was a vision. He was filled with a flood of emotion and pride as he looked at his daughter wearing her mother's wedding dress. He thought about how his Jane looked in that dress on their wedding day, and just as he had done for her, he made Mary a pair of satin shoes to wear on her special day.

As they entered the church, Thomas's mind turned inward as he thought about all the years gone by, and how their lives would be dramatically changed in the near future. He gazed at the people of the village who had come to witness and honor the event and felt sad that he and his family would most likely never see their faces again.

Mary and Benjamin were excited about beginning their life

together. They had surprised their families when they announced their engagement in February. Mary had surprised herself.

Mary hadn't expected to fall for Benjamin so fast. She had known him since school, but hadn't seen him for several years. Benjamin had unexpectedly re-entered her life during the previous Christmas season. She and Elizabeth had gone shopping in Delhi to buy some last minute gifts. The next thing they knew, they were in the middle of a snow storm. As they rushed to their wagon to hurry home, Mary slipped and fell. Elizabeth tried to help her up, but Mary had twisted her ankle. Benjamin was across the street and witnessed the mishap. He dashed to her rescue and swooped her up into his arms, and gently placed her into the wagon. He then insisted on escorting the young ladies home. He tied his horse to the back of the wagon and drove them to their destination. Mary had just found her knight.

Before agreeing to the engagement, Mary had to know if Benjamin would be willing to relocate to the other side of the nation. She wasn't prepared to separate from her family, and she didn't want to have to choose between her family and Benjamin. Fortunately, she didn't have to make that decision. Benjamin loved her so deeply, he was willing to go, even though it meant he would be separating from his family. What she didn't expect was for him to join her father and uncles on the voyage. This meant they would be separated for at least six months.

Now, as newlyweds, they had just a few months left together before Benjamin would be leaving her. He was torn about leaving Mary so soon after their marriage, but he felt duty-bound to join her father and uncle on the forthcoming voyage to Puget Sound. Despite his young age and inexperience, he had offered his support, insisting on going with them. He too, would stake and claim land to secure his and Mary's future. Thomas was impressed with Benjamin's courage and loyalty. He looked forward to getting to know his son-in-law.

Chapter 12

1854

Delhi, New York

*T*homas and Robert continued to communicate with Philip. Finally, in May, Philip sent a letter with the finalized plans for the voyage. Thomas shared the details with Jane.

"Jane, we'll be departing the first week of August on Philip's ship. He has made all the arrangements for you and the children to follow and he will contact you when it's time for you to leave. You'll be taking the shorter route through Nicaragua. You should reach San Francisco within two months' time. If you follow his instructions, all should go well. You will be under the care of his good friend Captain William Davis on his vessel, *Voyager,* where you will receive the best accommodations and services available. Captain Davis will take you as far as Greytown where you will transfer to the smaller steamer, *S.L. Tucker.*

"We'll be taking the longer route toward the southern tip of South America, which will take five to six months. We'll get word to you when we've settled and when you'll be able to leave San Francisco to continue on to Puget Sound." Then he handed Jane an envelope.

"Keep this safe, Jane. Philip has written a schedule for you and every detail you'll need."

Thomas pulled Jane into his arms and looked into her dark brown eyes. "And Jane, I want you to know how much it means to me that you're willing to go through with this. Throughout our life together, we've never been separated. My heart already aches for you, my love."

"This *was* a difficult decision for me, Thomas. I thought we had a good life, but I understand your heart. I have no idea how I'm going to handle being separated from you for such a long time. At least we'll each have family with us. Promise you'll write whenever you can so I'll know you're safe."

"I promise, Jane."

* * *

The month of June crept upon the Bennett party, marking two months remaining before the scheduled voyage to Puget Sound.

Mary had news for Benjamin. She was with child. Benjamin was elated and sad at the same time. He grabbed Mary's hands and clasped them into his, "Mary, do you want me to stay? If I go, I won't be here for you and the babe."

Mary looked into Benjamin's soft brown eyes. He had such a quiet and gentle spirit.

"No, dearest, you must go. I wish you could be here with me, but there's too much at stake. Remember, my mother, my sisters, my brothers, my grandparents, and aunt and uncle, are here to help me. Not to mention the whole village for heaven's sake! I'll be fine."

"Well, it helps to know that, but I'll still worry about you, my precious. I'll post a letter to you every chance I get. You'll be in my thoughts every day."

Mary looked at Benjamin with affection. Her husband possessed a strong but gentle spirit. She stroked his dark brown curly head of hair. "And you as well, Benjamin."

* * *

It was July before they knew it. With the departure time for the voyage only a month away, Thomas and Robert began the process of closing down Bennett Bros. Co. The villagers were disappointed to see the Bennetts leave. They had become dependent upon the products Thomas and Robert produced. Many of the customers had put in one last order for a new pair of boots or a fur hat for the upcoming winter months.

After the brothers completed their final orders, they wrapped their tools and supplies and secured them in wooden trunks. And finally, they took their company sign down, wrapping it in canvas. Their final act was to load everything onto the borrowed McKenzie wagon sitting ready in front of the building.

Robert looked at the heavily-loaded wagon. "Well, Thomas, there's our business all bundled and ready for our voyage."

"It's liberating, Robert. I feel like a new man."

Once the building was empty, they locked the door and stepped back and looked at it one last time. Robert took a deep breath. "This is it, Thomas. There's no turning back now."

"You're surely right, Robert, and I'm ready. Let's drop the key off to the landlord."

* * *

Two weeks later, Robert moved out of the boarding house. Since he had rented the room furnished, he had very little to take with him. The few possessions he owned fit into one trunk. Thomas arrived with the horse and wagon to bring Robert back to the McKenzie ranch. After they loaded Robert's trunk onto the wagon, he returned his room key to his landlady and settled up with her. She was disappointed to see Robert leave. She had hoped over time that Robert might show an interest in her, but there was no chance of it now.

"Thomas, before we leave, let's walk over to the general store and share a cold drink of cider with Abe," said Robert.

The familiar sound of the brass bells chimed when Thomas opened the door. He smiled at the store owner. "Good day, Abe. Have any cider on ice?"

Chapter 13

August 1854

Delhi, New York

The family had devoted several months of preparation for the journey. An abundant supply of fruits and vegetables had been laid out in the sun to dry during the summer. They cured meat by salting it down or smoking it. The McKenzies' smokehouse was filled with hanging hams that had been cured over a low, smoky fire for weeks, and the shelves held meat covered in salt, pepper and brown sugar. The salt drew the moisture from the meat, preventing it from rotting. Even though Thomas, Robert, and Benjamin would be cabin class passengers, and expected to be provided with food, they chose to be prepared in case of a food shortage. One could not know what might happen on such a long journey to their final destination.

***

It was the night before departure. All the trunks were packed with every necessity. They locked their trunks and lined them up in the front room near the door, ready to be loaded onto the wagon the next morning.

Jane's parents prepared a farewell dinner for the voyagers. The entire family gathered around the table to wish them well.

Edmund McKenzie clanged his wine glass and stood to make a toast. "Thomas and Jane, Ah remember a toast made tae ye on yer wedding day many years ago. Though ye hadn't planned tae live here in Delhi, Brenda and Ah have been so grateful tae the Lord for sending ye tae us. Watching ye grow together and create these wonderful children has been a blessing. Now that ye'r leaving for untamed lands, we're grateful for the time we've had together as a family. We wish ye Godspeed, health and happiness."

Then Edmund shifted his attention directly toward Thomas, and said, "And ye'll feel my furor if we don't hear from ye."

He continued. "Robert, ye'v been like a son tae us."

He turned to Benjamin, "Ye'r a good man, Benjamin, and we couldn't ask for a better husband for Mary. She made a fine choice. We'll miss each of ye."

There was a brief period of silence while a mix of emotions drifted around the table—love, excitement and exhilaration, uncertainty, fear, and sadness. It was a bittersweet farewell. Jane did her best to hold back a flood of tears, as did her sister and mother.

Thomas stood and returned the toast. He looked around the table at the people he might not see again. Jane's parents had welcomed them into their home when they were homeless, and he was jobless. Jane's sister, Abigail, and her husband, Charles, had been generous in their support of them. He glanced at Jane and saw she was on the verge of tears. *How will she fare without seeing her family on a daily basis to which she had become so accustomed?* It gave Jane some comfort when he offered their own house to Abigail and Charles, which was nearer to her parents.

Thomas raised his glass toward Jane's parents, "Mr. and Mrs. McKenzie, I thank you for everything you've done for us." He looked at their children sitting around the table, now grown up. "I must admit we have created a wonderful family, and I'm grateful for every moment of happiness they've brought to you. I pledge to you, I'll protect your daughter and our children with my life, and I make this promise to you today that we'll stay in contact with you despite the great distance between us. Transportation is continuing to improve, and I intend to send Jane back for a visit whenever possible. Cheers to you all."

Everyone raised their glass. "Cheers."

**

As the late summer sun rose from behind the hills the next day, the men prepared to leave and loaded the wagon with their trunks and baggage. Jonathan and Jeremy, who were to drive the wagon to take Thomas, Robert, and Benjamin to the New York harbor, harnessed the two horses to the wagon and waited on the front seat with reins in hand while everyone said their final goodbyes.

Thomas had made something special for his daughter, Elizabeth. He handed her a leather-bound journal, and said, "Lizzy, you seem to be the writer in this family. I'm giving you this journal so you can record your voyage to Puget Sound. Since I won't be with you, your journal entries will tell me how all of you fared."

"Oh, thank you, Father. I won't let you down."

"Open the journal, Lizzy."

Elizabeth opened the journal and saw an inscription inside:

August 1854

To my daughter, Elizabeth Bennett, from your loving father, Thomas Bennett.

Elizabeth hugged her father. "I'll treasure this forever."

Then Thomas turned to his wife. "I'll miss you, my dear wife. I'll miss everyone." Thomas gazed at Jane standing before him trying to be brave. He wanted to memorize that moment with the morning sun softly illuminating her face. He thought how beautiful she still was. He pulled her into his arms and kissed her, gently. They lingered in their embrace knowing it would need to last for several months.

It was time to board the wagon. They finished their final goodbyes. Robert shook hands with Mr. McKenzie and Charles. He kissed Mrs. McKenzie and Abigail on the cheek while he thanked them for their love and support during the past several years. Then he hugged his nieces. Thomas kissed Jane and each of his daughters one last time. Benjamin and Mary were locked in an embrace, eyes welling up with tears and apprehension.

Mrs. McKenzie handed Thomas a basket brimming with food. "Ye'll need to eat on yer way to New York City."

Thomas kissed her on the cheek and thanked her. No one could miss the aroma of fried chicken and freshly baked bread escaping the cloth-covered basket. She had included a crock of butter, preserves, a round of cheese, a berry pie and a bottle of wine. She had also thoughtfully tucked in utensils, which she had instructed the twins to bring back.

Thomas smiled at her as he peeked under the cloth covering the basket. "I'm going to miss your cooking, but I'll miss you most of all."

Saying goodbye to Jane's family was difficult. They would be so far away. Thomas hoped his words to them the night before gave them some comfort. Finally, the men boarded the wagon. Jonathan cracked the whip, and the horses jolted forward. The voyagers were on their way toward the beginning of a new life. The family watched the wagon and its occupants move away until they gradually disappeared into the distance.

Chapter 14

August 1854

New York City harbor

The *California II* lay at rest in the port while the crew prepared her for the upcoming voyage as the hour of departure rapidly approached. The Bennett brothers and Benjamin barely arrived on time to the loading dock and hurriedly unloaded their baggage to hand off to the handlers. The street was jammed with carriages and cabs delivering passengers to board the ship. Jonathan assisted while Jeremy calmed the nervous horses, which weren't accustomed to so much activity and noise. There was little time for long goodbyes. The men embraced Jonathan and Jeremy.

"Take care of your mother and sisters," Thomas said in a serious, fatherly voice.

"Yes, Father. Don't worry," said Jeremy.

"You can count on us," said Jonathan.

The three voyagers turned and waved to the twins as they wove their way through the crowds of scurrying people toward the pier at the end of Canal Street. They would wave at them one last time while standing at the rail of the ship as it departed. Jonathan and Jeremy struggled through the crowds and sought to find a vacant spot to wave goodbye to their family.

While the twin brothers waited for the ship's departure, Jonathan admired his uncle's ship, and envisioned being the captain of his own one day. The *California II* was two hundred three feet long, thirty-three and a half feet in beam, twenty feet in depth, and had a water draw of fourteen feet. Her capacity was one thousand fifty-seven gross tons, and she could hold two hundred passengers. She boasted two decks and three masts and sails that could be used as a secondary source of power. The ship was constructed of oak and cedar, and her hull was reinforced with diagonal iron straps. The steam engine turned two twenty-six-foot paddle wheels at the rate of thirteen revolutions per minute, which pushed her along between eight to fourteen knots. Salt water was used for the steam and five hundred-twenty tons of coal for fuel. Twelve firemen shoveled coal into her belly around the clock.

It was nearly noon. The ship's promenade deck was crammed with passengers squeezing close to the railing to wave farewell to those they were leaving behind. Thomas, Robert, and Benjamin stood on deck and leaned over the railing to catch a final glimpse of Jonathan and Jeremy. Jonathan watched the handlers hoist the baggage and mail up to the ship, the final task before departing. Jeremy spotted their family leaning over the ship's railing, shouting and waving to get their attention. Jonathan removed his red scarf from his neck and waved it high above the crowd. Thomas recognized his son's scarf and waved in recognition. They all waved and shouted as the ship moved from her berth and glided away from the wharf. It was a sight to witness. The paddle wheels splashed large water droplets into the air, glistening in the sun, and then the ship's loud throaty whistle blew a final farewell. The onlookers crowded onto the pier shouting their goodbyes while waving their handkerchiefs as they watched the mighty steamship's plume of steam billow from her tall stacks, leaving a cloud-like trail until the ship disappeared into the horizon.

***

Thomas, Robert, and Benjamin were anxious to check on their baggage. Robert pulled aside one of the crew members to inquire where baggage was stored. The man was in a rush to get on with his tasks but acknowledged them and quickly replied, "Aye, mates, yer baggage is stored below deck in the steerage compartment." He gestured toward the general proximity, then dashed off.

"Let's go there first before we find Philip," said Thomas.

They pushed through the throng of disoriented travelers and finally located the steerage area. The moment they climbed down to below deck, they realized their good fortune to be cabin class passengers. The space was dark and damp, and they grimaced at the unpleasant and lingering stench of vomit and bed pails. In stormy weather, it was necessary to batten down the hatches, contributing to the darkness and foul air. The passenger area was long and narrow, and the berths were tightly packed, one on top of the other. After squeezing through the crowded space, they found their baggage clustered together in a partition at the far end of the space. It looked satisfactory, so they lost no time in leaving the area.

Once they were back on deck, they sought out Philip. They worked their way toward the pilot house and found him giving instructions to some of his crew.

Philip saw them and smiled. "Brilliant, you found me. I saw you come aboard." He glanced over at Benjamin. "So, you must be my niece's husband, Benjamin. I'm sorry I wasn't able to attend your wedding. For that matter, I didn't make it to Thomas's wedding either. I guess nothing has changed over the years. I'm at sea most of the time." As Philip shook hands with Benjamin, he said, "Welcome to the family."

"It's good to finally meet you, Captain Bennett. Jonathan talks about you constantly. He wants to be just like you. I appreciate being included in this venture. I have to admit, I was apprehensive about coming. Mary is with child. She tried to put my mind at ease by assuring me she has plenty of family support and insisted I come."

Thomas and Robert nodded their heads in agreement.

"You don't need to be so formal, Benjamin. Call me Philip. Congratulations on becoming a father. My niece is a strong woman. I'm sure she and the babe will be fine. Now, let me show all of you to your quarters. I see you have your personal baggage with you. The rest of your baggage is in steerage."

Thomas replied, "Yes, we've already checked on it. It's hard to believe people can live down there on such a long journey. It's a dismal place, and there's no privacy. I hadn't realized how lucky we are to have our own cabin. What would we do without you, Philip?"

Philip motioned for them to follow him while he continued talking. "Yes, it's unfortunate for those who can afford nothing more than steerage quarters. For the benefit of the women, the space for them is segregated from the men. At least there is some privacy. Depending on the weather, I allow the passengers to be on deck as much as possible. Sometimes I let them sleep there, as long they're not underfoot. Unlike many ship captains, I provide them with basic food. On some ships, the passengers are expected to bring their own."

Benjamin was curious. "What kind of food do you give them, Captain—er, I mean Philip?"

"We provide potatoes, salt fish, beans and pork, hardtack, salted beef, and plum pudding, along with pea-coffee or tea as a beverage, and water of course. These are foods that will last without refrigeration. We give them fresh fish such as mackerel when we catch it. My chef will cook it up for them. You'll all see a big difference with the food provided for cabin class passengers."

They followed Philip down a hall past several cabin doors. When they reached a cabin at the end of the hall, he said, "Here's your room. I put you at the end to give you the most privacy. Now, I must take my leave. There's much to do. Come to the pilot house in an hour or two, and I'll tell you about our route."

The three men were exhausted and relieved to be settling into their cabin. It wasn't a large room, but there was enough space to hold two berths on one wall and a third on the opposite. The walls were lined with wood paneling, and the wood floor was covered with rugs. A chest of drawers sat at one end of the room, which held a bowl and pitcher. On the same wall, Benjamin noticed the bell pull and asked what it was.

Thomas answered, "That's how we ring for service."

Then Benjamin opened the door to what he assumed was a closet, but it was the privy.

"Look at this," he said, "we have our own privy!"

The privy was the latest model with an apparatus for pumping up salt water from the ocean. A privy in one's cabin was a luxury. Later, they learned from Philip that the people in steerage had to share the privies, and they were inconveniently located on the top deck; thus, the need for bed pails. Philip had been thoughtful and provided the women with a separate privy designated for them only.

After they finished surveying the cabin, they unpacked their bags. Each of them took a drawer in the chest. Besides a bag, Benjamin had carried in a case. Robert was curious.

"Benjamin, if I'm not intruding, may I ask what is in the case?"

"Of course, you're not intruding. Allow me to show you." He opened the case and brought out a violin, which he caressed with pride.

"This was handed down to me by my grandfather. It was made in Italy. With such a fine gift, it seemed fitting I should learn to play it. Mary hopes I'll teach our child one day."

Thomas was moved by his son-in-law's sentiment, then asked, "Would you play for us one night, Benjamin?"

"Yes, I'd be honored."

Thomas was nearly finished unpacking his bag when he discovered something on the bottom wrapped in a flour sack with a letter attached. The letter was from Edmund McKenzie. *A letter from Edmund McKenzie? What else could he possibly have to say to me?* Thomas anxiously read the letter.

Delhi, New York

August 1854

Thomas, ye said ye would protect my daughter and grandchildren with yer life. Ah'm giving ye something tae help ye keep yer promise. Thomas, ye've become like the son Ah've never had, and Ah want ye tae have something that belonged tae me. Guid luck on yer journey.

Edmund McKenzie.

Thomas was in a state of wonderment as he unwrapped this unexpected gift. His eyes widened when he saw a gun in a leather holster. It was a Colt Revolver multi-shot firearm with a long barrel, complete with a revolving cylinder, which could hold six bullets. The polished carved wood handle was trimmed in brass. Mr. McKenzie had also included a bag filled with a generous supply of bullets. Thomas was ecstatic. Money was tight, so he figured there would be no hope of purchasing a modern handgun. He owned a single-shot handgun given to him by his father when he left England years ago, along with a shotgun, and a hunting rifle. He held the Colt Revolver in his hand. It felt good, like it was meant to be in his hand. He yelled out to Robert and Benjamin. "Look what Jane's father gave me. She must have slipped it into my bag when she was helping me pack."

Robert asked in an envious voice, "May I hold it for a moment?" Thomas handed it to him, handle first. "This is really nice, Thomas. I'm going to have to get one of these someday, after we make our fortune that is."

Benjamin asked if he could hold it, and Robert handed it off to him. "This is what I call a gun!" He handed it back to Thomas.

As he cradled the gun in his hand, Thomas said, "This gift means a great deal to me. I've always felt Jane's father was disappointed that I'm his son-in-law instead of the other fellow who asked to court Jane."

"Well, Thomas," said Robert, "he's certainly making sure you don't forget about him, and in his way, he continues to put his protective arm around all of you. You never know, this gun may save your life. He's a good man, Thomas."

"You're right, Robert, and when I hold this gun in my hand, I feel a bond with him. I want Philip to see it. Speaking of him, shall we go to the pilot house and pay him a visit?"

Benjamin asked, "Can we explore a little first? I've never been on a ship."

Thomas smiled at his son-in-law. "Of course, we can, Benjamin."

Outside the cabin quarters, they followed a separate hall, which led cabin class passengers past a lounge area filled with comfortable chairs and settees. Next was a large dining saloon set up with several tables covered with white linen cloths and plush chairs for the diners. The room was lavish, and the dining experience could easily be compared to an evening at an elegant hotel in New York City. A typical dinner began with soup, followed by one of many varieties of freshly caught fish or roasted meat and roasted vegetables. A dessert such as pudding or pie and preserves was served afterward. The meal was topped off with fruit such as oranges, or dried fruit and nuts. Because there was a means of refrigeration on the ship, the chef was able to prepare any food he desired. Perishable food was stored in an ice room filled with large blocks of ice insulated with straw. Ice blocks had been loaded on to the ship while anchored in the harbor. The ice had been brought in by ship from Norway.

When they finished their tour of the dining area, Benjamin said, "I'm not going to mind eating in there. Never have I seen such a fancy place."

"No doubt, we'll be sitting at the Captain's table tonight," said Robert.

***

When the threesome entered the pilothouse, they were awestruck by the image of Philip in his captain's hat and uniform as he stood majestically next to the side of the giant wheel steering the ship. This was a much bigger vessel than the one they had traveled on to visit their parents in England. He looked distinguished in his uniform. His long slightly greying charcoal black hair was tied back at the nape. His sideburns, beard and mustache were manicured as always.

As he looked forward, he had an unobstructed view of the sea beyond. Nearby, there were bell pulls and speaking tubes ready for use. Then they noticed a dog sitting at attention next to him. It was a brown and white medium-sized Brittany spaniel. She had warm brown eyes and a light brown face with a white-patterned muzzle and pinkish tan nose.

Philip was excited to see them. With a sweeping bow, he announced, "Welcome to my world. We have a long voyage ahead of us. If all goes well, we'll be at sea for about five months. Depending on the weather, it could take longer."

They heard a whimper and turned their attention to the dog.

Surprised, Robert asked, "When did you decide to keep a dog on board?"

Philip chuckled. "I hadn't planned on getting a dog. It was fate, I guess. Several months ago, while making another trip to San Francisco, I saw her standing on the wharf when I disembarked. She looked lost and malnourished, so I asked around to see if anyone knew anything about her. They said they had no idea, but she'd been hanging around the wharf for several days. Some of the sailors shared their lunch with her. The poor thing just stood on the wharf waiting. I suspect someone dumped her there. How can the loyalty of such a dog be tossed away like that? How could I leave her behind? I call her Britta. She's become my faithful companion."

They all bent down to pet her, and Britta responded by wagging her short tail. Philip motioned to his first mate to take over the wheel.

"Now, let's take a look at the map." He led them to a small room and walked over to a slant-top table and unrolled a map he stored on a rack.

"You have our undivided attention," replied Thomas.

"Brilliant," said Philip. "We'll be traveling toward the southern tip of South America." He leaned over the table, and using his forefinger, traced the sixteen-thousand-mile journey on the map.

He continued, "We'll move along the Patagonian coast bypassing the Falkland Islands. We may experience some rough seas in this area. Then we'll enter the Strait of Magellan continuing our way west until we reach the Pacific Ocean.

"You'll have an opportunity to stretch your legs and post your letters at our first stop, Rio de Janeiro, where we'll replenish our water, food, wood, and coal. If the ship suffers any damage along the way, repairs will be made there. After we cross over to the Pacific, we'll stop at Valparaiso, Chile. As we continue on, our supplies will be getting low, so we'll stop at Callao, Peru, to replenish the ship at that port. Panama City will be our next port where we'll load supplies again. In about three weeks' time, we'll anchor at Acapulco to replenish any additional supplies needed.

"Our last stop before we continue on to Puget Sound will be San Francisco. Many of the passengers have chosen Frisco as their final destination and will disembark there. It's possible there will be some passengers waiting to board the ship who plan to go on to Puget Sound. We'll stay for a short time there while the ship is inspected again for any needed repairs, and mailbags and additional supplies are loaded. There is a post office there, so you'll be able to post your letters. The mail will be loaded on to the next vessel heading to the New York City harbor.

"While we're in San Francisco, I want to call on Captain Davis and introduce you. He'll play an important role in bringing our loved ones to us when we're ready for them to come.

"You'll see what I mean about the growth in San Francisco. I think it would be a good idea for us to acquaint ourselves with the city and establish connections. Once we depart, it should take us about a week to reach Washington Territory, where we'll land at the capital of the territory, Olympia.

"So there you are, the full itinerary. There may be a time or two that I'll take advantage of you being here and ask for your help. Nice to have family around. How's your first day on board been so far? Not seasick yet, are you? I hope not, you won't want to miss dinner. You'll sit at my table of course."

"We've had a good day so far, especially Thomas," said Robert.

"How so, Thomas?"

Thomas smiled, "I'll tell you about it tonight at dinner."

"I'm sure looking forward to eating in that fancy dining room," said Benjamin.

Philip heard his first mate calling out to him. "You'll have to excuse me, gentlemen. I'll see you tonight around six o'clock for dinner."

Chapter 15

*D*uring the voyage, the passengers found ways to occupy themselves. Thomas noticed many people writing in journals. He thought about Elizabeth and knew the journal he had given to her would help her pass the time. He observed people using their trunks as a surface to play cards, and during mealtime, using them as a table. There was a small group of musicians serenading the travelers, hoping for a tip now and then. A chaplain was on board to give a sermon on the Sabbath for any of the passengers who were interested. On occasion, he would lead the people in prayer if some poor soul's journey had ended. Their situation would suddenly become all too real as they witnessed the crew members slide a wrapped body into the sea.

The sea provided unexpected entertainment since it changed regularly. The passengers exclaimed in delight when they beheld the breathtaking appearance of a giant whale breaching the water. Sometimes they saw schools of porpoises frolicking in the waves. After viewing these spectacles firsthand, their spirits soared. They saw many types of sea birds flying above, displaying their agility or skimming the sea near the ship, waiting for a handout. Then without warning, the entertainment could be cut short in an instant. An angry squall might appear, ending a calm day.

During the second week of the voyage, a turbulent wind arrived like a ferocious lion, and the soft white ethereal clouds in the cerulean sky transformed into black storm clouds. The ship rolled and heaved on the foaming sea. The waves resembled giant rolling mountains and frothy valleys.

Storms like these challenged Philip and his crew. With the ship's large paddle wheels on each side of the vessel, it was critical for Philip to keep the ship balanced. In such turbulence, one paddle wheel could be spinning tumultuously in the air while the other wheel could be choking under water.

During this storm, many of the passengers experienced severe seasickness and desperately clung to their pails. The chests and trunks, which had been tightly secured in steerage, broke loose, rolling to and fro with the movement of the vessel. Many of the steerage passengers couldn't escape the rampant trajectory of the baggage, and sustained bumps and bruises, while others were jostled about along with the projectiles. Women and children were strapped into their bunks to prevent being thrown about or ending up in the path of the moving objects. There was mass chaos below deck. Because the latches had been battened down to prevent the sea from coming in, the passengers were left in total darkness.

The cabin class passengers who chose not to stay in their quarters dashed to the deck to hang their heads over the rail to heave. The cook keenly observed the sick and guessed he wouldn't be serving many dinners that night.

The next few days were calmer, providing a respite for the passengers. One day, a crew member cried out, "Porpoise!" Everyone on deck crowded the railing to see the sight. A group of torpedo-shaped porpoises shot out of the water like missiles twirling in unison and frolicked in and out of the sea as though performing a ballet. The passengers relished the scene and clung to every moment of the calm sea. Philip welcomed the jubilant sounds of friendly chatter and laughter among his passengers.

Thomas, Robert, and Benjamin spent time in the pilothouse visiting with Philip while watching him navigate the ship.

Thomas commented, "I wish Jonathan could be here. I'm certain we wouldn't be able to tear him away."

Eighteen days into the journey, Philip informed them, "We're now crossing the Equator heading south. When we cross to the Pacific Ocean and head north, we'll pass over it again."

Then he brought out the map and spread it on the table to show them the horizontal line representing the Equator, which ran across the upper portion of South America.

Thomas thought about Jonathan again, *I wouldn't be surprised if Jonathan knows all about this. He's always studying the maps his uncle sent him.*

Philip continued. "At the moment, we're in the tropics. We have been since we steamed past Florida, and it'll be awhile before we're out. I'm taking advantage of the prevailing winds common in this area."

He ordered his crew to unfurl the sails. Using the sails would cut down on the consumption of the coal and wood.

It was apparent Philip needed to give his full attention to navigate the ship, so his brothers and Benjamin left the pilothouse and strolled the deck.

Benjamin, fanning himself with his hand, said, "So this is what the tropics feel like. I'm about to start removing some clothes."

The tropic heat was oppressive, and the air muggy. The passengers who stayed below in steerage were close to suffocating, and some had passed out. Others were too listless to leave their berth. Many of them struggled to the deck gasping for any amount of fresh air.

Despite the uncomfortable heat, there were pleasant distractions. One day they were startled by splashes in the water.

Someone shouted out, "Look, there are hundreds of fish flying in the air!"

It was a magnificent sight. The passengers ran to the side of the vessel to witness the pageantry. Many of the passengers had never been on the ocean before this journey and were amazed at all the new and exciting experiences. And in the darkness of night, the voyagers were mesmerized as they gazed at the golden moon illuminating its reflection in the ocean, and the phosphorescence of luminous frothy waves that sparkled like gems.

Chapter 16

September 1854

Ports of Call

*A*fter a month at sea, the steamship chugged into her first port of call, Rio Harbor in the tropical city of Rio de Janeiro. The passengers were anxious and excited and looked forward to stepping on to terra firma.

As the vessel approached, the occupants saw their first sight of land. A grand range of mountains peeked through the clouds. The mountains were covered in rich green vegetation. At the base of the mountain range, white sandy beaches sparkled in the sun. In other areas, large craggy rocks dotted the shoreline. The voyagers marveled at the explosion of waves crashing onto the rocks thrusting large sprays of water into the air. The tropics bestowed a sensory experience of rich perfumes and exotic scenery, not unlike a temptress luring her visitors while satiating their senses.

As the *California II* entered the harbor, it glided past ancient Moorish-looking fortresses, towering palms, and cocoas. Robert, Thomas, and Benjamin stood at the railing absorbing every sight, sound, and mixture of fragrant aromas. They marveled at the rich coffee plantations of Praya Grande that stretched into long lines of green. When the vessel approached its anchor point, they could hear the babble of the Portuguese boatmen in their small boats loaded with tropical fruits to sell. Other vessels had come into port, creating a great deal of activity as the passengers disembarked. It was a scene of hustle and bustle. Everyone was anxious to stretch their legs and explore the Marble City.

Robert, Thomas, and Benjamin and the rest of the passengers disembarked. Benjamin lost his balance for a moment. "I'm on land, but I feel like I'm still moving."

Philip stayed behind to secure his ship and told his brothers and Benjamin that he and Britta would join them in a few hours. Since they would be in port for about two weeks, he asked Thomas to locate the *Hotel Imperial* and reserve a couple of rooms for them. "You won't have any trouble finding it, it's the yellow hotel on the main thoroughfare."

Soon, they spotted the hotel. There was a large sign on the front that read *Hotel Imperial. Cleanest sheets in Rio*! After settling into the hotel, they found a place to eat. There was no shortage of eateries and hotels. Since the Gold Rush in California, the inhabitants thrived on the tourism it had created.

They continued to explore the exotic city. They saw beautiful foliage and gardens filled with fig and orange trees, oleander, marigolds and sunflowers. They visited the Bishop's Palace. The exterior of the palace was quite shabby, but the interior was an unexpected surprise. It was majestic and adorned with beautiful fixtures.

The beauty they experienced, however, was a paradox to what they saw firsthand throughout the city—slavery. It was shocking to them. The streets were filled with blacks working in chain gangs. All of them wore a brand on their forehead, shoulder or back.

The source of water for the city came from an ancient aqueduct, which was considered to be the finest water source in the world. They saw hundreds of fountains from which the *Rio Negro* filled their containers and balanced them on their heads as they walked.

There were beautiful churches made of wood and plaster adorned with gilded trim. They also visited the Imperial Palace and Garden. Philip made plans to round out their experience in Rio. He had connections for tickets and took them to a bullfight.

Finally, it was time to depart the Marble City. Rio provided an exhilarating experience for the voyagers. Everyone was refreshed and ready to continue their journey. They had eaten plenty of fresh fish, fruits and vegetables, and drank the purest water.

After the repairs on his ship were completed, Philip made a final inspection to make sure it was ready to go. The ship was replenished with a new supply of coal and wood. Fresh fruits, vegetables, wine, and water had also been loaded. Many of the passengers had purchased their own variety of fresh food from the markets to bring on board.

Precisely at noon, the whistle blew, and the lines were cast off. As the ship left the sunny harbor and steamed toward the sea, the voyagers looked back at the city and admired Sugarloaf and Hunchback, the two sentinel mountains guarding the port.

* * *

With the course set southward, Philip guided his ship toward the Strait of Magellan, located at the southern tip of Cape Horn. It had been three weeks since they left Rio de Janeiro. He wanted to prepare his passengers for the next leg of the journey. He asked everyone to gather on the deck so he could speak to them.

"The closer we get to Cape Horn, the colder it will get. I guarantee you'll feel a drop in the temperature. Be prepared to dress in warm clothing and bring out your blankets. The tip of South America is separated from Antarctica by only about six hundred miles. We'll need to be on the lookout for icebergs, which can break loose and float in our direction. Also, the seas can be very high, making it difficult to see obstructions. The seas can be thirty to a hundred feet high, depending on the weather. I ask all of you to keep your eyes peeled to help us avoid a collision with icebergs. They are much larger than they look. Their actual size is hidden below the surface. Your safety is my highest priority."

The passengers were noticeably silent and nervous but nodded their heads in affirmation. Knowing the captain would have many sets of eyes on the lookout made them feel safer. They felt some control by being participants of the watch, albeit minimal. Philip knew this. His experience taught him to educate his passengers, which would give them a feeling of inclusion and confidence in him.

As he made eye contact to the group he thought, *I'm not about to allow panic on my ship.*

Thomas whispered to Robert, "Our brother is an impressive leader."

"Yes, I was thinking the same thing. We haven't had much of an opportunity to see him in action," Robert whispered back.

After Philip finished talking to his passengers, he dismissed them. They chatted amongst themselves and disbursed.

As the ship steamed along, the passengers saw sunfish, more porpoise and periodically, a shark. These sightings helped to distract their minds from what they knew might lie ahead of them. The crew put out some lines and hooks and caught a few fish to contribute toward the food supply. The fishing also provided some entertainment. The crew invited some of the younger male passengers to learn how to fish in the ocean. They eagerly accepted the invitation. After being at sea for several weeks since leaving Rio, fresh fish for dinner was a welcome addition. In the evenings, the passengers enjoyed looking up at the night sky where they saw the brightest of constellations, and the famous Southern Cross with its four bright stars composed in the shape of a cross.

The further south they traveled, the more the temperature dropped, and they were soon engulfed in fog. Benjamin, Thomas, and Robert stayed on deck to watch for any obstacle lurking in the ocean. Suddenly, Thomas thought he heard what sounded like slow breathing. He whispered, "Do you hear that?"

At that moment, the fog thinned, and though it was just barely visible, they saw a large black body slowly rise and break the surface, spouting a fountain of water into the atmosphere. The mighty creature was a sperm whale. Their eyes widened. "What a magnificent sight," said Robert, "It must be a hundred feet long."

* * *

Robert, Thomas, and Benjamin had just returned to their cabin after enjoying tea in the dining saloon when there was a knock on their cabin door. Startled, Robert responded, "I wonder if that's Philip?" He opened the door.

"Good day, *Messrs.* Bennett and Spencer. May I introduce myself?

I am Samuel, the Captain's first mate. He sent me to ask you to join him in his cabin. Follow me, if you please."

Curious, but happy for the opportunity to visit with Philip privately in his cabin, they followed Samuel. He tapped on the cabin door lightly. Philip opened it, and smiling, motioned for them to enter. He turned his attention back to Samuel. "That will be all for now, Samuel, thank you."

Thomas noticed a bottle of champagne and four glasses sitting on the table, and grinned, "What's this, Philip?"

"Well, gentlemen, we're very close to leaving the Atlantic behind, which means we're approaching the halfway point. Once we travel through the Strait, we will be on the Pacific Ocean side. I'd like to share a toast with you." He opened the bottle. There was a loud pop as he extracted the cork, and he slowly poured the bubbly golden liquid into the four glasses. "Let us toast to a successful venture, and to the success of our journey."

They clicked their glasses and enjoyed the champagne, along with the rare opportunity to spend some quiet time together. After his brothers and Benjamin left his cabin, Philip chose not to worry about what may lie ahead. *Maybe we'll be lucky.*

***

For awhile, the passengers enjoyed occasional moments of calm and were entertained by flocks of seabirds, which seemed to be following the ship. They watched albatross glide by. The snowy white birds had long hooked orange beaks and lengthy black flapping wings spanning nearly eight feet. Cape pigeons flew along both sides of the ship and landed on the water waiting for the passengers to throw food. Once rewarded, the pigeons dove down as the food sank.

Samuel called out to the passengers, "We hold these birds in high regard. Many ships have traveled between New York and San Francisco, and many ships have gone down taking all on board to a watery grave. There is a legend that the pigeons hold the souls of the sailors, and the albatross hold the spirit of the commanders."

Then the crew members, for a moment, took off their hats and put their hand on their heart as they gazed at the birds. Being superstitious wasn't uncommon among sailors on the high sea.

As the ship steamed further south toward the Strait of Magellan, the temperature dropped. The ship was besieged with squalls of hail and snow. Even the deck and railings iced up. None of the passengers ventured on to the deck. Hot tea was in demand. The days grew shorter, and the nights longer. The cabin class passengers had the luxury of small stoves in their cabin, but the passengers in steerage could only bundle up, clustering together to use each other's body heat for warmth.

The wind howled as they headed toward the Strait. The Strait of Magellan was a three-hundred-fifty-mile natural passage between the Atlantic and Pacific oceans situated at the southern extremity of South America. It was a natural wind tunnel with numerous twists and turns and varying widths and was susceptible to cold, violent, unpredictable winds and currents.

The ocean was choppy. As the winds and currents grew stronger, the steamship rode the sea like a bucking bronco. The passengers gripped their pails as they faced the possibility of seasickness again.

The blackness of night came early, but the sea calmed. The ship traveled along the Patagonian coast advancing toward the mouth of the Strait close to the latitude of forty degrees south. As usual, the crew members rotated shifts throughout the night to keep watch. They shared a special bond and looked out for each other.

In the half-light of dawn, a large black cloud rolled in. Squalls of rain and hail pounded the ship. The gales grew in intensity. Once the ship reached the latitudes between forty and fifty degrees, it entered the *Roaring Forties,* which were strong, persistent gale force winds blowing in from the west.

The first mate shouted out, "All hands on deck!" The crewmen scrambled and dressed in their oilskins and rushed topside to the deck. Some of the crewmen climbed up the icy, slippery masts to make sure the sails were furled tightly before the wind could rip them to shreds. They ordered any passengers remaining on deck to return to their quarters.

After the decks were cleared of passengers, the crewmen battened down the hatches above the steerage quarters. The passengers in steerage made preparations. The men lashed women and children to the berths, and then hung on to anything that was immobile. They kept bed pails close by.

The cabin class passengers also readied themselves for a rough ride. One of the crew members checked each cabin to extinguish any fire that might be lingering in a stove. A fire on a ship could spread rapidly and would result in a disastrous scene.

Thomas, Robert, and Benjamin were tucked away in their cabin dressed in their warmest clothes. Philip had asked Samuel to take Britta to his brothers' cabin so she wouldn't be underfoot. Everyone steadied themselves for a rough ride.

Suddenly, Benjamin felt sick. He remembered the stench he and his comrades smelled when they had gone down to the steerage area to check on their baggage. He didn't want to subject his roommates to the same unpleasantness. Without thinking about the power of the storm, he burst from the cabin with the door slamming shut behind him, and ran toward the deck, bending over the railing to heave. With the loud roar of the storm consuming their cabin, Thomas and Robert didn't hear the door slam shut when Benjamin rushed out. They were unaware that he had left the cabin. The room was dark since during a storm, candles and lanterns weren't allowed. Britta was upset. At first, they assumed she was afraid of the storm, but she kept scratching at the door and barking.

Then Thomas realized they hadn't heard Benjamin's voice lately. He called out. No response.

Robert worked his way toward Benjamin's berth. "Is it possible he's sleeping through all of this?" Benjamin wasn't there. "He's not here. I think Britta has been trying to tell us he's gone."

The storm gained momentum. The wind screamed, and the sky blackened. The giant swells were like rolling mountains, and the ship climbed to their peaks. Then the vessel plunged downward as though it were diving to the bottom of the sea. As the *California II* slid into the abyss with the sea breaking over her deck, the forward part of the ship was covered with water waist-high. The waves continued to build momentum and grew larger and stronger. Every man on deck worked to control the ship. It seemed as though they were breathing water instead of air.

Meanwhile, Philip and Samuel had their hands full in the pilothouse. The monster waves threw the ship off balance, causing one of the paddle wheels to whirl in the air and the other to choke under water. They fought to bring the ship under their control. The faithful lady eventually steadied herself for her master in the storm. Philip and Samuel had no idea what had been happening on deck but knew there was a possibility of casualties.

With knuckles white, Benjamin held on tightly to the rail as he heaved. He was so sick he hadn't paid attention to the waves increasing in size until the moment he lifted his head. His eyes widened, and he stood frozen when he saw a huge monster wave, which looked like a tall wall of water heading straight toward him. By the time he came to his senses from the shock, it was too late. The wave smacked him directly and flung him through the air so hard, he was in danger of being washed overboard on the opposite side of the ship—but instead—he slammed up against the main mast. His head took a direct hit, but he stayed conscious long enough to grab a rope that was tied to the mast and wrapped it around his wrist. This last-minute action saved him from being hurled straight into the out-of-control paddle wheel whirling in the air. Gallons of seawater washed over him as each wave hit the ship.

The crewmen had been clinging hard onto the railing with arms interlinked. The same wave that crashed onto Benjamin washed one of the crewmen overboard. He was inexperienced, and had panicked. When he saw the wall of water coming toward them, he broke loose from the other men and tried to outrun the wave. The men had been instructed to never try to outrun a giant wave about to hit the ship but to hang on tightly to a railing or anything immovable. The other crew members witnessed it, and yelled, "Man overboard!" It was so dark and the water so turbulent, they knew there was no saving him, especially wearing heavy oilskins. He would sink immediately.

Then, as the storm eased up, they heard Benjamin's intermittent moans and found him lying semiconscious nearly face down in three feet of water. If the water hadn't sloshed back and forth as the ship rocked, he could have drowned.

The storm eased, and there was a slight lull. Thomas and Robert left the cabin to look for Benjamin. The night was so black, they felt like they were wearing blinders. The brothers brought Britta with them. Thomas used a piece of rope that had been used on his luggage, and tied it onto her collar, letting her lead the way to find Benjamin. They had just come within earshot and heard the crewmen shouting that a man had gone overboard. They feared the worst.

Thomas moaned. "How will I tell Mary? She'll never forgive me for bringing Benjamin with us."

Suddenly, Britta broke away from Thomas and ran toward a group of men huddled around an injured man by the main mast. Robert and Thomas followed closely behind her. It was Benjamin. He was alive.

Robert asked the men tending Benjamin to carry him to their cabin. Thomas rushed to find the doctor on board and returned with him. The doctor examined Benjamin and ascertained he had sustained a concussion when he slammed into the mast. The mast had a protruding bolt which caused the large gash on his head as well. Benjamin shivered uncontrollably.

The doctor said, "He is suffering from hypothermia. We must get him into dry clothes and raise his body temperature immediately. Now that the storm is over, give him hot tea when he wakes."

Thomas and Robert rubbed Benjamin's body vigorously and wrapped him like a cocoon in wool blankets. After some time had passed, Benjamin regained consciousness. When he awoke, he was confused, and his head hurt.

With groggy eyes, he looked at Thomas and Robert. "What happened?"

"We'll talk about it later, Benjamin. You need to rest. Right now, drink this hot tea," insisted Thomas.

* * *

The first calm day after the storm, many voices prayed in unison:

Our Father, who art in heaven,
Hallowed by thy Name.
Thy Kingdom come,
Thy will be done on earth,
As it is in heaven...

All on board the ship gathered to participate in the prayer led by the chaplain for the lost crew member. Their eyes focused on the young sailor's belongings on display as they prayed. It was heart-wrenching to see young Timothy's belongings, representing his life. Benjamin, with his head still bandaged, stood motionless and stared at the orphaned belongings. Thomas and Robert stood next to him. He thought about how close he came to death's doorstep. *They could have been praying over me, too, had fate not stepped in to save me.*

After the memorial service, Captain Bennett was obliged to hold an auction for Timothy's effects. By law regulating navigation, a captain was required to allow the other crew members to bid on a deceased's belongings. The auction was somber, quiet, and respectful. Those crew members who purchased any of Timothy's clothes would not wear them while on board. They felt it would be disrespectful to Timothy's memory and, being superstitious, believed it would bring bad luck.

Philip was heavy-hearted to lose one of his crew members. He had always made an effort to know each member. He was a good captain, and his crew members had no desire to serve any other. Philip announced he would make sure that all the money raised would go to Timothy's young wife and babe. He was sorry he wouldn't be able to give her the news about Timothy in person. Instead, he would post a letter and packet to her at the next available mail stop.

That night when the crew retired to their quarters, even by averting their eyes, they couldn't avoid the presence of the empty berth. They were quiet and pensive for many nights to come.

Chapter 17

*C*aptain Bennett noted the date, October 21, 1854, in his log. They had been at sea since August. The captain navigated the *California II* through the unpredictable wind tunnel without any further hardship. The passage was cold and icy due to some williwaw winds, which brought in a few polar gusts descending from the mountainous coast.

Once the ship reached the Pacific Ocean side, the seas were calmer and the temperature warmer. The *California II* passed along the western side of the Patagonian coast at a safe distance from the coastline, but close enough for all to view the splendor of the majestic mountain ranges.

The next stop was Valparaiso, Chile. It was the first major stopping point after leaving the Strait passage and entering the Pacific Ocean. The city of Valparaiso was considered the springboard to the North American coast. While the ship rested and was inspected for any needed repairs, the passengers welcomed a much-needed respite, although brief, to explore the city refreshing body and soul.

The passengers embraced the opportunity to experience a different culture. They followed narrow cobbled streets past colorful one-story buildings built of adobe and sun-dried brick. There were no doors on the entrances, and the walls were four to six feet thick. The thick walls were necessary to withstand the frequent earthquakes common in that area. Several of the passengers visited the open markets and purchased fresh fruit and vegetables to carry on board.

They stayed at Valparaiso for two and a half days while the *California II* underwent repairs. By the end of the second day, she was ready to sail. The next morning fresh supplies were loaded and stored, and she was fitted out and ready to depart. At noon, the people of Valparaiso heard the ship's whistle blow and ran to wave farewell to the travelers as the *California II* steamed toward the open sea.

As the ship headed north toward the seaport of Callao, Peru, the travelers enjoyed more spectacles along the way. They saw whales again, still a magnificent sight, but no longer a shock to their eyes. The Pacific Ocean offered new excitements. They marveled at the display of swordfish, marlin, and sailfish leaping high into the air, bursting from the ocean's surface—a spectacular view with their long sword-like bills and dorsal fins. The sailfish were equally impressive with tall fins running the top length of their body in the shape of an elongated fan. The passengers scurried to the railings to witness the pageant of regalement. There was also tuna, which became prey to the sailor's harpoon. Everyone looked forward to enjoying tuna steak that night, and since the seas in the Pacific were calm, no one felt seasick, and everyone had an appetite.

One week after leaving Valparaiso, the *California II* glided into the protected bay of Callao, the port of call to the capital city of Lima, Peru. The weather was warm, but comfortable due to the cool ocean breezes wafting through the air. The bay was protected on the west side by the island of San Lorenzo. Many American, French, Chilean, and Peruvian ships occupied this port. With the business of loading and unloading so many ships, the wharf brimmed with activity.

When the *California II* passengers disembarked, they heard the mixed hum of voices in different languages of the passengers from other ships. Captain Bennett informed his passengers that the ship hadn't suffered any additional damage, so their sojourn would be brief, and they would only be in port long enough to replenish supplies. They would need to board the ship that night as soon as they heard the whistle blow. He planned to depart at daylight the next day.

The town was easy to find. The paved main road ran parallel with the bay. With little time to waste, the passengers rushed to leave the wharf to begin exploring. Thomas, Robert, and Benjamin separated as usual from the group of passengers and created their own itinerary. As they walked past the houses in town, they noticed a similarity to those in Valparaiso, but there were more varieties. The more affluent people lived in flat-roofed two-story adobe houses complete with beautiful balconies. The middle-class lived in single-story homes, which stood ten feet high. Some of these houses possessed grated windows. Some houses were built with a single doorway that opened into one room. The houses of the lower-class were made of dried mud with the ceilings, windows, and doors covered in nothing more than matting.

Anyone who wished to purchase food went to the market square. It wasn't as pleasant as the one in Valparaiso. The square was a dusty and disorganized environment. There was a selection of fish, beef, chicken, vegetables, and fruit, but not local. The food came from Lima on the back of donkeys.

The *California II* had arrived at the port on a Saturday. It was an opportune time for the passengers to become bystanders of a religious tradition, which took place every Saturday in the early evening. A priest and his devotees walked down the street chanting their prayer while carrying small portable alters decorated with tinsel holding a variety of colored lamps and a primitive painting of the Virgin Mary. During this time, the townspeople gave a tithing to their church.

Robert, Thomas, and Benjamin joined the other bystanders to watch the procession. Benjamin was moved by the sight and felt he had been saved by the hand of God. He turned to Robert and Thomas, "I'll be right back." Then he reached into his pocket and brought out a coin. He walked up to the priest and handed him the silver.

The Priest responded, "Gracias," and clasped Benjamin's hands.

As they watched Benjamin, Thomas and Robert expressed their gratitude that they wouldn't have to tell Mary she would never see her husband again. They looked at each other and nodded. They pulled out a coin and walked over to the priest and did the same. The priest bowed his head, thanking them.

The whistle blew, and everyone scurried to the ship. The next morning at first light, the *California II* left the port of Callao behind and continued north toward Panama City. As they approached the tropics, Captain Bennett ordered his men to unfurl the sails to take advantage of the trade winds. He instructed his crew to tell the passengers to meet him on the deck so he could give them an update of their route.

In a jubilant voice, he announced, "As you've probably noticed, we're back in the tropics. You'll find the tropical heat to be more tolerable on the Pacific side. There are some excellent trade winds, so we'll be sailing as long as they are with us. We will be crossing the Equator again shortly after we pass Ecuador. Our next stop is Panama City. We'll spend a few days there. And, you'll be happy to know we're on the last leg of our journey!"

Everyone clapped and cheered.

* * *

It was five days later, November 3rd. Upon entering the Panama harbor, Philip noticed a large group of rough-looking men gathered on the wharf staring straight at his ship. Not knowing what to expect, he gave the order to drop anchor a safe distance away from the wharf.

Philip assumed the men were waiting to board the first available ship heading to San Francisco. He figured the men had most likely taken the Panama route traveling over the Isthmus from the Atlantic side. He knew about that journey—it was rough. They would have disembarked from a ship on the east side of the Isthmus at the mouth of the Chagres River in Panama, traveled thirty miles in a dugout canoe to the city of Gorgona, and then traveled the remaining twenty-five miles on foot, or on the back of a mule, over the old Spanish trail to Panama City. They would have endured humid heat, sweat, insects, and the threat of malaria.

Philip recalled deciding which route Thomas's family should take. The Panama route would have been a much more dangerous and tortuous experience, and so he chose the safer Nicaragua route instead.

Philip's assessment was correct. These men had experienced such a trip, and they had been waiting for weeks in Panama City for the right ship to arrive. There was a local paper called the *Panama Herald*, which was published for the benefit of travelers landing in the city. There were ads for hotels, bars, restaurants, and most importantly—news of any ships. The group of men anxiously awaited the arrival of the *California II* and expected to board the vessel. Philip's ship was at full capacity. In fact, there were more passengers on board than usual. The food and water supply would diminish rapidly if he allowed any more passengers to board his ship.

When the locals saw the *California II* anchored in the harbor, a man rowed a small boat toward the ship. It was customary for the locals to approach a ship at anchor and charge a small fee to provide transportation to shore. Philip announced to the crew and passengers that he suspected trouble ashore, and to ensure their safety, he couldn't allow them to leave the ship.

He spoke privately to Samuel, "I want you to arm several men with rifles, and station them along the side of the ship facing the shore. Keep the rifles out of sight. If there's trouble, I'll signal you to have them show their rifles."

"I'll take care of it, Captain. Good luck," said Samuel.

Philip asked his brothers to go ashore with him and to bring their guns.

"This is one of those times when I need your help. Keep your guns out of sight unless we need them."

They strapped on their weapons, concealing them under their shirts. Benjamin wanted to go along, but they told him to stay on the ship since he was still weak.

Philip observed Benjamin's disappointment, so to help him feel more useful, he gave Benjamin a job.

"Benjamin, I'd appreciate it if you would keep an eye on Britta. She knows you. If we *all* left the ship, she'd probably jump into the water to follow us." Philip looked at Britta standing next to him, and commanded her to stay.

Benjamin grabbed Britta's collar. "Yes, sir, Captain, I mean Philip. I'll take care of her."

Britta was already straining at Benjamin's grip to follow Philip as he walked away.

When the small boat arrived, the Bennett brothers hopped on. Philip asked the boatman if he spoke English. "A little," he said.

Philip informed him that once they were ashore, he would like to immediately speak to the man in charge of supplying provisions for the ships. The man agreed to bring the supply manager to him. Minimally, Philip hoped to get fresh water loaded onto the ship. He had saved fuel by using the sails in the trade winds, so he figured he had enough to get to Acapulco. Food would need to be rationed, and they would rely more on catching fish.

When they arrived at the wharf, the boatman tied up his boat and hurried to fetch the supply manager. Philip and his brothers ignored the group of men while waiting for the manager. When the manager arrived, Philip quietly explained what he needed, and that time was of the essence. Then he discretely handed the man some cash. The manager nodded and said he would grant Philip's request expeditiously.

Meanwhile, Robert and Thomas had been listening to the rumblings of the unsettled group of men.

Robert murmured, "Thomas, there must be fifty to sixty men over there. From the sound of their voices, they remind me of those Irish gang members in New York City. They really *do* think they're boarding."

"They're also armed," replied Thomas. He laid his hand on his holstered gun.

Philip planned to act normal, and once the water was loaded onto the ship, they would make a quick getaway. He motioned to Thomas and Robert to walk to town with him. When they arrived at the town center, they found the local police. After they introduced themselves, Philip explained their situation to the commander in charge.

"Commander Valdez, I'm sure you're aware of the large group of men standing near the wharf. It's obvious to me they have every intention of boarding my ship. We've noticed they're armed. I'm sure they have endured a rough trip to get here and have been waiting for a ship to board to go to California, and I sympathize, but I'm afraid it can't be my ship. It's already at full capacity. They appear to be a tough bunch, and most likely won't take no for an answer. Once the fresh water is loaded onto my ship, we'll depart, but I'm certain we will need your protection to leave without them trying to board." After they discussed a plan, Philip reached into his pocket for some cash. "Here's something for your trouble."

When Philip and his brothers left the police headquarters, they stayed out of sight of the men but positioned themselves close enough to watch for the agreed signal from the supply manager when the fresh water was securely loaded onto the ship. About an hour later, they saw the manager wipe his brow with his bandana. That was the signal. The brothers approached the wharf, and as expected, the group of men confronted them with their demand.

"I'm truly sorry fellas, but my ship is at full capacity. I can't let you board. It won't be long before we reach our destination of San Francisco. I'll personally speak on your behalf and inform the shipping schedule manager about your situation and ask him to make sure a ship stops here for you."

The men didn't like Philip's answer and told him they knew of other ship captains who had taken on passengers regardless of being at full capacity. The lead man reached into his pocket and flashed a roll of bills. "We have money."

Philip was aware that some captains had risked the safety of his crew and passengers by sailing at over capacity. He also knew that many of those captains' actions resulted in tragedies. *It's always about money. Well, not this captain!*

Reacting to Philip's answer, some of the men pulled out their guns, and demanded, "We're boarding that ship!"

Thomas and Robert had been standing behind Philip and stepped forward to his side with their guns drawn. During the confrontation, the crowd of men hadn't noticed that several policemen had lined up behind them holding rifles pointed straight at them.

Philip said, "I'd put the guns down if I were you. Take a look behind you."

The men turned to see several rifles aimed at them.

"You have your choice. Spend your time in a saloon or a jail cell. It's up to you. We'll be leaving now. Despite your threats, I'll keep my word and report your situation. Believe me, I sympathize with you. I realize you've had a rough journey getting here, and you're anxious to continue on, but not on my ship."

At that moment, Philip pointed at his ship. That was Samuel's signal to let the firearms show. The men looked toward the ship where they saw shafts of sunlight glinting on gunmetal, revealing more rifles pointed toward them.

The men glared at Philip and his brothers, but they put their handguns back into their holsters and their rifles down. The Bennett brothers slowly backed away from the men and slipped into the strategically-placed boat. As the boatman rowed them toward the safety of the ship, Philip saluted Commander Valdez and his men. The Commander ordered his men to keep their rifles aimed at the group of men until Philip and his brothers boarded their ship. The whistle blew, and the stranded men could do nothing but watch the *California II* steam out of the harbor.

* * *

One week later, they were approaching Acapulco, Mexico, their last stop before reaching San Francisco. The steamer entered the deep, slightly hidden crescent-shaped bay, which was surrounded with wild, rugged volcanic mountains covered with lush vegetation. The towering mountain of Caravali was at the center, framed by golden beaches and an ornamental scene of various tropical trees and foliage. Cocoa, lime, and banana trees were abundant along with tall coconut palms topped with graceful crowns of giant feather-shaped leaves. Single-level adobe houses with tile or thatched roofs arranged in orderly layers covered the mountainsides. Still remaining as a reminder of the previous earthquake that shook the city two years earlier, the ruins of crumbled buildings remained, dotting the landscape. It was a picturesque scene, with the ruins contributing their own beauty and mystery.

Captain Bennett told his crew and passengers they would stay for four days in this charming harbor and city to compensate for the disappointment in Panama City. The leisurely stay would allow more than enough time to replenish the ship with the much-needed supplies. Philip was quick to take advantage of the abundance of Mexican textiles available for purchase, knowing he could easily resell them for a handsome profit in San Francisco.

Thomas noticed many of the buildings in the city looked newly built, and yet, the city was old. He asked Philip if he knew what had happened.

"Yes, I do. Acapulco has been through several transformations with its troubled past. It was a busy port with a thriving economy, but it attracted pirates.

"To defend their city, the Spaniards built Fort San Diego in 1616. Then a few years later, Dutch pirates attacked and overran the fort, leaving the city helpless. There were many notorious pirates. Have you ever heard of Sir Francis Drake?"

Thomas nodded. "I have heard the name."

"Not so long ago, I believe it was around 1814, Acapulco was burned to the ground during the Mexican War of Independence. The city suffered until the California gold rush began about six years ago in 1848. It became a regular stopping point for ships carrying thousands of people on their way to California hoping to strike it rich. Now the city has been rebuilt, and once again, it is prospering."

Thomas was impressed with Philip's knowledge. "Acapulco has endured a rough time. How do you know all this?"

Philip shaded his eyes from the bright sun while glancing at his ship anchored in the port, and replied, "I make it a practice to learn as much as I can about the ports I enter."

Then he turned his attention toward Robert and Benjamin wandering around in the marketplace. Benjamin stopped at a vendor's stand. "Speaking of learning, I see Benjamin is about to lose money to an unscrupulous vendor over there. I've already learned my lesson with *that* thief. I'd better rescue him before *he* learns the same lesson."

The four days passed too quickly for the passengers. They reveled in everything the city had to offer. The markets were clean and well organized and filled to the brim with fresh fruits and vegetables. Many of the passengers bought a quantity of bananas, limes, oranges, and coconuts for their personal supply on the ship. They frolicked on the beach and laid out their newly purchased Mexican blankets on the warm sand while the sun bathed their bodies. The children ran shoeless and waded in the surf and squealed with delight as the waves chased them back to the beach. The four days invigorated and rejuvenated the voyagers, and for that, they could thank their Captain Bennett.

Chapter 18

December 1854

San Francisco, California

*G*t was December 5th when the *California II* slid into the Golden Gate harbor. Thomas, Robert, and Benjamin strained to see San Francisco Bay for the first time. Through the mist, they saw hundreds of masts in the harbor and long wharves extending out into the water. Hillsides covered with houses layered one on top of the other surrounded the bay. They passed by Telegraph Hill proudly displaying the American flag from the top of its wood-framed structure. Telegraph Hill was the vantage point to send signals when ships entered the harbor. Seeing the American flag proudly waving, was a reminder that just four years earlier, in 1850, California had become the thirty-first state to join the Union.

The large wharves were crowded with throngs of people awaiting loved ones to arrive from their long journeys. Others eagerly anticipated the arrival of the mail ships, and when those ships arrived, they watched for the mailbags to be unloaded and delivered to the nearby post office building. It wasn't unusual to stand in line for hours for mail. It was a small sacrifice if there was a letter waiting from a loved one, separated by land or sea. The mail was their only connection. Curious onlookers contributed to the commotion, along with draymen and cabmen who hastened to the scene hoping to pick up a fare.

Cargo, trunks, and bags dotted the wharves. Ships filled with an abundance of products waited in line to be unloaded. Vessels from Puget Sound brought netted bags of oysters and shiploads of wood cut specifically for the innovative two-foot by four-foot box frames used for building houses, as well as wood that had been cut specifically for flooring. Wood was in constant demand. Whaling ships carried whale oil for use in lamps and boxes of whale baleen needed for making buggy whips and the frameworks of umbrellas. Cargo ships arriving from the inland part of California brought large bags of wheat. Some vessels transported silk and fabric from China.

When Robert, Thomas, and Benjamin disembarked from the ship onto the busy wharf, they found themselves exhilarated by the frenzy of activity and new surroundings. They inhaled the essence of the harbor. Oysters released the smell of kelp, and the smell of fresh cut lumber and bags of harvested wheat lingered in the air. Smelling the wheat reminded Thomas of the fresh bread Jane's mother had packed into their basket for their one-way trip to the ship.

Philip caught up with them and suggested they spend a little time exploring the city.

"Meet me back here at the wharf in three hours. That should give me enough time to tend to the ship, and for Britta and I to pay a visit to a friend. When you come back, we'll catch a cab and go to the home of Captain Davis."

After they left, Philip sent a messenger to alert Captain Davis of their arrival and to expect them later in the day. Then he checked on the ship and gave final instructions to Samuel. He hadn't forgotten about the promise he had made to the men in Panama City and walked over to the shipping office to inform them about the stranded men desperate for a ship to transport them to San Francisco.

Now that he had taken care of business, he was free to visit his friend, Margaret Dawson. Margaret made her living in San Francisco by running a boarding house and cooking meals. Philip met her two years earlier when he rented a room from her for a few days. Margaret and Philip were instantly attracted to each other. The chemistry between them was undeniable, and they rapidly developed an intimate relationship. During that two-year span, Philip stayed with her whenever he landed in Frisco. He liked calling her Maggie.

When Philip arrived at the boarding house, he walked directly to the main dining room. The room was filled with several tables bedecked with red checked tablecloths. Lanterns lit with glowing candles took center stage of each table. The enticing aroma of freshly baked apple pie permeated the room.

Maggie was finishing up with her final customers for the day when she felt someone's eyes on her. She turned and saw Philip. Surprised and happy to see him, she flashed him a warm smile. She felt her neck and face redden. She hated that—it revealed her feelings. Maggie feared her feelings for him were stronger than his for her. *He's never told me how he feels. He travels from port to port. How do I know there isn't another woman in another port? Or several!* He looked so rugged and handsome. When she looked into his slate blue eyes, her heart pounded. *I love him so.*

A slow grin spread across his face. As his gaze traveled over her body, her heart raced, causing her face to turn scarlet. Philip knew she wished she could hide her crimson glow. He took pleasure in knowing how she felt. From the moment he met her, he was mesmerized by her beauty. He admired her hourglass figure and alabaster skin, both of which he had longed to touch. He credited her burnished red hair and flashing green eyes to her Irish origin.

With the diners still in the room, the couple greeted each other with pleasantries. Philip was anxious for the customers to leave and even found himself counting how many bites of food were left on their plates.

Maggie finally noticed Philip's dog standing by his side. Britta had been so quiet, Maggie hadn't seen her yet.

She bent down to pet Britta. "How are you, Britta? Such a sweet dog."

Philip patted Britta's head. "She's my constant companion." Then he leaned toward Maggie and whispered in an impatient tone, "Are they ever going to finish eating?" He was anxious to talk to her.

Finally, they heard the chairs scraping the floor—a signal the diners were finished. Since the customers had already settled up with Maggie, they thanked her and left.

Maggie rushed to lock the door and flew into Philip's open arms.

After a long embrace and passionate kiss, Philip pointed to one of the tables. "Let us sit, there's much to tell you, but before we talk, I must have a slice of your irresistible apple pie. It's aroma has been driving me crazy."

Maggie scurried to the kitchen and returned with a large slice of her pie. The warm juices oozed through the sugar and cinnamon-sprinkled crust. As he brought the first bite to his mouth, he held it in midair on his fork and stared at it for a moment. He had an idea. Maggie wondered what that was about. *Has he changed his mind about my pie? Everyone loved it today.*

"Is there something wrong, Philip?"

Jolted from his momentary trance, he put the piece of pie in his mouth and closed his eyes, savoring the mouth-watering morsel. "This is so delicious, Maggie. I think about your pie even after I leave."

She breathed a sigh of relief. Although, she had hoped he would have been thinking about her when he left.

"Maggie, I'm curious. How did you happen to come up with the name *Lady Kay* for your pie?"

"I named the pie after my dear deceased mother. It's her recipe."

" I think your pies would be in heavy demand in Puget Sound."

"What are you saying, Philip?"

"I'm saying I want you to come to the Sound and sell your pies there. You would probably be the only person for miles around who could provide pies like this. Possibly even the entire Territory. There are very few women out there right now. You would have a line of men as long as the post office line here in Frisco waiting to buy a Lady Kay apple pie!"

Maggie wondered if this was what he wanted to talk about. He always asked for pie when he came to visit her. She had hoped for something more romantic. *I guess he wants me for my damned pies!*

"But Philip, where would I put my kitchen? Where would I live?"

"You'll live with me, of course. Your business would be on my land." His excitement escalated. "We'll build you a bakery and maybe a restaurant. My family will be there with me. I want to establish roots, and I want my own place to live, and I want you to be there too, Maggie. I'm tired of staying at hotels and boarding houses." Before he got himself into trouble, he smiled and added, "Except, when I stay here of course."

Maggie stood and briskly placed her hands on her hips. "Philip Bennett! Are you offering me a business proposal or a marriage proposal?"

"I want us to be together, Maggie."

Maggie leaned forward and rested her hands on the table. Her blouse gaped open revealing her ample bosom. He was distracted by the view.

She said, "And?"

Philip hadn't really thought about the word marriage before, but he realized if he didn't say it at this moment, Maggie might walk away. He knew she loved him, and he knew he wanted her to be with him for the rest of his life. *Yes, I do love her, and I want to marry her.*

"And, yes, it's a marriage proposal. I'm sorry I don't have a ring. This kind of snuck up on me."

Maggie stood back up with her hands on her hips again and responded in a sarcastic tone. "Well, that *sounds* romantic." Then she sat down and leaned toward him. He was distracted again with the view. "Philip, if we're going to be married, isn't there something we should say to each other?"

Philip knew he couldn't make another mistake. They were both sitting, each across from the other. He grasped her hands and pulled them close to him, and said softly, "Maggie, I love you."

"My Philip, I love you too, with all my heart. I *will* marry you." Maggie was ecstatic. Then her past drifted forward into her mind overshadowing this moment of happiness. There was something she had to tell him. Her smile faded, and she was suddenly quiet.

"Maggie, what's wrong?"

Tears filled her eyes and overflowed down her cheeks. She busied herself for a moment to brush off imaginary food crumbs on her side of the table. "There is something you don't know about me. You may not want to marry me after I tell you."

Philip remained silent and let her continue.

"I'm a divorced woman and—"

Philip interrupted her and grabbed her hands again, "Maggie I don't care about that."

"But there's more, Philip." Her voice faltered, and a look of worry veiled her face. "I was born and raised in Kentucky. My father raised horses, and I loved going to horse auctions with him. I met Winston at one of those auctions. He was charming and swept me off my feet. Before I knew it, we were married. After our first year of marriage, his personality changed. In his mind, I should have been carrying his child by then. My flow was irregular, and I hadn't been able to conceive. When he took me to bed, he was rough with me. He had begun to drink regularly, and one night when he was dead drunk, I refused him. He responded by beating and raping me. From that time on, my monthly flow stopped.

"He was obsessed with having children. All he cared about was making sure his family name carried on. When we realized I couldn't conceive, he became furious. He grew cold toward me, and over time, I suspected he had begun a relationship with another woman. I was no longer of any use to him, and he wanted a divorce. I gave him no argument. Divorce is difficult, but he found a way. The courts in Indiana are more lenient, so we traveled there where the divorce was granted. Now you know my tarnished story, Philip. I'll understand if you don't want to marry a barren woman." Tears streamed down her face.

Philip was stunned. It shook him to learn how much this beautiful woman had suffered. He walked over to her side of the table, took her hands, and gently coaxed her to stand. Then he wrapped his strong arms around her and held her tightly.

Seeing Maggie so hurt and vulnerable moved him, and it was then he realized *how much* he loved her. "No one is ever going to hurt you again, Maggie. I would die protecting you. Maggie, I love you. Nothing else matters. If we decide we want children, we'll find a child that needs a home." He grinned and looked over at Britta lying by the warm cookstove. "I rescued Britta, and I can rescue a child. What matters is that we'll build our life together. I've missed you. It's been harder and harder to say goodbye to you each time I leave. I'll say it again. Marry me, Maggie."

Maggie looked up at him—eyes no longer filled with tears of sadness, but with happiness. "Yes, oh yes, Philip. I'll marry you."

Philip pulled her close to him again, and she laid her head on his beating heart. Then they shared their most passionate kiss. As he pressed against her, their bodies melted into the other as though they were one. Philip never felt closer to her than this moment and told himself he would never let her go.

"This is splendid. I came to tell you about *my* plans for Puget Sound and now it's *our* plans. I'll keep you abreast of my progress, Maggie, and I'll come for you when we're both ready, with a ring in hand. I shall take my leave, for now, my love. There's so much to do. I'll be back tonight to tell you more about Puget Sound, and you'll be *happy* to know I'll be in town for two more days. Until tonight, my darling," he said as he took a sweeping bow.

"Yes, until tonight, my Philip." She watched him leave, and sighed, *My knight in shining armor.*

* * *

The two brothers and Benjamin had set out on foot to explore the city. The streets consisted of dirt, which meant they were either dusty in dry weather or muddy in wet weather. It was the rainy season, and they saw people sinking in the mud past their ankles, and horses' hooves stirring it up, splattering mud everywhere. They were grateful for the board sidewalks available on some of the streets. During their exploration, they discovered the four quarters—Spanish, French, Italian, and Chinese—each with its own distinct personality. After they walked through the Spanish quarter, they came upon the Barbary Coast, famous for fast living. Prostitution and gambling were rampant and available, as was the secret practice of shanghaiing unsuspecting men into forced labor. The El Dorado gambling house was nearby. They chose not to spend any time there.

Thomas was amused to see shoeblacks stationed on every corner. There was a sign showing a charge of twenty-five cents to polish a pair of shoes. He chuckled, "How can anyone keep their shoes clean with streets like this?"

They continued, circling back to meet Philip. Along the way, they noticed several businesses lined up side by side along the street. The wood-framed buildings were covered with clapboard siding and designed with a flat façade and flat roof. One type of structure stood out from the others. It was the *ghost* of a sailing ship that had been converted into a hotel. The hull of the ship was used for the front portion of the building with a door cut into it for an entrance, and there was a flight of steps located on the outside of the hull providing access to an upper level. The remaining section of the ship was fabricated into a slightly stepped back two-story structure integrated with a deck.

Thomas laughed, "The lower section looks almost like a wooden shoe. Maybe we should consider staying in it, and I could tell Jane I slept in a shoe."

Sitting next to it, was another ship, which had been converted into a single-level structure, with the masts on the ship deck still intact.

* * *

When they met up with Philip at the set hour, he had a cab waiting to take them to Captain Davis's home. Philip waved them over. Britta was pinned to his side making sure she wouldn't be left behind. "Ready to go, mates?"

The three had done enough walking for the day and eagerly climbed into the cab. The driver cracked the whip, and the two matching black horses moved into a trot. Philip told the driver to take them to Rincon Hill, giving him the specific address.

Rincon Hill was considered to be San Francisco's most fashionable neighborhood. Captain Davis became wealthy during the 1849 gold rush era due to the demand for supplies and building materials needing to be brought into the port.

Many other people made their fortune during the gold rush, but not in the gold fields. Instead, they opened businesses in the city as merchants, or they provided services to the people who came for gold. Other businessmen opened gambling houses and brothels, affording easy temptations for the gold miners to spend their newly found riches.

During the cab ride, Robert reflected back to the oddity they saw on the city streets, "Philip, how did ships end up as buildings on the street? I couldn't believe my eyes. I certainly never expected to see a ship out of the water like that."

"It's because of the gold rush. Throngs of people came here either overland or by ship. When the ships came, there were hundreds anchored in the harbor. I might add, I had one heck of a time finding a slot to drop anchor. Not only did the passengers run to the gold fields, but the ship captains and crews as well. The ships ended up abandoned and sat clogging the harbor while they rotted. Some of the ships were salvaged so the wood could be used, and others were drug onto land to be turned into buildings such as those you saw today. Many ships were purposely sunk to help fill in the cove."

"I'm impressed with their ingenuity," said Benjamin as he recalled the image of the *ship* hotel.

Thomas was curious about Philip's mysterious visit. "By the way, Philip, how was your visit with your friend? You appear quite happy. Was it a lady friend, by any chance?"

Philip grinned, "As a matter of fact, yes. My future wife. I've known her for a while. I visit her every time I come to Frisco. She's going to join me in Puget Sound. I will tell you more about that later."

Robert chimed in. "You son of a gun. You've been holding out on us. Congratulations, brother. To be truthful, I thought it would never happen. This is big news to pass on to the family."

Chuckling, he replied, "Yes, it is big news. I didn't realize it myself until today."

The ride was bumpy as the cab wheels maneuvered through the ruts on the muddy street. When they approached the neighborhood, the driver turned onto a cobblestone street that led them up to a hill overlooking the bay and city. The community had been strategically located to be a safe distance from any of the city's unsavory influences. They rode past several public gardens surrounded by elegant houses. The current architectural styles of Greek Revival, Gothic Revival, and Second Empire were displayed throughout the area. The next block revealed a large private gated park where a windmill had been installed to pump water to the garden. The gentle *whoosh* of the windmill blades exuded a sense of calm. This garden was surrounded by beautiful Italianate row houses. The cab driver slowed the horses and stopped in front of the Italianate residence of Captain Davis. Philip paid the fare and asked the driver to return in two hours.

They stepped down from the cab and followed the hedge-bordered stone path to the ornately carved wooden front door. Philip tapped the bronze lion's head door knocker. A servant, dressed in a black dress and a crisp white pinafore apron and cap, answered the door. She was a petite woman with flaming red hair in her mid-twenties. Despite her age and size, she possessed an air about her of a gatekeeper. "May I help you, gentlemen?"

Philip replied. "Yes, miss, I'm Captain Bennett. I believe Captain Davis is expecting us."

"Please come in. May I take your hats?" She noticed Philip's dog. "You're welcome to bring your dog in. Make yourselves comfortable while I let the captain know you are here."

Momentarily, the captain entered the foyer. Captain William Davis was a tall, stately handsome man in his fifties. His dark brown hair was peppered with grey as was his trimmed beard and mustache. His skin was tanned from exposure at sea, and the crease lines around his amber brown eyes and forehead revealed a history of hard decisions. His eyes brightened when he saw Philip.

"Ah, my old friend." He grabbed Philip's hands and clasped them in his with a firm shake. Britta wagged her tail impatiently waiting for Captain Davis's attention. He bent down to pet her. "How are you, Britta? I haven't seen you in awhile." Then he acknowledged Philip's brothers and Benjamin with a nod.

"May I introduce my two brothers, Thomas and Robert, and the newest member of our family, Thomas's son-in-law, Benjamin Spencer. I must say, we're quite happy to be back on dry land. It was a challenging trip. As you well know, many things can happen on the open sea."

The Captain nodded, "Yes, I'm quite aware." Then he extended his hand to each of the newcomers. "I'm pleased to know you, welcome to my home." He turned his attention back to his friend.

"Philip, be assured that I'll care for your family as if it were mine. Now, my wife insists you are all to stay here with us until you are ready to sail."

"Thank you, William. You are a good friend."

"Let's go to the library where we can be more comfortable." He rang the bell for his servant. Barely a minute passed before she appeared.

"Yes, sir?"

"Bridget, please bring us a tray of the usual."

"Very good, sir." She curtsied and left the room.

After she left, Philip asked, "William, is your servant Irish? Her accent is charming. She seems young but appears to be in complete control of your household."

"She is young. You might say I rescued her off the wharf in New York City. She was an Irish immigrant and had just arrived alone at the port of entry in New York harbor. I saw a thief attack her and steal her bag, which contained all her money in the world. Unfortunately, I wasn't able to move fast enough to stop the thief.

"Bridget, along with many other young Irish women, left Ireland to find work as a domestic over here. I felt sorry for her, bought her a lunch, and learned more about her. The next thing I knew, I was offering her a job. She is fortunate to be working here in Frisco. Due to the scarcity of women here, she makes ten times more than what is offered in New York City. For me, she was the answer to my prayers. I needed someone immediately. She has proven to be a hard worker and speaks enough English to readily follow my wife's instructions."

Bridget returned holding a tray with tea and coffee accompanied with several slices of shortbread. She set the tray on the center table.

Captain Davis smiled, "Thank you, Bridget. That will be all for now."

"Yes, sir." She curtsied, and left the room closing the door behind her.

A few minutes later, there was a light tap on the library door, and a slim, attractive woman glided into the library. The men stood as she entered.

"Gentlemen, I trust you are comfortable. How are you, Philip?" She bent down to pet Britta. "I see you brought your faithful companion."

"Yes, she is always with me. It is good to be back in Frisco. Victoria, allow me to introduce my brothers, Robert and Thomas, and Thomas's son-in-law, Benjamin Spencer." Each of them smiled and nodded.

Her blue eyes sparkled, "I'm charmed to meet all of you." She looked over at William and back at Philip, "Has my husband extended our invitation for you to be our guests during your stay here in the city?"

"Yes, he did. We appreciate your hospitality."

Victoria chatted a few moments and stayed a proper amount of time. Then she excused herself, knowing the men had serious business to discuss. As she stood up, the men rose to their feet again, and bid her good day. William walked her to the door and kissed her on the cheek, closing the door after she left.

"You still look happy, William," said Philip. He thought about Maggie. "I might as well tell you, Maggie and I got engaged today."

"I knew it was going to happen long before you knew it, Philip. The last time we all dined together, it was pretty obvious how smitten the two of you were."

"I have to admit, it took me by surprise. Enough about me. Let's talk business."

William listened intently as Philip described their journey to San Francisco, and about the one still ahead. Then they discussed the subject at hand—the upcoming Nicaragua route for the rest of the family under the care of Captain Davis.

William had vital information to relay. "Philip, I must tell you what's going on in San Francisco right now. The last time you were here, the city was growing at an accelerated pace. But it has been in a bubble that has finally burst. Real estate values have dropped, and some of the banks are in trouble and struggling to hang on."

Thomas and Robert were quiet as they listened to Captain Davis. They looked at each other. Each knew what the other was thinking. They were feeling a sense of panic and hoped they hadn't made a mistake. Benjamin felt queasy.

William continued. "There's still some demand for lumber here, but there are other places with higher demand. A lumber company has established a large sawmill in Puget Sound, and they have an office here in Frisco. It's important you pay them a visit tomorrow. They're a strong, reputable company, and you need to make a connection. I've already talked to them about you. They want a meeting and are expecting you."

"Thank you for paving the way, William. I'll go there first thing tomorrow morning. In fact, it will be easy to do so since I will already be in the city. I was about to tell you, only my brothers and Benjamin will be returning this evening. I will be staying with Maggie. I would be in big trouble if I neglected her right after proposing to her!"

William laughed. "Yes, you don't want to start out wrong, my friend." He glanced out the window. "I see your cab is here. I'll see *most* of you tonight."

They hopped into the cab and instructed the driver to take them back to the city.

Philip had sensed his brothers' and Benjamin's uneasiness during the conversation with Captain Davis about the downhill spiral of the city.

"No worries, mates, I am not going to let you down. I know how to make things happen."

* * *

Benjamin and the Bennett brothers were hungry and found a place to eat in the Spanish Quarter. The aroma of the food drew them in. When they walked in, a black-eyed senorita with bluish black hair swished past them in the process of delivering a plate of steaming hot tamales to a customer. They could smell the enticing spicy aroma still lingering in the air as she passed by. The room was brimming with gaiety. Musicians briskly strummed guitars accompanied by singing Spanish vocals. There was a melodious hum of voices speaking the language. A colorful mixture of cultures of Mexicans, Spaniards, Chileans, Peruvians, and Hispano-Americans filled the eatery.

They spotted a table and sat down. The same stunning senorita they saw earlier approached them to take their order. She introduced herself as Consuelo. Since none of them knew much about the cuisine and didn't speak Spanish, they kept it simple and pointed at the table with the plate of tamales on it. Consuelo nodded and whisked away. Shortly, she returned with the aromatic steaming tamales. They thoroughly enjoyed this new taste sensation and the stimulating atmosphere.

Philip sighed. "I must say, this is the first time I've eaten Mexican food. I'm used to Maggie's cooking when I come to Frisco."

Just as they were about to leave, they heard a jangling sound. *Jing, jing, jing.* They looked toward the door. A striking gentleman cowboy, known as a Caballero, entered the room. The silver spurs on his high-heeled embroidered leather boots emitted the tinkling metallic sound. They were in the form of large circular spiked wheels fringed with tiny silver bells.

Benjamin and the brothers couldn't help but stare. The Caballero's black trousers were embellished with silver medallions down the entire length of the leg. His black jacket was cut and ornamented in the likeness of a bullfighter's jacket, and beneath his jacket, he wore a white ruffled shirt finished with a red neck scarf. His black felt hat was decorated with silver embroidery. He had sharp dark eyes and a manicured mustache and goatee. They watched the Caballero's eyes scan the room until they landed on Consuelo. She had already seen him, and their eyes locked.

"Hmm," Philip mused, "I think something is going on between the two of them. Too bad we don't have time to hang around and see how it plays out."

When they left the eatery, they noticed a beautiful grey Andalusian stallion tied to the hitching post. The horse was fitted out as ornately as the Caballero inside.

Benjamin remarked, "I think we can guess who owns this horse."

Robert smiled, "Delhi seems like another world compared to all of this, doesn't it? Now that we've had a good meal, let's find a saloon and treat ourselves to a drink."

As they strolled along on the wood plank boardwalks, they passed several shops with wares, such as Mexican clay pottery, displayed in the windows. In contrast to the buzzing activity of the eatery located only a few blocks away, this part of the community exuded a slow-paced life. People leaned in open doorways, and others lounged on porches, while some used a handy barrel as a seat. Flowers and plants, and screeching parrots living in cages hung from balconies.

As the foursome continued, they found a saloon located near the Barbary Coast. When they walked in, it was obvious they had entered a rough environment. Feeling adventurous, they decided to stay. They grabbed a table near the back and sat down. The room was rowdy with loud voices, and every card table was full. The place was dimly lit and smoky, and cobwebs hung from the ceiling. There was an enormous smudged mirror behind the bar reflecting a lineup of bottles of hard liquor. Most of the men were drunk. Philip noticed a man leaning against the bar with a drink in his hand. It was evident by his body language he was the man in charge, and probably the owner.

While they waited for someone to take their order, they discussed their plans for departure the day after next at noon. A man appeared out of nowhere and approached them. He directed his attention toward Philip who was wearing his captain's hat. Britta growled, and Philip gently but firmly restrained her, patting her head. He could feel her hairs bristle, which didn't happen very often.

"Greetings, Captain. I couldn't help but overhear you have a ship in the harbor. Did I hear you are departing in two days? I didn't get the name of your ship? Need any sailors? I can help you out if you do."

"No thanks," replied Philip. "We lost one of our men on our way here, but we're on the last leg of our voyage so I can get by. My ship is the *California II*." Philip scrutinized the man, *He seems awfully suspicious.* The shifty man acquiesced and walked away, then looked toward the man standing at the bar, and shook his head.

Philip patted Britta, "Good girl. I didn't like him either."

A young boy, who had been lingering nearby, came to their table and asked for their order. His appearance was unsettling. He was shabbily dressed, had a cut lip, and his arms were covered with bruises. He seemed insecure, and his voice trembled when he spoke. Britta sniffed him.

"Hello, young man. We'll try a bottle of Tequila," said Thomas. The boy nodded and left the table. They noticed he went out of his way to avoid the man at the bar.

"That lad looks like he's in a bad way," Benjamin commented as he watched the boy walk away.

Robert saw the boy returning with their bottle of Tequila and four glasses on a tray, and said, "I see our Tequila is on its way."

As the boy walked past a crowded table, a man's outstretched leg was in the pathway. Not seeing the leg, the boy tripped and spilled everything onto the floor. There was a loud crash. He froze with fear. The owner charged over, cuffed the boy on the side of his face, and slung him across the floor. The Bennett brothers and Benjamin witnessed the scene. They didn't like what they saw and stood up. Philip walked up to the owner. Benjamin followed.

"Leave the lad alone. He didn't deserve that. The man slumped in the chair over there had his leg sticking out in his path," said Philip in a disgusted voice.

Robert walked over, "We'll pay for the damages."

Meanwhile, Thomas went over to the boy and helped him up off the floor. "Are you all right, young man?"

The imprint of the owner's hand was still visible on the side of the boy's face. The boy glanced at the owner, and nodded that he was fine, and hastily left the room.

The owner glared and yelled, "Mind your own god-damned business. Get out of my saloon now, and don't come back!"

Robert threw some cash on the floor, and they left. They quickly exited but felt bad about the plight of the unfortunate boy. As far as they were concerned, it was time to leave that part of the city. They hailed a cab.

Philip gave the cab driver two addresses. The first stop was Maggie's place, where he parted from his brothers and Benjamin for the night.

He waved goodbye to them, "I'll meet you in the morning at the captain's house. I'll bring a cab."

Then the cab driver took Robert, Thomas, and Benjamin to Captain Davis's house.

* * *

Early the next morning, after kissing Maggie farewell, Philip followed Captain Davis's suggestion and sought out the lumber company representatives. The meeting proved to be fortuitous, and he left feeling confident about working with the sawmill in Puget Sound. He and the sawmill leaders struck a good deal. He was anxious to tell his brothers and Benjamin. *This should set their minds at ease.*

As promised, Philip arrived at Captain Davis's home with a cab to fetch his brothers and Benjamin. On their way back to the city, he was pleased to tell them about his successful meeting at the mill office. ". . . And mates, I know where we're going to settle. The sawmill is a godsend for us. After we leave Olympia, we'll be heading to a place called Teekalet."

Robert and Thomas looked at each other, and then to Benjamin. They all nodded their heads in affirmation.

Thomas said, "We feel a little more relieved with what you've told us. I have to admit we were concerned, but we're ready to follow you, Philip."

"Brilliant! I had sensed your anxiety and hoped my news would inspire all of you. Now, shall we carry on with our plans for the day?"

They had planned to spend their day scouting the business side of the city and making connections. The first priority for Thomas and Benjamin was to post letters back east to the family. A ship carrying mail to New York City would be leaving the harbor the next day.

Benjamin was desperate to know how Mary was doing. She was always on his mind. Thomas was also concerned about how Jane and the children were coping. It felt unnatural being separated from his wife. They missed their family and were anxious for the time when they could be summoned. They knew the family would be relieved to learn they had all arrived safely to San Francisco. Benjamin chose not to tell Mary or the rest of the family about his near-death experience.

After they finished their day, they hailed a cab and left the city to return to the captain's house. They would be enjoying dinner with William and Victoria that evening, and then turn in early. Tomorrow was the beginning of the rest of their journey, and their future.

* * *

It was the morning of departure. The Bennett brothers and Benjamin thanked their hosts for their hospitality and said goodbye. Captain Davis had his own carriage and insisted that his driver take them to the port.

When they arrived at the wharf, they witnessed the same scene of activity and confusion as before. The cargo, supplies, and baggage were loaded onto Philip's ship, as well as mailbags with the destination of Puget Sound. Philip promptly boarded the ship. Robert, Thomas, and Benjamin followed shortly.

Finally, at the appointed hour, the throaty whistle blew, and the passengers boarded along with a few new arrivals. The first mate called out, "Weigh anchor!" The onlookers on the wharf watched the steamer glide out of the San Francisco Bay, and the passengers on the *California II* watched the city and the bay disappear into a foggy cloud in the distance.

Chapter 19

December 1854

Pacific Coast

*T*he weather was fair, and the sea was calm. As the *California II* steamed northward, the coastline began to take on a different personality. Lighthouses dotted the shoreline marking the hazards along the way. The travelers tasted the salty essence of the ocean and relaxed to the euphoric sound of the sea lapping against the ship. They watched with wonder as surf waves crashed into the irregular rocky shoreline flinging foamy sprays of water high into the atmosphere. They listened to the cries of the seabirds such as terns, gulls, pelicans, and cormorants flying above the ocean searching for food, while some birds rested on nearby rocky perches. They saw expanses of sandy beaches, and large coves carved out by the persistent waves. The uplands consisted of rolling hills with patches of woodlands and stands of pine. The lowlands were filled with windblown Sitka spruce, Douglas fir, Western hemlock, alder, and the mighty Redwoods.

The vessel continued north, and as it approached the Oregon coast, the sky greyed and the shoreline gradually changed. Giant sand dunes stood tall on fine-textured sandy beaches. Sea lions bathed on large outcroppings of rocks while sea otters skimmed the ocean surface. The coastline was fringed with lodgepole pine, cedar, hemlock, alder, and madrone spreading up to the mountain ranges. Grasslands and areas of brush covered the slopes interspersed with wild flowers, rhododendrons, and azaleas.

About a week after leaving the Golden Gate, Philip announced to the crew and passengers, "We're approaching the mouth of the Columbia River, and you'll be pleased to know that since our departure from San Francisco, we are over half way to our final destination."

Everyone cheered.

"The Columbia River is another route to Puget Sound, but it involves going over the ferocious bar, nicknamed the *graveyard of ships.*" He pointed in the direction of the Columbia.

Many of the passengers appeared nervous, and murmured among themselves, wondering what dangers might lie ahead.

Philip noticed their reaction.

"If I may continue. Once the ships cross the bar, they stop at Portland where the passengers change to canoe travel, then paddle up the Columbia and switch over to the Cowlitz River where the rivers converge. When they arrive at Cowlitz Landing, they will change from canoe to horses, or horse and wagon, and if necessary, go on foot until they reach Olympia.

"While I have been talking to you, you may have noticed we have bypassed the mouth of the Columbia. We are not taking that route."

The passengers turned their heads in the direction of the Columbia and were relieved to see they had indeed, passed by.

"We will continue up the Pacific Coast until we enter the Strait of Juan de Fuca, then we will head east and turn south into the Puget Sound, which ends at our final destination, the Olympia harbor."

* * *

When the weather was agreeable, Philip allowed Britta to enjoy some freedom on the ship. One calm day, Robert, Thomas, and Benjamin had joined Philip in the pilothouse to finalize their plans when they were interrupted by Philip's cook, Meng.

"Captain Bennett, your dog has been sniffing around the hold where the food and water are stored. I know you keep Britta well fed and watered, so I don't understand what she's doing there. She's been sniffing at the door for several days."

"Hmm," let's investigate," said Philip. They walked toward the hold with Britta rushing ahead of them. As they approached the hold, Britta sniffed at the bottom of the door, wagging her tail vigorously. The cook came prepared with a lantern and handed it to his captain. Guardedly, Philip opened the door. Britta sped past him, ran down the steps, and headed straight to a dark corner. Philip followed her to the corner. He lifted the lantern high above his head slowly swinging it back and forth, and in the dim light saw a young lad crouched in the corner, trembling. They had just found a stowaway. Philip shined the light closer onto the boy. He recognized him.

"Why, you're the young waiter from the saloon! How did you get onto my ship undetected?"

Before the boy could answer, Philip grasped the boy's arm to lead him out of the hold. As he did so, the boy grimaced in pain.

"It's my arm, sir. I think it might be broken."

Philip turned to the cook, "Meng, please tell Dr. Bradley to be prepared to tend an injured arm, possibly broken. We'll be there shortly."

"Lad, you're going to be okay now," Philip said reassuringly.

Robert grimaced as he looked at the boy's bruised and cut face. Even in the dim light, he could see the boy had taken a beating. "You're among friends, lad." He smiled compassionately. "I have a feeling you have quite a story to tell us."

Benjamin gazed at the beaten face. He shook his head in disgust and murmured to himself, *I think we can all guess who beat him.*

Philip interjected, "But first, lad, let's get your arm taken care of, and I'd venture to say you wouldn't mind a good hot meal?"

"I'd be beholden to you, sir. I've been living on hard tack and water since your ship left San Francisco."

Philip and Thomas helped the lad up the stairs to the deck. As they led him to the doctor's cabin, Robert said, "I'll stay in case the doctor needs my assistance." He turned to the boy, "I'm Robert Bennett. What's your name, young man?"

"My name is Christopher, sir. Christopher Taylor."

* * *

After the doctor finished tending Christopher's injuries, Robert led him to sickbay. "Get some rest, Christopher. If you feel like you can eat, I will tell Meng you are ready for a meal. In a little while, we'll come back, and you can tell us everything."

"I'm beholden, Mr. Bennett." As he watched Robert leave, his eyelids drooped, and he fell asleep. He was safe now.

* * *

A few hours later, Christopher's bruised face lit up as the Bennett brothers and Benjamin entered the room. Philip smiled at him. "I trust you're feeling a little better, Christopher?"

Christopher looked down at his arm in the sling. "The doctor said I was lucky. He said my arm isn't broken. It's fractured, so it'll heal faster."

"Yes, Robert mentioned that."

Thomas asked, "How did you end up at the saloon?"

"I'm all alone. My father and I had taken a ship from Sidney bound for San Francisco. Then he took sick and died."

Robert wondered what had happened to the boy's mother. "What about your mother, Christopher?"

"My mother died when I was born. It's just been my father and me. He wanted to make a fresh start in California." Christopher's voice faltered. "When my father died on the ship, the captain said he knew someone who would help me and give me shelter and a job. That was the man you met at the saloon.

"He is a cruel man. He gets men drunk with a drink mixed with whiskey, gin, brandy, and opium. I saw the bartender make the drinks. He calls it his special drink and tells the men it's on the house. After they pass out, they carry the men to a ship where the captain gives the saloon men money. I heard the owner laughing about how the men will wake up and find themselves on a ship far away out to sea and forced to work. None of their family ever finds out what happened to them.

"After I fell with the tray, I ran and hid so he wouldn't beat me, but he found me, and beat me so hard he hurt my arm. Later, I overheard him talking to one of his men about selling me to that same ship captain. He bragged about how he would be rid of me and get paid for it. I heard you talking about your ship, so I waited until nightfall, and ran to the harbor to find the *California II*. It was dark, so no one saw me slip onto your ship. Please forgive me. I'll work for passage. I'll do anything. I can use my good arm to scrub the deck."

Philip interrupted him. "Christopher, you poor lad. We didn't like leaving you there when we left, but not knowing the circumstances, we didn't get further involved. You will have a safe passage with us, and you can perform some light labor. How old are you?"

"I'm fourteen, sir. Thank you, sir. I swear, I will find a way to repay you someday."

Thomas thought to himself, *Why he's just a year older than my youngest child and on his own. Poor laddie.*

In a firm but kind voice, Philip said, "When you are ready to leave sickbay, we have an empty berth you can take. Your first duty will be to help entertain Britta. She obviously recognized you. You are already off to a good start with her. She's a good judge of character."

* * *

Despite the rain, the passengers spent as much time as possible on the deck. Those who had umbrellas kept them handy, which when opened, portrayed a kaleidoscope of color. The people filled their lungs with the fresh marine air. For steerage passengers, it was like breathing in new life.

There was a mélange of activity on the deck. The newest passenger, Christopher, entertained Britta by throwing a small ball back and forth. Excited, she ran to retrieve the ball as fast as she could run, and brought it back to Christopher. Sometimes she chose to tease him and didn't release the ball from her mouth. As Philip watched this lively scene, he thought, *What's to become of this boy? I feel responsible for him. I must speak with my brothers. Perhaps they will have an idea of what to do.*

The Strait was due north and close-by. The wind picked up in strength, causing the sea to become choppy. As they entered a thick fog bank, common to the area, the air was dense and moist. Philip was concerned, but even if he chose to anchor until the conditions were more favorable, it was impossible. The entire route from San Francisco to the Strait of Juan de Fuca was known as an ironbound coast. It was a continuous rocky coastline, and finding a calm harbor for refuge in bad weather was not in the offering. The winds that blew in from the southwest not only caused strong currents—which could run at a velocity of six miles per hour resulting in huge swells—but also had the power to push a ship into the dangerous rocks along the coastline.

At this point, Cape Flattery was a short distance away. The Cape was the most northwestern point on the mainland of the United States, and it marked the dangerous rocky entrance to the Strait. Philip strained through the fog to spot the famous landmark, Fuca Pillar. Then in the distance, he saw the outline of a mammoth rectangular-shaped rock towering over the rest. It was the Pillar. *Thank the Lord. We are close to Cape Flattery, then onward to the mouth of the Strait.*

With the fog growing thicker, Captain Bennett instructed the crew to hang the ship lanterns on the outside rails of the vessel, hopeful that the swaying shafts of light would pierce through the thick haze. Then he sounded the fog bells to warn any oncoming ship of their presence. Ships could easily collide in the dense fog, and nightfall could also cause collisions.

Suddenly, a small steamer appeared, coming toward them. It passed at a comfortable distance but was close enough for Philip and his crew to notice structural damage to her side. It did not appear to be significant or alarming, and no signal for assistance had been given. The ship continued on without incident.

A storm front was moving in. Gusts of wind swept the sea into turbulent, tall, white-topped waves. As they progressed forward through the storm toward Cape Flattery, they spotted something ahead. Philip slowed the ship. They strained to see through the thick fog and saw the faint image of wreckage. It appeared to be the remains of a vessel. They saw debris floating everywhere. Remnants of a ship and the belongings of its passengers now belonged to the sea. There appeared to be little hope that anyone was still alive when they saw so many life jackets floating, each empty of its intended recipient.

As they crept in closer, they heard the screams and cries of survivors desperately hanging on to slippery rocks projecting from the water. Captain Bennett immediately sounded the whistle letting them know they had been seen, but he wasn't sure how he would maneuver his ship to reach the survivors, due to the momentum of the huge waves and the danger of the rocks. The crew identified two men, two children, and one woman.

Captain Bennett positioned his ship as close as he dared, while it jostled about in the rolling sea. He instructed his crew members to throw out ropes with life rings, but just as they were about to do so, a monster wave crashed onto the rocks and the survivors. Those on the ship's deck heard the shrieks of terror, and when the water receded, there was only the sound of the crashing waves. The people were gone, as though they were never there. The crew and the passengers who witnessed the horrifying scene, would never forget the screams, nor the image of the people washed away in an instant.

It was an off-chance, and Philip was aware of the wind and waves growing stronger, but he couldn't leave without searching for any other survivors. Time was running out, then one of the crew members spotted two men hanging on to some wreckage, yelling for help. Philip cautiously brought the ship closer, making it possible for the crew to throw the life ropes out to the men and pull them onto the ship.

While the ship was at a halt for the rescue, one of the crew members spotted a corked bottle floating in the debris. He held out the lantern to take a closer look and noticed there was a note in the bottle. He scooped the bottle up with a long-handled fishnet and took it to the captain.

* * *

The two hypothermic survivors had been immediately taken to the Purser's cabin where the doctor awaited. Philip was concerned about the men and paid them a visit.

"They're in a bad state, Captain, but they'll live," said Dr. Bradley.

The survivors were conscious and able to talk. Dr. Bradley's assistant helped them out of their wet clothes and into dry ones. While they clung to the wool blankets wrapped around them and drank hot tea, Philip sat down and introduced himself. He asked the older man his name.

"My name is Peter Crandall. I am, er, I was the second mate on the ship *Theodora*. This young boy, Billy, was one of the passengers, the only person I was able to save. We were struck along the side of our ship by another. The ship that struck us didn't appear to have much damage, so we figured our ship had sustained only a glancing blow. The real damage to our ship didn't show up immediately. I have to believe in my heart, that the other ship captain assumed we weren't in any danger since the damage on both ships appeared minimal, or surely he would have turned around to help us."

Philip's mind flashed to the image of the ship that had passed them earlier.

Peter continued. "Soon after, the crew from below deck yelled that water was rushing in and the ship was breaking apart. There were over two hundred passengers and thirty-five crew members on board. We were over capacity. Of course, everyone panicked and tried to get to the lifeboats. No one had been told where the life jackets were, so they boarded the lifeboats without them. The crew members rushed to lower the lifeboats already overflowing with people. Many things went wrong. Some of the lifeboats being lowered were at the mercy of the ropes lowering them. With the weight of so many people, the ropes broke, and the people fell into the ocean and drowned. Some of the boats capsized the moment they landed on the rough sea. I saw boats filled with people sink because the drain plugs were missing. They all drowned. Some of the lifeboats couldn't be used because they had been filled with water—the captain's idea of using the filled boats to ballast the ship."

Philip cringed at such a thought.

"When the other ship struck us, the first mate and I tried to persuade the captain to find a safe place to anchor to inspect the ship for any damage. He refused and continued to try to go around Cape Flattery. The sea was so rough. It is my belief the ship was weakened and couldn't withstand the rough seas. Once she started breaking up, she sank within minutes, and all those poor souls went with her. We were doomed from the beginning."

Peter stopped, lowering his face into his hands, overcome with emotion.

"Do you want to rest, Peter? Continue later?"

"No, I'm alright now. I need to tell it. I heard horses screaming and witnessed a man from first class run to his two prize horses that were secured in a stall. They were trying to break free. Their eyes were white and filled with fear. The owner didn't take the small window of time to try to save himself. Instead, he went to his horses and shot them in the head rather than let them drown. Then, knowing there was no hope of survival, he shot himself.

"I knew the ship was going down, so I jumped into the sea and swam away as fast as I could to avoid being sucked down. I found a piece of wreckage floating from one of the lifeboats, and grabbed onto it. Then I saw Billy floundering in the water near me. While I hung onto the rubble, I swam toward him and pulled him to me. By the grace of God, we were able to cling to that piece of debris until you found us. We owe you our lives, Captain.

"I'll never forget the screams of those horses, the cries and panicked voices of the passengers, and then, the eerie silence when the ship took them down with her."

Philip knew Peter and Billy needed to rest. He stood up, signaling he was leaving. "You've been through a harrowing ordeal. Get some rest. We'll talk later. You're in good hands with Doctor Bradley."

***

Philip quickly returned to his cabin where he had stored the recovered wine bottle. It was empty of its original contents and held a note instead. He coaxed it from the bottle. He was shocked at what he read.

He called out to Samuel, who was never far from his captain, and asked him to tell his brothers and Benjamin to come to his cabin. When they arrived, he held the recovered bottle in his hands.

"I requested you here to show you a note found in this bottle. I suspect there is more to what happened than what Peter Crandall knows." He laid the crumpled unfinished note of scribbled words onto the table. "Read this."

I'm Daniel Bly. I'm the first mate of the Theodora under the command of Captain Lars Jensen. I write this in the hope it will be found. I know I am about to die. I want it known that Captain Jensen is the cause of our death. He bought this ship out of the bone yard in San Francisco. He covered rotten wood with paint and claimed the ship was fit to travel on the sea. We are all lost. Tell my wife and children I love them and

They were all stunned. After having heard Peter's account, Philip had already formed his opinion about the captain—he was reckless.

The description of the lifeboats was evidence alone. The ropes used to lower the lifeboats were most likely rotten, and *why were there no drain plugs in some of the boats?* His careless act of filling the lifeboats with water for ballast was unforgivable. His recklessness deprived the passengers and crew of any chance for survival.

Two days later, Philip asked Samuel to bring Peter Crandall to his cabin.

Samuel escorted Peter to the captain's cabin, tapped on the door as usual, and opened it allowing Peter to enter. Philip saw a different man. "You're looking much better, Peter. How are you feeling?"

"Much better, Captain Bennett. I am forever in your debt."

"We were fortunate to have come along in time, Peter. I asked you here because I would like to talk to you about your captain and the first mate. Did you know much about their relationship?"

"Well, Captain Bennett, I know there was something between them. It was obvious that Daniel disliked and distrusted him. He held no respect for the captain. I always felt Daniel held a secret about him, which he couldn't reveal. The captain seemed to have something over on him. None of us respected Captain Jensen. Daniel was a good man though. Why are you asking about them?"

"We found a corked bottle floating in the wreckage. There was a note inside, written by Daniel before he died. In the note, he reveals he knew the ship was unfit for travel." Philip handed it to Peter.

Peter balked at the offered note. "If you don't mind, Captain Bennett, would you mind reading it? I don't feel quite up to it."

After Philip finished reading the note out loud, Peter commented, "The captain must have bribed an inspector."

Philip remarked, "Between the other ship striking it, and the rough sea, the *Theodora* fell apart. Captain Jensen's luck ran out, and he and those people lost their lives on his gamble. Do you know anything about Daniel's family?"

"Yes, they live in San Francisco."

"I will deliver his message to them if you'll give me the necessary details to contact them. Do you know what you're going to do now, Peter?

"No. I have been pondering on that myself. I also feel a responsibility to help Billy. While we were recovering in sickbay, I got to know him. His given name is Ying Chan, but he likes to go by Billy. When he and his family arrived in this country, he learned to speak English. His family and other Chinese families migrated because of the gold rush. Very few of them were successful. Billy's family and the other Chinese families were all lost on the *Theodora*. They had heard about a large lumber mill in Puget Sound that needed workers and was hiring. He's eighteen years old. I have been to China many times working on different ships and learned their language. I've come to know the Chinese people well, and intend to honor their ancient Chinese proverb—*he who saves a life is responsible for it.*"

After listening to Peter, Philip judged him to be a good man. "If you're interested, Peter, you can work for me. I'm short one crew member. If necessary, I may ask you to accompany me when I visit Mr. Bly's family in San Francisco."

"I would be honored to work for you, Captain Bennett, and of course I'll accompany you to visit Daniel's family."

***

Philip was saddened as he thought about so many people dying because of the carelessness of Captain Lars Jensen. At the first available stop, he reported the wreck of the *Theodora*, and the details surrounding it, including information about the smaller steamer ship that struck it. He insisted on being informed of any findings.

Weeks later, Philip received a report along with gratitude for his efforts. He was reminded of the tragedy as he read the report that many bodies had washed ashore along the Strait, and there were still many bodies missing.

A newspaper reporter wrote a story about a father who had said goodbye to his daughter. She was going to visit friends in San Francisco and was to return home to Victoria two weeks later on the *Theodora*. The reporter quoted the father, "Somehow, as I waved goodbye to her, I felt I would never see her again," he said. It was later reported the young lady's body had floated back to the shoreline of Victoria very near to where she lived. It was as though she made one final effort to go back home to her father's loving arms.

The debris from the *Theodora* had been collected and studied. The wood from the timbers of the ship was indeed rotten. It could be pulled apart with one's fingers. The nails in the wood were rusted and brittle and could be easily expelled from their position with any small amount of pressure. Ropes had floated ashore, many of them rotten and frayed. They found pieces of the hull, deteriorated and covered with chipped paint.

∗∗

Cape Flattery would never be forgotten. As the *California II* continued onward toward the Strait, the silence on the ship was deafening. The crew and the passengers had witnessed a failed rescue and the watery gravesite of so many souls. Even though the people who died were strangers, the crew and passengers grieved and prayed for them. There was an unexpected courtesy displayed among the passengers for the remainder of the trip. Many people made an effort to develop friendships of those who had been strangers alongside them. Suddenly, life seemed so much more precious.

The *California II* continued her final leg of the voyage through the Strait and finally, into Puget Sound. The inland passage of water was protected from tempestuous winds resulting in calm, serene waters. Instead of rocky shorelines, there were green wooded shorelines and pebble beaches. Curvaceous waterways stretched into inviting little coves and snug harbors.

They marveled at majestic snow-capped mountain ranges. To the northwest were the Olympic Mountains situated on the Olympic Peninsula, which was an arm of land bound by the Pacific Ocean to the west, and the Strait of Juan de Fuca to the north, and to the east, Puget Sound. If they looked to the east from the Sound, they saw the Cascade Mountain range that ran from the southern end of New Caledonia (which became known as British Columbia four years later, in 1858) all the way to Northern California. Rising from the Cascades was the tallest of the peaks called Mount Tacoma (later changed to Mount Rainier in 1890). Mount Tacoma was impressively visible from Puget Sound. Everyone stayed on deck as long as possible to experience the splendorous beauty of this new territory. It was like traveling through the Garden of Eden.

Chapter 20

December 18, 1854

Olympia, Washington Territory

*E*veryone strained at the ship's railings to see Olympia in the distance, the capital of Washington Territory, named in 1853. It sat at the head of Budd Inlet, the southern-most extension of Puget Sound. It was one of the main stops for mail. A steamboat mail route had been established between Olympia and all the other points along Puget Sound including Port Townsend and Victoria. Regular travel between the towns and mills was either by canoe or steamboat.

Now that they were close to their destination, Philip asked his brothers and Benjamin to meet him in the pilothouse to finalize their plans.

He was also concerned about Christopher's well-being. "If I get Maggie's approval, I am going to tell Christopher he will be welcome to live with the two of us. Once we have settled here, I'll be going back to Frisco. I plan to see Maggie then, and if she is still willing to marry me, I will ask her about Christopher." He felt sure she would go along with the decision since she couldn't have children of her own.

Robert stepped in closer to his brother. "Philip, are you crazy? Are you sure about asking her that? Did you ever think Maggie might want to be alone with you for a while? I'm alone, let me take him."

"I feel so responsible for him, but I guess you're right. It might be too soon for Maggie to accept a young boy living with us. What *was* I thinking? You might have just prevented our first argument, Robert."

"Then it's settled, I will take the lad," said Robert.

Thomas patted Robert's back. "This may work out well for you, Robert. You can teach him the furrier trade, and he can become your assistant."

"Yes, I had thought of that," said Robert.

Philip chuckled, "You're both as obsessed with business as I am. He will be fortunate indeed to be a part of the Bennett family."

***

The *California II* slid into the port of Olympia and anchored next to the long wharf extending out into the harbor. The whistle blew, signaling the moment had come to disembark. Suddenly, the population of Olympia expanded. Straight ahead in walking distance was a large two-story building. In its past life, it had been the Customs House where ship captains came to register their ships. The headquarters had been relocated to Port Townsend, which was a more convenient location for the ships entering and leaving Puget Sound.

The lower level of the former Customs House building was partitioned off to include a small store and a post office, and the second level was used as a residence. Thomas and Benjamin were eager to post their letters to the family back east letting them know they had arrived safely to Olympia. The next ship leaving for San Francisco would be carrying their mail, where it would be transferred to a mail ship heading to New York City.

Not far from the building, they saw twenty Duwamish Indian huts lined up on the shoreline along with several canoes drawn up to the beach. Philip pondered about the Indians. *Their heads look deformed.* He asked one of the locals about them.

The man answered, "The Indians are from the Duwamish tribe. They're called *Flatheads.*"

Philip asked, "I see why they are called *Flatheads,* but how did their heads end up like that?"

The man explained. "From birth, their foreheads are weighted down with a board fixed in a slanted position until their forehead forms into a flattened angle, like what you see."

The new arrivals had never seen such a sight but were quite happy to learn the Indians were friendly. They had heard frightful stories back east about *wild* Indians in the new territory.

Several of the passengers found the store as soon as they landed. The store offered a variety of merchandise. The passengers found soap, sperm whale candles, hoop skirts, patent medicines, axes, powder, shot, whiskey, and smoked fish.

They were overwhelmed by the stark contrast of these new surroundings compared to their previous environment. Most of them had come from the big city. In New York City, they were accustomed to loud noise, the smell of sewage, large buildings, beggars on the streets, rampant crime, and extreme weather conditions.

Here, they were surrounded with giant evergreens, verdant foliage, and the salty scent of the sea from the sparkling waters of Puget Sound. They reveled at the spectacles before them—the rolling pastures and patches of gardens, and the panoramic view of the surrounding snow-capped mountains and hills. The weather was moderate, and when it rained, it not only kept the land verdant and green, but cleansed the air.

Despite the beauty and closeness to nature, the new arrivals had expected Olympia, the designated capital of the territory, to resemble something more of a city. Instead, it was a city of stumps, and the narrow roads turned into thick mud when it rained.

The typical residence was a single-story cabin with split cedar siding. The inhabitants were industrious, enterprising, and always ready to offer a helping hand.

As the newcomers removed their rose-colored glasses, they realized the living conditions were going to be rough and crude at the beginning, and there would be fewer conveniences while settling on raw land. They also knew the Donation Land Grant would make it all worthwhile.

Chapter 21

*T*he next morning Philip marveled at his group of adventurers standing before him on the ship's deck. He had started out with his two brothers and Benjamin, and now Christopher, Peter, and Billy had become part of the entourage. Soon, Maggie would be with him.

He gazed at them with reverence, and said, "Gentlemen, our moment has come. Our land awaits us! We've come a long way since I first sent that letter to you, dear brothers. My crew will be looking for land along with us. They all want to settle here.

"We'll be traveling along the Sound as we explore the land while working our way to Teekalet where the sawmill is located. It is near the entrance of the Hood Canal, and I understand there is a good harbor to drop anchor. I expect it will be about an eight-hour trip."

* * *

Eight hours later, the adventurers reached their destination, the Hood Canal entrance. They navigated through the opening and along the northwestern shore of the heavily forested peninsula that jutted out forming a sheltered bay.

Instantly, Philip spotted the mill on the sandspit at the mouth of the bay. He pointed and said, "There's the Teekalet Lumber Mill. I will be meeting with the owners as soon as we tie up to their wharf."

On the opposite side of the bay, they noticed an Indian village.

Near the mill, they noticed bunkhouses and individual cabins for the mill workers, along with a cookhouse. The general store was nearby. They had entered the small company town of Teekalet. They saw a hotel and restaurant, and a long wharf set up for ships to drop anchor. Up above on a bluff, a neighborhood was visible with houses constructed in the familiar New England style, each with a yard surrounded with a white picket fence. A park had been strategically located providing a buffer from the lower section of the town. They also noticed a large blockhouse located on the fringe of the town, which made Thomas uneasy. *Was this a place for refuge?* He wondered if there were problems with the Indians. His wife and children would be coming soon. He needed answers.

The *California II* slowly eased in next to the wharf. After the crew tied her off, everyone disembarked. They were happy to stretch their legs.

Thomas looked toward the hotel and turned to Philip. "Philip, while you talk business with the mill owners, we'll walk over to the hotel and check in."

"I was going to suggest that myself. I will meet you at the hotel when I'm finished. I have no idea how long the meeting will take."

Robert yelled out, "Good luck, Philip."

* * *

The meeting with the mill owners went well. It was agreed Philip would be the captain of their vessel and would sail to a specific port with their venture shipment. His duty, as captain, was to sell the cargo to an agent and lay the groundwork for future relationships. Philip's payment would be a percentage of the sale. If he used his own ship, he would receive half of the sale proceeds.

Philip decided to utilize their ship most of the time since deck space for freight on the *California II* was more limited, but he insisted on using his own crew. They recognized the value of a captain with a loyal crew, and agreed to hire Philip's men. They shook hands.

"Welcome to our community, Captain Bennett. You will be

pleased to know that we have cabins available for you and your crew to occupy for as long as you wish," said one of the mill owners.

"Thank you, I look forward to our success."

Philip's first assignment was to take a shipment to San Francisco, which worked out to be good timing for him to visit Daniel Bly's family and to see Maggie. He would leave in one week's time.

The crew happily settled into the cabins. Peter and Billy also stayed in one of the cabins, but only on a temporary basis.

After the meeting, Philip joined his brothers and Benjamin at the hotel. That night they celebrated their arrival by sharing a meal in the hotel dining room. The menu offered a selection of seafood. They learned from the waitress there was a superabundant supply of salmon, oysters, and clams throughout the Hood Canal.

Robert smiled at the waitress and said, "Miss, we will start out with a bucket of clams!"

"Yes sir," she said as she smiled at him flirtatiously.

While they waited for the clams, the owner of the hotel stopped at their table and introduced himself.

"Greetings. I am Silas Johnson, the owner of this hotel. You fellas are new in town. You don't look like the type to work at the mill, so you must be planning to settle. Am I correct?"

They, in turn, introduced themselves and told him he was correct.

"Well, you are settling in God's country. The area is abundant with fertile farmland. Because of the temperate climate and rich lowlands here, the conditions are perfect for cultivating orchards and vineyards."

Thomas inquired about the blockhouse.

Silas responded and pointed east across the bay, "That's Point Julia, where the S'Klallam tribe resides. We don't have to worry about them causing us harm. But the Haida Indians from up north are dangerous and terrifying. From time to time they come as raiding parties to kidnap our Indian neighbors for slave labor. They will kill anyone who gets in their way. We do the best we can to protect them from those predators.

"The Haidas' dugout canoes are impressive. They can travel a great distance, and they are fast and sturdy. We've seen as many as a hundred Indians in one canoe! The mill has a lookout man, and he can see them when they come toward the bay. If you hear the mill's whistle, grab your guns and run like hell to the blockhouse. We let the S'Klallam Indians come across the bay for shelter, so don't be alarmed when you see them coming across in their canoes. You will learn to know and recognize them. You might run into them at the store, and some of them even work at the mill."

***

Philip hadn't expected the mill to send him on a business trip so soon. Since he would be leaving in seven days, he laid out a detailed agenda of what he hoped they could accomplish in the week before his departure. Finding their land was the first priority.

After a couple of days of rigorous exploration, the Bennett party found suitable land located a couple of miles south of the mill. Very few people had settled in the area, so there was an ample amount of land still available. They felt fortunate to find land abutting the shoreline. It was ideal for Robert and Thomas to load their goods onto Philip's ship for him to sell in San Francisco, and other places such as the Hawaiian Islands. Each one-hundred-sixty-acre tract was adjacent to the other. They rushed to file their claims and began preparations to settle on their new land.

Their next priority was to make specific arrangements with the mill owners. The mill would clear timber from the owners' parcels, trade their timber for dry lumber, and construct their houses and buildings. In exchange, the mill's payment would be in timber.

Additionally, the Bennett Bros. Co. would wholesale their products to the mill's general store. The array of products would include shoes, gloves, belts, vests, hats, and leather breeches, as well as fur products such as hats, collars, muffs, gauntlets, and capes. The mill owners were quick to recognize that the mill workers and their families would enjoy access to such a variety of products in the general store.

The week passed quickly. It was time for Philip to leave on the venture trip. He and his crew boarded the mill's ship, *Tahoma*, and departed for San Francisco. He had decided to leave Peter behind, believing he would be more valuable at their settlement.

Philip left Teekalet feeling confident this first venture trip would be successful. Since he had previously established several contacts during his many sojourns to Frisco, selling the shipment would be easy. He had a busy schedule ahead of him, including seeing Maggie and visiting Mrs. Bly. Meanwhile, the rest of the group forged ahead with their plans.

The Bennett party's next step was to procure a workboat from the mill for regular travel on the canal to and from the mill. The mill built boats in various sizes. Philip left Peter in charge of selecting and navigating the new boat. Peter chose a medium-sized boat equipped with a sail. There would be goods to deliver to both the mill and the general store. They would also be purchasing supplies from the general store for which they would be granted a credit account using their timber as collateral.

Finally, the time came to check out of the hotel and move to their new land. The group loaded their boat with the supplies they had purchased from the store. Then they loaded their cargo that had been stored on the *California II*. They were fortunate to have access to the ship while it sat tied to the wharf during Philip's absence.

Everyone boarded the new boat. Britta hopped on first. She wasn't about to be left behind. They navigated their boat for the first time down the Hood Canal until they reached their destination—their new settlement.

It was early morning when they arrived. They would need every hour of daylight to set up some kind of camp and shelter for the night. They fabricated two lean-tos, each up against a tree. The trees surrounding them were approximately two-hundred-fifty feet tall and six to eight feet in diameter. They used the sail canvas they had borrowed from Philip's ship to stretch over the tree limbs. Then they set up a campfire, ready for nightfall. For their first meal, they planned to dig some clams from their beach and bake them on the open fire. The clams would make a nice fresh addition to the food they brought with them.

After a few hours, Britta's excited barking startled them. They looked up and saw several Indians coming toward them in canoes. Their eyes darted about the campsite. *Where did we set our guns?* They had been so busy working on their shelter and campsite, they neglected to keep their weapons close by. There wasn't time to retrieve them. They stood motionless.

Peter, the most seasoned of the group, said, "Just stay calm, and don't make any sudden movements—especially not toward your guns. Try to act natural. Christopher, calm Britta down. They eat dogs you know."

Christopher took control of Britta.

"Calm, you say? Easier said than done. I'm shaking in my boots," said Benjamin.

The Indians slid their canoes onto the beach. Peter counted four men and two women. He stepped forward, using a hand motion signaling hospitality. The Indians nodded. Peter learned they were from the Suquamish tribe, and had come to trade. They brought salmon and clams. Peter looked sideways toward Thomas, "What do we have to offer for trade?"

"I suppose we could give up one of our kettles." Thomas cautiously nodded to the Indians as he walked over to their supplies and pulled out a shiny new kettle. The lead Indian stepped forward and took it from Thomas. Examining it, he seemed pleased.

Then the Indians, through signs and gestures, insisted on showing their new friends how to cook the salmon and clams. They enjoyed showing off their skills to these naïve white men.

One of the matrons of the Indian party walked over to the campfire on the beach, which Peter had built and lit earlier in the day. On one section of the fire, she laid several handfuls of pebbles on to the embers. Once the stones were hot, she added a new layer of stones and placed the clams on top, and then covered them with small twigs. After the clams were sufficiently cooked, she removed the steaming morsels and set them on a piece of nearby driftwood, and indicated the clams were ready to eat.

One of the male Indians skewered the salmon onto sharp green sticks. Then he inserted the sticks into the ground in a vertical position next to the campfire. Soon the salmon was cooked. The Indians stayed and ate the food with the homesteaders.

Benjamin rubbed his stomach, "That's one of the best meals I have ever eaten. I could eat clams this way every day."

Peter, who had spent time in Maine many years prior, was accustomed to clam bakes. He chuckled, "I take it you have experienced your first clam bake?"

Robert and Thomas had relaxed, and as usual, were thinking about their business. They realized they had a trading opportunity standing before them. If they established a relationship with these Indians, perhaps they could lead them to nearby trading posts. The brothers started using hand motions.

Thomas touched his shoes rubbing the leather between his fingers. Robert did the same except with his beaver hat. The Indians were used to traders and immediately understood. Then one of the Indians stepped forward and spoke in French. Thomas and Robert didn't speak French but were pleasantly surprised when Peter stepped forward speaking fluent French to the Indian. He helped seal the relationship.

With nightfall coming on, the Indians bid them goodbye. They hopped into their canoes and left as quietly as they had arrived.

As they watched the Indians leave, Thomas commented, "We've had a productive day, and what an unexpected feast!"

Peter commented, "Our little clambake reminded me of the time I spent in Maine."

Robert said, "You sure came in handy for Thomas and me. Appreciate it. I am curious, where did you learn to speak French so well?"

"I was born in Montreal, and of course, while growing up among the French, I learned quite naturally. My parents had emigrated from England to Quebec and settled there."

"Well, we sure are glad you're here, Peter. It's obvious Philip has confidence in you since he offered you a position on his ship. He is pretty particular," said Thomas.

"I am beholden to Captain Bennett. I've spent most of my adult life at sea. For awhile, I worked on a ship that sailed to and from England and the York Factory. The Factory needed fresh supplies of trade goods, and in return, sent back furs to England. It was good while it lasted since I was close to my home base."

Robert asked, "How did you end up so far from home, and then on the *Theodora?*"

Peter hesitated. "Sometimes, you have to choose a different path. I heard about the land grant out here and decided to give it a try. The *Theodora* was a bit of bad luck. I was supposed to have been on the same ship as Daniel Bly before it hit a reef and had to be put in dry dock for repair." Peter quickly changed the subject. "We're losing daylight. Let's prepare our camp for the night."

Chapter 22

*I*t was Philip's first business trip to San Francisco for the mill. He navigated the *Tahoma* into the fog-shrouded harbor, easing her up to the long wharf. He sounded the whistle and gave the order to drop anchor. As usual, the wharf was a flurry of activity. Philip instructed Samuel to delay unloading the cargo until he returned with a buyer.

He had a full agenda for this trip. He would make a quick stop at the post office to mail the letters Thomas and Benjamin had written to Jane and Mary informing them of their safe arrival to Puget Sound. Afterward, he planned to visit Maggie, check in with Captain Davis, and finally, pay his respects to Daniel Bly's wife and children.

Visiting Maggie was first on Philip's agenda. She happened to be alone when he walked in, and with eyes flashing, she flew into his arms. They kissed passionately. As always, he planned to stay with her while he was in Frisco.

"I can't stay at the moment, my love. So many tasks, and so little time. I'll catch up with you tonight. There's much to tell you." Just then a thought flashed through his mind, *I must return with a ring, but I don't know her ring size.*

"Before I leave, may I take my bag to your bedroom and use your privy?"

"You know the way," she said.

He knew she kept her jewelry in the top drawer of her dresser. He quickly rummaged through the drawer until he found a ring and slipped it into his pocket. Pleased with himself, he emerged and kissed her. "I will see you tonight, love."

She kissed him back. "Until tonight, my Philip."

***

After several hours of footwork and cab rides, Philip sold the cargo and established several firm commitments for future shipments. He also found buyers for merchandise that would soon be available from the Bennett Bros. Co. He would use his own ship, the *California II,* for Bennett Bros. shipments.

He rushed back to the ship to tell Samuel to prepare the cargo for the buyers. Next, he hailed a cab to take him to the residence of Captain Davis. He didn't intend to stay long, so he asked the cab driver to wait for him. When he knocked on the door, he learned from the servant, Bridget, that Captain Davis wasn't there. He was on a voyage to the Hawaiian Islands.

"I see. May I speak to Mrs. Davis then?"

Victoria appeared and saw Philip standing in the doorway, "Philip, do come in. Are you well? It is wonderful to see you again. How are your plans coming along? I imagine you and your party have settled in Washington Territory by now?"

"Yes, we are officially homesteaders, and that's why I am here. I wanted to let William know it's time to schedule the voyage for Thomas's family. September would be timely if that works for him. May I write him a note?"

"Of course, you can use William's desk. You'll find everything you need there."

"Thank you, Victoria. I will give him Jane's address as well. In our last conversation, he indicated he would like to contact Jane directly about the schedule. I'll assume September is agreeable unless I hear differently. He can always leave a message at the post office for me.

Now that I'm working with the mill in Teekalet, I'll be coming to Frisco on a regular basis."

"I'll make sure William sees your note. So, Philip, how is Maggie? You must have already seen her by now."

"Indeed I have, Victoria. In fact, perhaps you could help me out with an important task. While I am in Frisco, I need to buy a wedding ring, but I don't have any idea of where to find a trustworthy jeweler. Can you recommend anyone?"

"I am absolutely elated, Philip. And yes, I do know of a good jeweler. I have used his service for years. Just give me a moment, and I will get the address for you."

She returned with the address. Philip thanked her and bid her goodbye. "Please give my regards to William when he returns. I will try to see him on my next trip back."

He went back to the waiting cab and instructed the driver to take him to the jeweler's address. When they arrived, Philip asked the driver to wait for him again. At first glance, Philip was impressed with the façade of the jewelry store, which gave him confidence about the quality of the establishment. When he opened the front door, the brass bells jingled alerting the storeowner someone had just entered.

"May I help you, *Monsieur*?"

"Yes, Victoria Davis referred me to you. I am on a mission to buy a wedding ring."

"Ah, Madame Davis. She is a valued customer. I will take special care of you. Do you have a design in mind?"

"I have no idea. To be truthful, I'm a little nervous."

"Please, allow me to show you my private collection." The jeweler directed Philip to follow him to another room. As he approached the doorway, the jeweler parted a pair of heavy red velvet curtains.

Philip followed him to an alcove that was home to an ornate glass case filled with solid gold bands.

"Monsieur, you are viewing my most superb rings. The difference between these rings and those in the other room is the weight of the gold and the intricate engravings." He brought out a ring for a closer inspection. "Do you see the delicate engraving encircling this ring?"

Philip took the ring from the jeweler and examined it. "Yes, this is fine work. May I see some of the other designs?"

"Oui, Monsieur, do you know her ring size?"

Philip reached into his pocket and brought out the borrowed ring and handed it to the jeweler.

"You came prepared, Monsieur. I'll take a measurement. Please, examine as many rings as you like."

Philip continued to survey the case. There were so many choices. He finally decided on a ring with an engraved design of a rose and leaf spiraling the band and bordered with diamond and emerald chips. There was an accompanying ring of the same design except without the stones to join its companion on the wedding day.

"This is the set!" They negotiated a price.

Philip extended his hand. "Done!"

The jeweler exclaimed, "Tres bien! You are a shrewd buyer."

He put the ring set into an emerald green velvet ring box, and with great finesse, presented the box to Philip.

With his tasks completed for the day, Philip instructed the cab driver to take him to Maggie's address—the final stop for the day. He planned to devote his last day visiting Daniel Bly's wife and family before his final departure. He had previously contacted Mrs. Bly by mail about her husband's passing and that he planned to visit her on his next trip to San Francisco.

Maggie continued to watch out the window for Philip's arrival. When she saw him step out of the cab, her heart raced. *Will he have a ring for me?* It was after hours, so the restaurant was closed. She scurried and checked to see that the desk clerk was at his station in case any of the boarders needed assistance. All the doors would be locked soon. The dining room was separated from the public space with a set of locking doors. Her private living space was situated on the opposite side of the dining area. She planned a quiet, and hopefully romantic, dinner together. She made a special dinner— roast chicken, potatoes and vegetables, and bread fresh out of the oven. For dessert, she baked Philip's favorite, her Lady Kay apple pie. The pie sat cooling in the pie safe in the kitchen area.

When Philip walked in, he could smell the delicious mingling of aromas wafting through the air. Maggie was wearing one of her most seductive dresses. When she saw him coming, she quickly removed her apron and brushed a few stray strands of hair away from her face. She smoothed her dress with her hands to eliminate any possible wrinkles.

Philip savored the vision, and his senses were well rewarded. *Look how beautiful she is, inside and out, and what a good cook! I'm a lucky man.*

She had skillfully set the scene. The table was covered with a white linen cloth in place of the more casual checked cloth, and a candle flickered in the center of the table. There were two crystal glasses placed on the table, accompanied by a bottle of fine wine she had purchased from the French Quarter that afternoon. When she had returned with the bottle, she wondered, *Will there be something special to toast to tonight?*

After they embraced and kissed, they sat down at the table. Philip was nervous. He could see by the ambiance she had staged, she was expecting something. *I would have been a fool not to have come with a ring tonight.*

He took her hands into his, and said, "Maggie, you mean everything to me. I want us to spend the rest of our lives together. I love you, Maggie. Will you marry me?" As soon as he said the words, he brought out the velvet ring box and presented it to her.

She opened it and saw the beautiful gold rings. She was happy and crying at the same time. "Yes, yes, Philip, I will marry you!"

Philip smiled and took the engagement ring out of the box and slipped it on to her finger.

"Oh, Philip, it's so beautiful. You remembered how much I love roses. This is such a special ring. I have never seen anything like it. But, how did you know my ring size?"

Philip answered with a sheepish grin as he pulled a ring out of his pocket. "When I went into your bedroom earlier today, I went to your jewelry drawer and borrowed this." He handed the ring to her.

Maggie smiled with eyes flashing, "You are certainly resourceful, Captain Bennett. Would you like to pour the wine while I return this to my drawer?" She returned shortly, and they clinked glasses to toast the moment.

They relaxed together and enjoyed the delicious dinner topped off with the Lady Kay apple pie. Afterward, they spent a memorable romantic evening in the bedroom.

***

The next morning, Philip was anxious to bring her up-to-date.

"Maggie, so much has happened since I saw you last."

He told her the story about the orphaned stowaway they had discovered on board after leaving San Francisco.

"His name is Christopher. He's a good lad. I believe Robert is going to take him in."

Maggie's heart went out to Christopher. "That poor boy, how good of Robert to offer him a home."

Philip thought about his earlier conversation with his brothers when they advised him *not* to ask Maggie about allowing Christopher to live with the two of them. He thought about their romantic evening together. *Was I crazy? Disaster averted. Thank you, brothers.*

He continued to tell her about the rest of the journey. He told her about the shipwreck and the rescue of the two survivors, about Daniel Bly's message in the bottle. "I feel duty-bound to visit Daniel Bly's widow."

"*So* sad. I'm happy you're going to visit her, and I know you will be a comfort to her, Philip."

"I plan to visit her tomorrow morning. I believe there is more to find out, and I want to get to the bottom of it."

"I know you will, Philip."

"I hope so, Maggie. Now, let's talk about you. I have plans. Construction of your bakery building on my parcel will begin immediately. We will be able to deliver your pies to the other settlements nearby. We now have a smaller vessel that is perfect to sail from port to port all along Puget Sound. When we traveled to Teekalet, I noticed a port every few miles with settlements."

Maggie was overwhelmed with everything Philip told her. She felt a little uneasy about producing so many pies. "Philip, I don't think I could keep up with the volume without help."

"Don't worry, my darling. I'll make sure you have help. And Maggie, it won't be long before I come back for you. You will love Teekalet. When we are finally there together, I will take you by the hand, and lead you up the hill that overlooks the Hood Canal. The view is spectacular. That is where our house shall be built, and where I would like us to be married, Maggie."

"It sounds wonderful, Philip."

"Now, love, I must take my leave and check in with Samuel to see if the cargo has been unloaded. I'm meeting the buyer at the wharf to receive payment. I will be back after the meeting. I'm afraid this will be our last night together, my sweet, until my next trip."

Chapter 23

The next morning, Philip and Maggie woke up in each other's arms. They chatted about their future together. It wouldn't be much longer before he would whisk her away to join him in Teekalet.

"I'm afraid we cannot tarry any longer, my love." Philip began to dress. "I will be visiting Mrs. Bly this morning, and I plan to leave the harbor by noon."

Maggie cooked a hearty breakfast for Philip. Afterwards, they said their farewells with an embrace and one last lingering kiss.

Then Philip drew her ring hand to his lips and kissed it softly. "Goodbye, my darling."

As Maggie watched Philip walk away, she smiled like a little girl who had won a prize. She extended out her left hand, which had been so gently kissed, and admired her ring as it glinted in the morning sun.

Philip walked to the nearest cab stop and hired a driver to take him to the address of Mrs. Bly. He walked up the gravel pathway to a modest but tidy house and knocked on the door. A petite woman he judged to be in her thirties answered. She was dressed in black, and her dark hair was pulled back to form a bun at the nape of her neck. Her mahogany brown eyes stared back, sorrowfully, and she could only offer a faint smile when Philip introduced himself.

"Come in, Captain Bennett. I received your message by courier yesterday that you were coming this morning. It is so kind of you to visit. Do sit down."

Philip politely doffed his hat. "Mrs. Bly, please accept my deepest condolences."

She interrupted. "Please, call me Rachel if you like."

"Of course. Rachel, as I mentioned in my earlier communication to you, your husband wrote a letter and secured it in a corked bottle for the chance of someone finding it. We found the bottle wedged in some floating debris. I do hope it gives you some comfort when I tell you his last thoughts were of you and your children."

Tears filled Rachel's eyes. Philip lowered his eyes giving her a private moment.

"Where are my manners, Captain Bennett? Allow me to serve you some refreshment. If you will excuse me, I will be back momentarily."

Philip stood and nodded. He was sure she needed some time to compose her emotions.

In Rachel's absence, Philip gazed about the room. The drapes were drawn closed, contributing to the melancholy mood. He noticed a man's coat laying on a chair, and a table next to the chair on which a framed picture of a man held a place of honor. The picture was illuminated with a flickering candle. Across the room was another table. A single wine glass and a nearly empty bottle of red wine were set on the table.

Philip was startled when the front door swung open. The Blys' adolescent son and daughter had come home after running errands for their mother. He stood and introduced himself.

The daughter spoke first, "Hello, I'm Annie Bly, and this is my brother, Matthew Bly. You must be here about our father?"

Philip answered. "I am pleased to meet both of you, and yes, I am here about your father. May I ask, is that your father's picture on the table next to the candle?"

Matthew answered, "Yes, and that's his coat on the chair. Our mother is so lost. She takes the coat to bed with her every night and holds it close to her to smell his scent. Each day, she brings the coat out here and lays it in his chair and lights the candle next to his picture. That was our father's favorite chair. Do you see the bottle of wine over there on the table? Our father bought that bottle of wine, and our parents made a toast to our new beginning in Washington Territory. It was the night before he sailed. We never saw him again."

That's *her* glass. Every night she drinks a small portion of wine, and as there is less wine left in the bottle, she drinks a smaller portion, and then the portions turn into sips, then tinier sips, for fear of emptying the bottle too soon."

Rachel entered the room with a tray holding a pot of coffee and a dessert cake. She set it on a small table near their chairs. "I'm pleased to see you have met Annie and Matthew."

She turned her attention to the children and asked them to excuse themselves. Then she motioned for Philip to sit next to the table.

Philip seated himself. "Rachel, Daniel wrote something else in his letter. He said the captain was the cause for the ship sinking. He wanted it known he had knowledge of the ship, *Theodora,* to have been one of the abandoned ships rotting in the harbor here, which the captain had purchased on the cheap. One of the two survivors told me the *Theodora* was struck by another ship, and because the wood was so rotten, it didn't withstand the blow, and broke apart. Do you know anything about that? I am puzzled why he would have been on the *Theodora* if he knew its condition. And why didn't he report it to anyone?"

The look on Rachel's face was telling. A revelation shot through Philip's mind. *She knows something.*

She replied, "Daniel was under contract with Captain Jensen on a different ship, but the ship had struck a reef and was being repaired. The captain forced Daniel to work on the *Theodora* instead. Daniel *was* stressed about taking the voyage."

Philip was sure there was more to the story, so he prompted Rachel to continue. "Rachel, there was a survivor by the name of Peter Crandall. He told me he felt the captain was holding something over on Daniel, and it was obvious Daniel was afraid of him. I think you know more than you are saying. I would like to help if I can, but Rachel, you need to be more forthcoming."

Rachel's voice trembled. "I know of Peter. Daniel liked him. Daniel despised the captain. You see, the captain knew Daniel had witnessed his purchase of the *Theodora,* and that he also knew the rotten wood on the bottom of the ship wasn't replaced, but covered with paint instead. When Daniel learned the ship was scheduled to sail, he confronted the captain and told him the ship wasn't fit. It was then that he threatened our lives. Daniel felt our only hope was for him to claim land in Washington Territory once they reached Puget Sound. He knew it was a gamble. If he reached the Sound, he planned to send for us when he was ready for us to come, and we would be free of Captain Jensen."

"Please, go on, Rachel."

"The captain told Daniel he couldn't say anything about what he knew, and he expected him to be on the voyage, or else."

"Or else what?"

Rachel looked toward the hallway to make sure Matthew and Annie were out of earshot. She leaned forward and whispered, "The captain threatened both of our children. He said he would have Matthew shanghaied and sold to a ship captain for labor and have Annie kidnapped and sold into the white slave market. He said we would never see either of them again. I think one of his connections is an owner of a saloon next to the Barbary Coast."

Those last words struck a nerve. Philip's mind flashed back to the saloon where Christopher was nearly shanghaied. *I actually met that scoundrel in person.*

Rachel stood and poured the coffee. "The coffee will get cold." Then she handed Philip a piece of cake.

Philip was deep in thought as he drank the coffee. But when he took a bite of the cake, it stole his attention. As he savored the flavor, an idea slowly formed in his mind.

"Rachel, what is this cake called? I have never tasted anything like it. It's especially good with this coffee."

Rachel was now more relaxed with the pleasant change of subject, and replied, "It is called coffee cake. Coffee is one of the ingredients. My mother made it every time we had guests. I wanted to honor your visit, so I made it for you, Captain Bennett."

"I am honored. Rachel, how are you going to live? Do you have any form of income?"

"I don't know what I am going to do. I have very little money. Daniel took most of it with him to settle on the new land. Everything is gone, he is gone." She began to weep.

Philip's first reaction was to go and comfort her, but he checked himself. He realized she might feel uncomfortable with a man she had just met.

164

"Rachel, I am so sorry for your loss, but I *am* in a position to help you, and I insist you allow me to do so."

Rachel dabbed her eyes with her serviette and looked at Philip with a puzzled expression. "What do you mean, Captain Bennett?"

"I would like to offer you and your children the opportunity to join our settlement in Washington Territory. You can think of it as keeping your husband's dream alive.

"You will be safe with us." Philip took another bite of the cake. "In fact, I think I have an idea. Please allow me to explain. My fiancée and I plan to settle in Puget Sound in a town called Teekalet. Her name is Maggie. She lives here in San Francisco. Maggie is an excellent cook and baker, and bakes the most delicious apple pie. I came up with the idea to build a bakery for her to sell her wares. We will be located near the lumber mill and community, and it will be the only bakery in the entire Puget Sound.

"Rachel, why not offer your coffee cake too? I am sure you and Maggie would work well together *and* enjoy each other's company. Women are outnumbered by men twenty to one. What do you think, Rachel?"

"But how would we get there? I don't have money to pay the fare."

"Fortunately, Rachel, I own my ship, and on my next trip back to Frisco, I want you all to be packed and ready to leave this place." Philip leaned forward and lowered his voice. "I'm concerned about your children still being in danger. Make sure not to let them out of your sight, don't venture out at night, and keep your door locked."

"I—I, don't know what to say."

"Say yes, Rachel," said Philip.

Just then, Matthew and Annie rushed into the room. They had overheard a good portion of the conversation.

Annie threw her arms around Rachel. "Oh, Mother, say yes. I can help."

Matthew begged, "And I can chop wood. I want to come, Captain Bennett."

Rachel smiled and looked at her children. "Thank you, Captain Bennett, for this opportunity. Yes, I believe we will take you up on your offer. We *would* like to join your settlement."

"Brilliant. Rachel, one more thing. I have a friend here in the city.

His name is Captain William Davis. If you have paper and quill I may use, I will write down his address for you."

Rachel pointed to the desk against the wall. Philip sat down for a moment to write the address down. Then he also wrote a brief note to Captain Davis explaining Rachel Bly's situation.

"If you and the children need any help before I return, I know you can count on him. I will send him this note by courier in the next hour. And with that, I shall take my leave now."

Tearing up, Rachel thanked Philip and said goodbye. For the first time since he had met her, he saw a faint smile. She extended her hand, and he obliged with a cordial grasp. As she watched him leave, she closed and locked the door.

Philip hailed a cab and instructed the driver to take him to his ship, and then to deliver the note to Captain Davis.

When Philip arrived at the *Tahoma*, Samuel had finished loading the new supplies to take back to Teekalet for the lumber mill. Their business in San Francisco was finished. They sounded the whistle and weighed anchor. As they steamed away, Philip looked back at the Frisco Bay, ruminating about the events of his trip.

Chapter 24

Early February 1855

Teekalet, Washington Territory

The Teekalet harbor lay straight ahead. Philip eased the *Tahoma* alongside the wharf. At ninety feet long and four hundred feet wide, the mill wharf extended out far enough to allow the ship to remain in deep water while the crew unloaded the cargo. Philip's first venture shipment for the mill was a success. The mill owners were pleased with Philip's results, both in selling their cargo for a higher price than expected, and purchasing the much-needed supplies under budget.

After Philip finished his business meeting with the mill owners, he and a few of his crew members walked further down the wharf to where the *California II* sat anchored, waiting for her master. They boarded the ship, weighed anchor, and sailed her further down the canal toward the Bennett land claims. As the ship glided around the bend, Philip fixed his eyes upon their new settlement and wharf. *What a magnificant sight it was to behold.* The last time he saw their land, it consisted of just beach and trees. *They've accomplished so much more than I expected.* He sounded the whistle, and for the first time, Philip positioned his ship next to the new wharf. Samuel called out, "Drop anchor and tie the lines!"

The crew unloaded the remaining stored baggage while Philip jumped onto the wharf. When they finished, Samuel waved to Philip as he navigated the ship back to Teekalet. The crew looked forward to settling into their new cabins.

As Philip walked toward the settlement, Britta charged toward him. Her barking escalated into a high-pitched whine in her excitement to see him. "There's my sweet girl." He bent down and loved her up.

Thomas heard the commotion and looked up from his task. "Philip! I thought I heard the whistle. It's so good to have you back! How did you like pulling up to our new wharf? We have a lot to catch up on. We have been busy, and we are not alone."

Thomas pointed over to the lumber camp set up in a large cleared area. The sound of axes cutting into the giant trees reverberated through the forest.

Thomas led Philip to the bunkhouse. "As you can see, we have improved our sleeping arrangements, and we have even attached a temporary kitchen. The cookhouse building should be finished soon."

The group had done well during his absence. Thomas was proud to show off the completed building for the Bennett Bros. business. As planned, it was strategically located near the shoreline to facilitate loading their products onto the smaller vessel for delivering to the mill's general store. Once they increased their inventory, they planned to send their products to the San Francisco merchants on the *California II.*

"Thomas, these buildings have gone up remarkably fast."

"Yes, your plan for us to be situated near the mill has worked out well. We've been able to take advantage of their balloon framing method using pre-cut lumber. We are trading our green wood for their air-dried wood. Once each site is cleared, we're able to frame a building in one day, two at the most. Come, take a closer look at one of the buildings."

Philip was knowledgeable about the new framing method and looked forward to seeing it in action. He followed Thomas to one of the buildings. The walls consisted of sawn studs and then covered with split cedar siding, while the roof was covered with split cedar shakes. Philip inhaled the woody, spicy-resinous scent of the cedar still lingering in the air. Next, Thomas led him to one end of the building and showed him the large brick fireplace and chimney.

Thomas was especially proud of the multi-paned wood sash windows. "How do you like these windows, Philip? They're the latest design and purchased straight from the mill's general store."

"I am impressed with everything, Thomas. You have been busy. I have been busy as well. There is much to tell you. Where is everyone?"

"They're working on the cookhouse."

They walked toward the work party. Britta trailed close behind. The group saw them coming and were excited Philip had returned.

After Philip greeted them, he retrieved two letters from inside his jacket. "Thomas, I have a letter for you from Jane, and one for you, Benjamin, from Mary. Benjamin, aren't you about to become a father soon?"

"Yes, about another month. Mary is constantly on my mind."

"You two take some time to read your letters. You must be anxious. Then we can all talk."

Thomas and Benjamin couldn't wait to tear open the envelopes. While waiting for Thomas and Benjamin to finish reading their letters, Philip chatted with the rest of the group.

"Thomas gave me a tour of the buildings. Looks like the balloon framing method worked out well."

Robert updated Philip with his news. "We've made a connection with the local Indians, and they've been helpful in providing us with information about other traders. We've decided to trade directly with the Indians once we have something to trade with."

After Thomas and Benjamin finished reading their letters, Philip recounted his experience in San Francisco. "... and I'm bringing Maggie back to Teekalet. We will be getting married as soon as the rest of the family arrives."

"That is wonderful news," said Thomas.

"Thanks. I am a happy man." Then he revealed his idea about Maggie selling her pies and other bakery items to the local restaurant in Teekalet. "I plan to build a bakery building for her on my parcel.

"There is something else. As you all know, I made plans to visit Mrs. Bly. During my visit, I learned that she and her children are vulnerable and in danger, so I offered to bring them back to Teekalet. After some persuasion, she accepted my offer. I plan to bring the family back here on my next trip to Frisco."

Peter was keenly interested. "So, you're going to bring them here? I'm all for that, but we don't have a place for them to live. We can't keep them at the hotel forever. The mill cabins are out of the question with all those mill workers around. In case you haven't noticed, there are very few women around here. Looks like we had better get busy building them a house." He thought for a moment. "I'll volunteer my parcel."

Peter felt protective over Daniel's family. He had met them once when Daniel had invited him to supper. He liked the family instantly. Mrs. Bly was a sweet, gentle woman. Daniel had shared so much about her, Peter felt like he already knew her. *I will take good care of them, Daniel.*

The brothers nodded in agreement.

Thomas said, "Tomorrow we will tell the lumber supervisor to move his crew over to Peter's parcel and start clearing for a small house. When do you go back to Frisco, Philip?"

"In two weeks. I will take my ship. The mill owners have granted me flexibility. And by the way, you'll be happy to know I have plans to come back with two cookstoves. One for the cookhouse and one for the bakery. Our group is expanding with Maggie and Mrs. Bly and her children returning with me. Peter, I suggest you have the house built large enough for all of them to live together until we get our permanent quarters built. Now that I think about it, I had better purchase a third stove."

Chapter 25

February 1855

San Francisco

Two weeks passed before he knew it, and Philip was on his way back to San Francisco. This trip was more than business—he was on a mission.

Thomas and Robert used the workboat to transport Philip back to his ship, still anchored at the Teekalet harbor. The mill's cargo had already been loaded onto the ship under Samuel's supervision. He and the crew were waiting to weigh anchor when Philip arrived.

He boarded his ship and yelled out to his brothers, "I'll see you in three weeks' time."

They waved and watched the *California II* leave the bay.

Meanwhile, the group had much to accomplish. According to the rules of the Donation Land Act, it was mandatory that each of the parcels claimed show signs of settlement. This meant land needed to be cleared, dwellings built, and signs of having worked the land evident. Everyone worked hard, and a spirit of camaraderie evolved.

***

The *California II* steamed into San Francisco Bay and Philip positioned her next to the wharf for his crew to offload the shipment. This time, due to Philip's business acumen, the shipment was pre-sold.

His first priority was to see Rachel Bly and let her know he was back in Frisco and to be ready to leave the next day.

She greeted him warmly. "Captain Bennett, I'm so relieved to see you. Please, come in. I began packing the day after you left. We're ready to leave. You were right about my children still being in danger. I hadn't noticed before, but there is always someone standing across the street watching us. When I think back, I believe we were being watched even before you came. News of the *Theodora* hasn't reached the city yet, and I haven't told a soul. Those men must be waiting to hear from Captain Jensen for word to carry out his threat. The children and I have been *so* frightened. We have been careful not to make our packing obvious."

Philip walked over to the window and slowly parted the curtain enough to peer out. He saw the men across the street watching the house. He didn't like it.

"Rachel, can you be prepared to leave tonight? I'm going back to my ship to instruct some of my men to keep an eye on you. Under cover of darkness, we will get you and the children out of here. Then, you will finally be safe."

"Oh yes, Captain Bennett, we'll be ready. The rent is paid for the month. I'll leave a note for my landlord. Do you think Captain Jensen might have planned to double cross my husband, and still have our children taken?"

"It wouldn't surprise me in the least. He was a greedy and unscrupulous man. My men will be close by, but please *do* stay inside. I will see you at nightfall."

Tears welled up in Rachel's eyes while she extended her hand to Philip. "Thank you, again, Captain Bennett."

Philip bid the Blys goodbye and hurried back to his ship. He instructed two of his crew members to watch the Bly house, but to stay out of sight of the men spying on the family.

"Even if the men leave at nightfall, I want you to continue guarding the Blys until I return to take them to the ship."

He hailed a cab and instructed the driver to take him to Maggie's boarding house. When Philip arrived, he told the driver to wait. Maggie saw Philip arriving. The moment he walked through the door, she pulled him into her arms and kissed him over and over. "You're here! I have finalized everything! I am ready to leave with you. How soon are we leaving?"

"Soon, my love. We will be weighing anchor by tomorrow afternoon. I have some news, Maggie. You'll have company. There's been a new development."

Then he told her about the Bly family being in danger if they stayed in San Francisco, and his idea for her and Mrs. Bly to work together in the bakery.

"The idea came to me when I tasted her coffee cake. She'll be able to help you, Maggie, and we will be helping her."

"It's a wonderful idea, Philip. I'm actually relieved not to be taking on this project alone."

"It makes me feel better about it too. And now, I have a surprise for you."

"Oh? Whatever could it be? You know how I love surprises."

"How would you like to accompany me to pick out your new cookstove? I need to purchase two other stoves as well, but they won't be as special as yours."

Maggie could barely contain her excitement. She hadn't thought that far ahead about how and when she would get a stove.

"Yes, oh yes, thank you, Philip!"

"Shall we go now, my love?" Philip extended his arm to her as they walked out of the boarding house. She waved goodbye to Arthur at the front desk as she left. Philip assisted her into the cab, and off they went to the stove company.

When they walked into the Babbitt Stove Shop, Maggie was in awe.

Philip smiled. "Pick out anything you desire, my darling."

Her eyes scanned the room until they stopped at a particular stove. After close scrutiny, she said, "This is the one, Philip!"

The black cast iron cooking stove was described as having been recently tested and introduced to the market. It was made with an oven that extended underneath the hearth, making it a much larger oven than most. It had double action reversible flues beneath the stove, which made for perfect baking results. There was a large firebox and an extra firebox behind. The stove even had a broiling feature. The top had four hearth plates, and there was a handy apron tray located midway down the front and sides. The stove had just enough embellishment to please the eye.

"It appears you have made your choice, Maggie. That didn't take long."

Philip turned to the owner who was also the sales clerk. "We'll take it." Then Philip asked Maggie to help him select two more cooking stoves. With three stoves selected, Philip paid the owner and asked him to have the stoves delivered to his ship and loaded on board before noon the next day.

"Yes, sir, Captain Bennett. My men and I will have the stoves loaded on to the *California II* before noon tomorrow. It's been a pleasure doing business with you."

The owner couldn't stop smiling as Philip and Maggie left the shop, and thought to himself, *I'll be danged, I've never had such a large sale happen so fast from a walk-in. I'll be buying my wife that new dress she wants from that fancy French boutique.*

Philip took Maggie back to the boarding house.

"Maggie, I still have some business details to take care of about future deliveries, so I'll take my leave for now. I'll be back tonight, but it'll be late. As soon as it's dark, my men and I are taking Rachel and her children to the ship. They'll sleep on board tonight."

***

It was nightfall, and Philip arrived by cab to the Bly house. The watchers who had been lurking in the shadows had left at dusk. Inside, the Blys nervously waited for Philip. They had followed his instructions and dressed in dark clothes to blend into the night. Finally, they heard Philip's coded knock on the door. Philip saw the window curtain move, and the door opened.

"Oh, Captain Bennett. I thought the hour would never come."

"You're safe now, Rachel."

Philip helped carry their baggage and escorted them from the house. Matthew assisted his mother and sister into the cab while Philip and the driver loaded their trunk and bags onto the back of the cab. Soon, Rachel and her children would board the *California*

II, their safe haven. She caressed a small bag she kept close to her. The bag held her husband's picture. A tear trickled down her face. She clutched the bag, holding it next to her heart. She looked sadly at their little house that was once a home. Moments before leaving, she had taken her final sip of the wine. She could still taste the lingering bitterness of the wine, which had gone bad weeks ago.

* * *

The following morning marked the beginning of a new life for Maggie. While she and Philip ate a quick breakfast, Philip wanted to make sure Maggie knew what to expect.

"Maggie, at the moment, life in Washington Territory isn't what you are accustomed to here in Frisco. We're striving to develop our land, but it is going to take some time. To be honest, life will be a little primitive for awhile, but I promise, that'll change.

"Rachel Bly and her children are now safe on my ship. They're excited about joining us. Peter Crandall has offered his parcel to have a house built for them to live in. The house is being built as we speak. At first, you'll need to live there too, so the size of the house is being built large enough for all of you. I'll be sleeping in the bunkhouse with the men. I'm positive you and Rachel are going to get along and enjoy working together in the bakery. I imagine the two of you will be grateful to have each other's company? There are very few women in the entire territory. Now, that I've laid it all out, my love, are you still willing to go?"

Maggie grabbed Philip's hands, "Yes, my darling, I am ready to begin our new life together. I'm looking forward to meeting Rachel, and I welcome the opportunity to offer her my friendship. I'll miss not being with you on a private basis, but I will be patient and be *respectable* until we marry and have a house of our own."

"That's what I wanted to hear, my love. Now, if you are ready, darling, let us walk out this door, and begin a new chapter together."

"Oh, yes, Philip, I am ready." Then she cupped his face in her hands and kissed him gently.

Maggie said goodbye to the people taking over the boarding house. The happy couple stood on the boardwalk listening to the steady clip-clop, clip-clop sound of the horses' hooves striking the cobblestone street as their cab approached. The driver arrived at the appointed hour. Philip assisted Maggie into the cab and stepped in behind her. There was no baggage to load since Philip had already arranged to have her belongings taken to the ship the day before.

Philip signaled the driver. "The wharf please, driver."

Chapter 26

February 1855

$\mathcal{P}$hilip helped Maggie board the ship. She was overwhelmed with excitement. As the *California II* steamed out of the Frisco Bay, Maggie looked back at the city she was leaving behind, and exclaimed, "Philip, is this really happening? I feel like I am dreaming and I don't want to wake up."

Her flaming red hair flew freely in the wind. He gently brushed it away from her face. "It is happening my love. I can't wait to introduce you as my fiancée to my family."

"You have told me so much about them, I feel like I already know them. How long will it take to get to Teekalet?"

"It should take about ten days. Plenty of time for you and Rachel to get to know each other. I've arranged for each of you to have a private cabin. She will share hers with her daughter, Annie, of course. Samuel has offered to share his cabin with her son, Matthew. Now, let's get you settled in. I'll invite them to dine with us this evening, and you'll be able to meet them."

She brought his face close to hers and kissed him softly. "I look forward to this evening then."

He offered his arm to escort her to her cabin, and with a tilt of his hat and a half bow, said, "This way, my lady."

* * *

On the second day of the voyage, Maggie invited Rachel and her children to her cabin for tea. This marked the beginning of a budding friendship between Maggie and Rachel. Both women realized they would need and appreciate each other's support.

During the visit, Rachel opened a small box she had brought with her and took out a few pieces of her coffee cake. "I was saving this for later, but this seems as good a time as any to share it. I always serve it with coffee, but tea should be just fine."

"Philip told me about your coffee cake, Rachel. He's very fond of it."

"He told me about your Lady Kay apple pie as well. I'm looking forward to tasting it."

"I think we are going to have a good time working together, Rachel." Maggie chuckled, "With our two specialties, I fear we will have more business than we can handle!"

The next day, Rachel tapped on Maggie's cabin door. She opened the door and was pleased to see her new friend.

"Maggie, there's a bit of sun peeking through the clouds, would you like to join the children and me on the deck for some fresh air? You'll need warm clothes. It's a little nippy."

Maggie quickly donned a warm cloak and joined Rachel on deck. She could see they enjoyed more than cooking in common as she learned more about her new friend.

During the voyage, Maggie and Rachel continuously spent time together on the deck. Each shared about her own life, and Rachel poured her heart out about the loss of her husband. Maggie was a comfort to her, and by talking, Rachel felt a great weight gradually lift. Day after day as the weather allowed, they stood next to the deck railing, chatting. They breathed in the crisp marine air, and as the *California II* steamed northward, they gazed at the splendorous ever-changing coastline.

As the ship approached the Teekalet port, Maggie and Rachel marveled at the majestic timbered snow-capped mountains fringing the bay. Then they saw a small town built around a lumber mill. There were long wharves and piers, and several ships anchored next to them.

The *California II* took her place alongside the wharf, and the crew unloaded the mill's supply order. Philip reported to the owners and handed them a *very* full money parcel from the sales of their goods.

"Excellent job, Captain Bennett. By the way, we have an update on your house projects."

Philip thanked them for the news, then re-boarded his ship. Most of the crew had disembarked, but a handful of crewmen stayed on board to navigate the ship down the canal toward the Bennett settlement. When the settlement was in sight, Philip sounded the whistle, easing the ship next to the wharf. Samuel resounded the usual command, "Drop anchor and tie the lines!"

The crew unloaded the heavy cookstoves, which required several strong men. Next, they set Maggie and Rachel's baggage onto the wharf. Philip assisted both women off the ship while Matthew helped his sister. After everyone had disembarked, Philip signaled Samuel to take the ship back to Teekalet to its assigned berth.

Everyone hurried toward the activity to greet the newcomers. Britta took the lead, barking and jumping with excitement now that her master was back. Philip greeted Britta, then introduced the newcomers.

Maggie and the Bly family received a warm welcome from the group. Thomas and Robert couldn't stop smiling at Philip. They finally believed him when he said he was getting married. Benjamin smiled quietly. He was happy for Philip, but it made him mourn the absence of his bride even more.

Peter gravitated toward Rachel. She didn't seem to show any recognition of him. Could it be because he now had a full beard and long hair? She was as attractive and demure as he had remembered from his visit to the Bly home. He and Daniel Bly had sailed on several voyages together for over two years and had become close friends. Daniel had shared a great deal about his life with Rachel and always brought out her picture. Through Daniel's reminiscence of his wife, Peter came to know and care for Rachel, and found himself thinking about her more than he should. On their last voyage together, Peter realized he envied Daniel. Now, fate had swept Rachel into his life. Peter welcomed her and reminded her of his friendship with her husband. After his short conversation with her, it was obvious why Daniel loved her so much. For Rachel, it was a comfort to know someone who had been close to her husband.

Philip crouched down to pet Britta again. She had been impatiently nudging at his hand. While petting her, his mind drifted as he watched his little group of travelers chatting with one another. Maggie and Rachel were fully engaged in conversation. Annie stayed glued to Rachel's side while Matthew was already forming a friendship with Billy and Christopher. Philip thought about how he had affected each person's life. It all began when he convinced his brothers to leave England. Now, here they were, and along the way, by mere happenstance, he had touched the lives of all these people standing before him, bringing them to Teekalet for a new beginning.

***

The house on Peter's parcel was nearly complete. Finishing the interior had taken top priority to make the house livable in time for Maggie and the Bly family's arrival. Maggie and Rachel immediately began setting up the household. Four bedrooms provided private space for each person. Despite the bakery building not being finished, the two women planned to move forward with their baking business by utilizing the house kitchen.

Each cookstove was moved to its proper location. First, the stove chosen for the house was placed.

Next came the stove for the cookhouse. Billy had volunteered to be the camp cook and he couldn't wait to use it. It would replace the Dutch oven and iron skillet he had been using over an open fire. His true cooking talent would soon be revealed.

Finally, it was time for Maggie's stove. She nervously watched the men transport her precious stove to the storage section of the cookhouse, where it would have to remain until the bakery building was completed.

She couldn't help but hover as they moved it. "Now be careful of my stove, it's heavy. Are you sure there are enough of you?"

With the new stove installed in the house, the two women wasted little time. They baked pies, bread, and the coffee cake to sell to the mill's cookhouse and general store. Peter delivered the goods using the workboat. On the same trip, he purchased flour from the mill's flour mill, and any other supplies needed from the general store and brought it back for the bakery business.

Before long, Maggie and Rachel weren't able to keep up with the demand for their baked goods in such a limited space. The bakery building needed to be finished as soon as possible. The large population of mill workers couldn't get enough of their bakery goods. There was also another customer right under their nose. The logging camp cook was always in need of good food, and the loggers had a ferocious appetite. They expended an enormous amount of energy and consumed hundreds of calories to keep up their stamina.

As soon as the lumber camp cook heard about bakery items being delivered to the mill cookhouse, he approached Maggie and Rachel about providing pies, cakes, and cookies for his loggers. He was a husky man with a bushy beard, and he wore suspenders to hold up his pants, which hung below his extended belly.

"Li'l ladies, the whole camp has heard about your pies and cake. Loggers love pie and cake! If I don't come back with the answer they want, they'll likely throw me in that thar canal. By the way, m'name's Bart, short for Bartholomew. Guess my ma thought I should have a fancy name. Not for me though. So, how 'bout it? Do we have a deal, li'l ladies?"

Maggie responded. "Bart, you make it awfully hard to say no. I have to tell you, though, we're already having a difficult time keeping up with the demand. I'll have to get creative, I guess. Yes, we have a deal!" She chuckled, "After all, we don't want to be responsible for you being thrown into the canal!"

"That's a good gal. Now, here's how we gotta do it. As we finish clearing each parcel and work the next, we gotta move our camp to stay close to the work. If we can work out a schedule, I'll send m'driver with m'wagon to pick up our order."

"We will do our best," replied Rachel.

With the new commitment to the lumber camp cook, Maggie was sure they would need help. She thought of Billy and summoned him to come and talk to her and Rachel at the house. Billy was shy and a little nervous. *What do they want with me?* He knocked on the door.

"Come in Billy," said Maggie. "I understand you've become the cook for our men. Captain Bennett tells me you are quite talented."

Billy relaxed and beamed with pride at her praise.

Maggie smiled, "How would you like to learn to bake? We could use some extra help and making use of that second stove would be most helpful. As soon as we start showing a profit, we will pay you. What do you say?"

"Yes, ma'am. I'd like that."

"Good, then we have a deal! You will start tomorrow!"

Rachel added, "And Billy, if you begin to feel overwhelmed, please come talk to us. Maybe Annie and Matthew could help you out. We can be flexible. Even a little help will be better than nothing at all."

Billy thanked the ladies and left. He walked away with a jaunty stride. He was excited about his new job. He would soon be a baker along with being a cook. He would have a regular income. *My family would be so proud of me. If only they were here.*

Rachel also recruited Annie and Matthew to help. She promised to pay them once the business began to show a profit.

Annie loved the idea of learning how to bake. *I'm seventeen years old now, and I might marry at any time. There are so many men here.* Besides helping with the baking, she milked the cows, churned the butter, fed the chickens, and gathered eggs.

Matthew wasn't sure in what way he could help, but he liked the idea of earning money. He yearned to buy a rifle. With a rifle, he could learn to hunt and help provide food for the table, but most importantly, keep his mother and sister safe. He was nineteen. *With Father gone, I need to be the man of the family. The provider, the protector.*

***

Philip was consistently on call for the mill's business ventures. When he returned from his latest trip, he arrived with a gift for Maggie. It was a music box he had purchased in San Francisco. It had caught his eye in the jewelry store on the day he bought her rings. *I'll surprise her with an unannounced visit.* She didn't know he was back yet. They hadn't been able to see much of each other between his time spent at sea and her baking schedule. He felt guilty about being gone so much and luring her into this bakery business frenzy. *I hope she hasn't been upset with me.*

He knocked on the door, and Annie came to answer it. She opened it and responded, "Come in, Captain Bennett."

Philip thanked her, and as he stepped in, the aroma of the bakery items swept over him. His mouth watered. It reminded him of the days when he came to see Maggie in Frisco. He strolled into the kitchen area where he saw pies lined up on every surface. Some of them were baked, and others were waiting to be baked. Rachel was on the other side of the room at a table stirring the batter for her special cake, which was next in line to go into the oven once the pies were finished. She smiled at Philip and could see he had something for Maggie. Philip grinned. She found an excuse to leave the room, giving him a private moment with his fiancée.

Maggie was a sight to behold, which amused Philip. She was wearing a blue apron, but she was covered in so much flour, it looked more white than blue. There was also flour on the tip of her nose. Her cheeks were flushed, and although her hair was tied back, stray tendrils had escaped onto her cheeks and forehead. He stood quietly enjoying the vision. *My God, she's beautiful, even when she's covered in flour.*

Maggie sensed his presence and looked up. Her hands were covered with pie dough. She wanted to fix her hair but couldn't use her sticky hands, so she pursed her lips and tried to blow the hair off her face with a big *whoosh*. He chuckled.

"Philip Bennett, what are you laughing at? I know I'm a mess. You gave me no warning that you were coming. I—."

With the box hidden behind his back with one arm, he used his free arm to pull her in close to him. "Stop talking and kiss me," he said, his voice husky with desire. They kissed fervently.

Maggie chuckled. "Now there's flour all over *you*. It's my turn to laugh!"

He spoke to her in a very soft mysterious voice, "I have something for you." Then he brought out the box from behind his back and handed it to her.

"Oh, I love presents!" She wiped her hands on her apron and quickly opened the box. Inside was a beautiful music box embellished with porcelain roses. She opened the lid and turned the key, and it played Longfellow's serenade *Stars of the Summer Night*. "Philip, it's so beautiful. I love it, and I love the melody. Thank you!" She hugged and kissed him.

"I'm gone so much, Maggie, and we hardly see each other. I wanted you to have something to remind you of me. Actually, I'm feeling a little guilty. I brought you here, and now you're working harder than I had ever imagined. You're not upset with me, are you?"

"I must admit I'm slightly overwhelmed. We're so busy, there's hardly any time to think about being lonely. You have no reason to feel guilty. I'm a big girl. Neither of us knew what would happen."

"I'm relieved you aren't upset with me, but I think I'm a little disappointed you haven't been thinking about me."

"Don't worry, my darling Philip. I adore you and love you. Of course, I think about you too, and I do wish you were here more." She caressed his face. "I must confess, however, it's rather enjoyable when you bring me gifts," she said with a coquettish grin.

Philip grinned. "I'll have to make sure I don't disappoint you, my love. Now, tell me everything. How are you and Rachel doing?"

Maggie updated Philip on the latest bakery news.

As Maggie talked, Philip noticed she kept turning her head back toward the stove. He figured that was his cue to leave. "Maggie, I can see you have your hands full at the moment, so I shall take my leave for now."

She nodded. "Yes, this is our first order for the logging camp, and they're coming later today to pick up whatever we have made. The loggers are insisting on eating pie for breakfast tomorrow morning. I ran out of fresh apples, so I used canned peaches instead. I don't think they care if it's apple pie or not, as long as it's pie!"

They shared a quick embrace and kiss, and Maggie dashed back to the pie-making. Philip missed their tradition of her walking him to the door. *She didn't even watch me leave.* He had to admit to himself this whole project was his idea, so he'd better get used to it. She definitely needed help. *I'll check the progress on her building. While I'm there, I will pass on the news from the mill owners. I wanted to have a meeting anyway. It might as well be there.*

While Philip walked to the bakery building, he thought about how proud he was of Maggie. He was impressed with the way she handled pressure and took control. She had even been checking on the construction of the new building to make sure it was just the way she wanted.

He was happy to see the building nearly finished. Robert and Thomas were up on the roof installing the shakes, and Peter and Benjamin were working on the interior. Philip waved at his brothers and motioned for them to come down and join him inside for a short meeting. He greeted Peter and Benjamin and told them he had some news.

"I have news from the mill owners. They gave me a brief update about our parcels. Benjamin, I learned your parcel is nearly cleared enough to start building your house. When Mary and your new babe arrive here in a few months, we'll want to make sure you have a house waiting for them."

Then he addressed everyone. "The mill's architect and builder will be coming to meet with all of us about our houses soon, so keep in mind what style of house you would like. I've noticed the houses on the bluff at Teekalet are designed similar to what we were used to seeing back home. Most of the mill workers are from the East and New England. The mill is making sure their workers don't get homesick."

Benjamin said, "That's wonderful news. I know exactly what Mary will want. She'll want our house to be just like the one she grew up in at Delhi. I'll post a letter to her and tell her it's time to send me her design ideas. She will be so excited to be involved. Frankly, I'm a little nervous to be the one making all the decisions about our house."

Mary was always on Benjamin's mind. The baby was due at any time. He wished he could be with her. At least he could have a beautiful home waiting for her and their babe.

Chapter 27

March 1855

Delhi, New York

*I*t's a girl! She's a little towhead," exclaimed the midwife. It had been a difficult delivery. The midwife had been with Mary for two days. The babe was born earlier than expected and was quite small, which concerned them. The midwife told Mary to put the baby girl to her breast as often as she would feed. Building up the babe's strength was important. Mary named the baby girl Mollie, the name she and Benjamin had chosen if a girl was born.

Jane said, "It is good we still have a few months left before we start our journey. We'll post a letter to Benjamin with the news of his baby girl right away, and to your father that he's a grandfather! I don't think there's any need to mention how small and weak Mollie is. No need to worry them. We are going to take good care of her, and we'll build up her strength and size."

Mary agreed with her mother. She held little Mollie in her arms and nursed her. Mollie bonded well and sucked aggressively.

"I hope Benjamin won't be disappointed I didn't give him a son. I'm sure we will have more children, and I'll present him with a son one day. I can't wait to see Benjamin and show him our little girl."

"She will capture his heart, and he'll fall in love with her. Just look at that cute little rosebud mouth. Who could resist her?" said Jane.

"I am so anxious to introduce Mollie to her grandfather. You and Father are grandparents now!"

"Indeed we are, Mary. You have given us a special gift."

Chapter 28

March 1855

Teekalet

*T*he bakery building was finally completed, and the ladies lost no time setting it up. Maggie's crowning moment was when the men carried in her prize cookstove.

"Where to?" they had asked.

She pointed to the end wall opposite the entrance. Once the stove was operational, Maggie set her cast iron teakettle on one of the hearth plates. She celebrated by brewing some of her special tea to share with Rachel.

Maggie had planned every detail of the building. She specified it to be rectangular in shape. The door was centered on the entrance wall, and paned operable windows were positioned on each side of the door. These windows would allow the ladies to have a clear view of what was going on outside, and who might be about to enter.

She also had windows placed on the two longer side walls, set high to allow useable space below. The windows would bring in natural light and fresh air.

Several shelves were installed on the walls, and two large rectangular tables were placed in the center of the room accompanied by long moveable benches. Maggie had brought all of her cooking and baking ware with her, and she and Rachel were ready to put it to use. All the wares of a baker were lined up on shelves, and Maggie's unique collection of yellow ware bowls and pie plates were on full display. Soon the aroma of freshly baked goods filled the building.

Other shelves held freshly baked pies and cakes waiting to be transferred to the wood pie safes, which Benjamin had built for her. The pie safes provided safe storage for the bakery goods while cooling, and protection from any insects that might slip into the building.

As a finishing touch to the room, there was always a cheerful bouquet of herbs or flowers in Maggie's yellow ware pitcher sitting on one of the window sills.

A small storage building, which would also function as a pantry, had been added on to the rear of the building. The building had two doors, one door opened directly into the bakery building, and the other was located on the opposite wall to be used as an exterior entrance for ease of unloading supplies from the wagon. She also specified an opening in the floor with a hinged lid allowing access to stairs leading down to a root cellar. This permitted Maggie and Rachel to keep some goods cool.

The logger cook's wagon came on a regular basis, and Peter made weekly trips delivering orders for the mill's cookhouse. For his return trip, he loaded up with supplies from the general store and flour from the flour mill. On one of his trips, he spied a beautiful butter mold for sale in the general store. He thought of Rachel and bought it for her using his credit account. It seemed like the perfect gift. Something practical, but not too personal. He was sure if it appeared practical, she would accept it. He had made the right choice. Rachel was moved by his gesture and graciously accepted the gift.

Maggie and Rachel finally took a moment to give their business a name. They named it *HOOD CANAL BAKERY*, and Maggie asked Philip to help them get a sign hung as soon as possible for their prized building.

* * *

Thomas and Robert were ready for business. For the final touch, the brothers unwrapped their company signs and installed them on the front of their building. They looked forward to trading with the

Indians for hides and pelts, and with their tools of the trade set in place, they were ready to begin production of their goods. The mill's general store was an anxious buyer, awaiting the leather and fur products to be fabricated by the Bennett brothers.

Philip was proud of his brothers. "I still have a bottle of champagne waiting to be opened. With your signs up on the building now, it is time for a toast to the *Bennett Bros. Co.*"

The business progressed well. The Indians visited regularly with canoes filled to the brim with pelts and hides. Trading with the Indians helped elevate the Bennett brothers' business beyond their expectations. They couldn't keep up with the pace. It was time to bring in help. Robert had an idea.

"Thomas, we need help. I've noticed Matthew and Christopher have become good friends. Why don't we bring them in as apprentices and pay them a wage? I already had plans for Christopher to learn the trade. I'm sure he'll enjoy Matthew's companionship."

"I like the idea, Robert. They do seem to have bonded. I'm sure they'll get along well."

Matthew and Christopher eagerly accepted the Bennett brothers' offer. The twosome had developed a strong friendship with the Indians, and had started learning their language. This would benefit Robert and Thomas, who were limited in their communication proficiency with the Indians.

The Indians also taught Matthew and Christopher many skills, such as how to make a knife from mussel shells, and a spear from yew wood using a shell or bone point attached to the end. Thomas and Robert considered Matthew's and Christopher's friendship with the Indians as a boon to their business, and everything they learned was useful for the settlement.

One day when the Indians came to trade, they extended an invitation to Christopher and Matthew to visit their village. Christopher turned to Thomas and Robert, "Do you mind if we accept?"

"Go ahead. I wouldn't mind hearing about their village, but have them bring you back before nightfall," said Thomas.

When Matthew and Christopher arrived at the Indian village, they were surprised to see the Indians not living in teepees as they had always heard. The Indian dwellings were large cedar structures measuring several hundred feet in length. They were invited into one of the longhouses, in which several families lived together. The longhouse was divided with partitions allowing each family to have its own space and fire hearth. There was a hole in the ceiling just large enough to let the smoke escape.

Matthew and Christopher happened to look outside and saw smoke in the distance, and thought the forest was on fire. No one seemed to be concerned, though.

Matthew exclaimed, "We need to warn them!"

They alerted the Indians as they pointed to the smoke in the distance. The Indians laughed and explained. Every year they burned their field land purposely to renew the earth, which helped keep the forests at bay.

After their initial visit to the village, Matthew and Christopher returned often by hitching a ride with the Indians when they came to trade. When it was time to leave, the Indians took them back to the settlement. As Matthew and Christopher continued their visits, the Indians presented them with many gifts. The wealthier Indians enjoyed bestowing gifts to show off their wealth. Each time the two visited the Indian village, they came back with another prize.

On one of their visits, a wealthy Indian approached them. He motioned them to follow. They shadowed him to a small cove where there were several dugout canoes lined up on the beach.

The Indian pulled one of the canoes out of the row and said, "For you." They were shocked to receive such a generous gift and thanked him profusely. Then the Indian told them to hop into the canoe. He climbed in with them and gave them a short lesson on maneuvering it. The time on the water passed quickly. Daylight was fading, and the Indian told them if they were going to leave in their new canoe, they should go before dark. They bid their Indian friend farewell and paddled toward the settlement. No more hitching rides back and forth.

While paddling home, they talked about how guilty they felt for receiving so many gifts and giving nothing back. What could they give? Even if Maggie and Rachel were willing to let them have some of the bakery goods, there wouldn't be any to spare due to the demand from their customers.

Suddenly Matthew had a thought. "Christopher, we've taught

some of the Indians to speak a little English. What if we teach all of the Indians in the village to speak English?"

"Yeah, I like that idea. We can start on our next visit!"

"It's getting dark, and we're so slow," said Matthew.

"We must not have much further to go. Let's try paddling faster."

"We can try. I don't think we will ever be as fast as our friends. We probably have everyone worried."

* * *

Back at the settlement, Thomas and Robert were concerned that Christopher and Matthew hadn't returned yet. It was nightfall.

Peter volunteered to watch for them from the wharf. "If they don't come soon, I'll take the workboat out to look for them."

Several minutes later, Peter heard the familiar splash of canoe paddles dipping into the water, but it wasn't the quiet rhythmic sound he usually heard. He could barely see the silhouette of two people in a canoe paddling in a zigzag motion coming up the canal. *What on earth? I've never seen Indians paddle like that. They must be drunk.* But as they moved closer, he saw Matthew and Christopher paddling their new canoe.

Chapter 29

Mid-March 1855

Teekalet

*I*t was the season of new beginnings. Once the warm spring sun softened the frozen ground, the homesteaders plowed their land and planted their crops. Now they were ready to travel to town to purchase a few supplies, a couple of cows, some horses, and a large wagon. Thomas, Robert, Benjamin, and Peter planned to make the journey using the workboat. Once they completed their transaction, the brothers and Benjamin planned to travel overland back to the settlement using the newly purchased wagon and horses. Peter would return in the workboat.

Teekalet offered a good selection. The men loaded the supplies onto the wagon along with several bales of hay and feed for the animals. Then they harnessed four horses to the wagon and tied the two cows at the rear to follow along. Thomas and Benjamin would ride the remaining two horses while Robert drove the wagon.

Peter loaded the workboat with additional supplies and was ready to leave. Climbing aboard the workboat, he shouted. "Good luck on the trip. I'll see you back at the settlement."

Robert waved and settled in the seat for the long ride. He shook the reins and the caravan moved forward. This was their first trip overland between Teekalet and their settlement. It wasn't a well-traveled road, which was brushy and narrow. They felt uneasy and stayed alert. As they moved along, they noticed the sky was dense with smoke. Thomas looked in the direction of the Indian village and commented to Benjamin.

"I see the Indians are burning their land again. The first time I saw the smoke, I panicked and thought the forest was on fire, but Christopher and Matthew told me not to worry. It was just the Indians' method of clearing their land."

Suddenly, they heard a gunshot, startling the horses. Robert held the reins taut to settle them down. Then they heard something crashing through the brush toward them. It was a huge black bear charging from the forest, running across the road in front of them. The horses panicked and reared up, and the cows bayed as they tried to free themselves from the wagon. Robert retook control of the horses. The two horses Thomas and Benjamin were riding reared up, throwing them both. Despite the wind being knocked out of him, Benjamin managed to quickly pick himself up and grab the reins of the horses before they could run off. He secured them to the back of the wagon. Then he saw Thomas still on the ground. He was holding his shoulder in excruciating pain.

Robert turned in his seat as he held the reins in a firm grip, and shouted, "What's happened back there? Are you two all right?"

Benjamin helped Thomas to his feet and led him toward the front of the wagon. "Thomas is injured, Robert."

Thomas interjected. "Something's happened to my shoulder, and it hurts like hell! What in Hades happened!?"

The horses and cows were restless again. They heard dogs barking, coming closer and closer. Two black and white dogs burst through the same brushy opening where the bear had exited. Close behind the dogs, a rough-looking hunter appeared, running behind his dogs. Robert was still trying his best to control the horses.

The hunter stopped momentarily and spoke to Robert. "So sorry, Monsieur. I'm chasing that confounded bear." He glanced at Thomas holding himself up against the wagon, grimacing in pain. "I see one of you is hurt. My apology. Stay here, so I know where you are when I shoot. I'll be back after I catch him!" He headed out as quickly as he appeared.

Robert turned to Thomas. "We're not waiting long. We need to get you to a doctor."

Benjamin interjected, "I can still ride. I only have a few bruises. I'll ride back to Teekalet and bring the doctor here. It should save time, and Thomas won't have to be moved around as much. Better for the doctor to come with us back to our settlement."

As Benjamin mounted his horse, Robert answered, "Yes, good idea."

Robert put the brake on the wagon. The horses began to settle down.

"Thomas, let's get you into the wagon." He climbed into the back of the wagon to make a comfortable place for his brother. He broke apart one of the bales of hay, spreading it out for Thomas to sit on. Then Robert helped him into the front of the wagon and propped him up against a corner, covering him with his coat.

Just then, in the distance, they heard the dogs howling and barking. Next, they heard a gunshot, startling the horses again. Robert quickly settled them down.

"Well, Thomas, I'd say that hunter got him. He'll probably show up pretty soon."

"Better keep your gun handy, Robert. He might not be trustworthy. He looked pretty rough."

A few minutes later, the hunter and his dogs returned. He was a rugged sight dressed in buckskins, and he wore a coonskin cap. Around his waist, he donned a leather belt with a sheath holding a large hunting knife. His long scraggly mop of brownish grey hair was tied back at the nape of his neck with a leather strap. His lower face was covered with a bushy beard, not quite hiding a long scar on the side of his face.

His dogs didn't look like typical bear-hunting dogs. Their coats consisted of straight, stiff guard hairs, the undercoat was thick, and the color was mainly black with white markings. They had short pointed ears, bright intelligent eyes, and stood about two feet tall at the withers. Their white-tipped bushy tails curled in a circle over their backs in the shape of a ring.

Robert cautiously walked toward the hunter, his hand on his holstered revolver.

The hunter set his rifle down at his side, and acknowledged Robert with a half-bow. Speaking with a thick French accent, he said "Ah, *monsieur*, you were in the wrong place at the wrong time. Do not worry about that bear. He's lying dead back there at the bottom of the big fir. My dogs had him treed. I'm Pierre Mallet, mountain man, hunter, and guide. At your service, if you so desire." He looked back at Thomas in the wagon. "How bad is your friend injured?"

Robert was incensed. *The nerve of him asking if I need his services!*

Robert's first reaction was to answer in anger. But looking at the hunter's rifle and the large knife hanging on his hip, not to mention the two bear dogs, he checked himself.

"He's my brother, and it seems his shoulder is injured. The other rider got banged up but was able to ride back to Teekalet to fetch the doctor."

"That's unfortunate. My apologies again. You have me at a disadvantage, *monsieur*. You know my name, but I don't know yours."

"I'm Robert Bennett. My brothers and I recently claimed land along the canal."

"Ah, I canoed past your place a few days ago. I saw your sign *Bennett Bros. Co.* on your building."

"I'm a furrier, and Thomas back here works with leather. I suppose his injury is probably going to slow him down now."

Robert wondered if Pierre hunted for the Hudson Bay Company. He was wary about how much to reveal to this French mountain man. The Hudson Bay Company didn't want settlers competing with them. He had heard they were a tough bunch.

"So tell me, Mr. Mallet, do you hunt for the Hudson Bay Company?"

Thomas's ears perked up when he heard Robert's question, and quietly listened for the Frenchman's answer.

"Call me Pierre. Yes, I started working under contract for them in Montreal, Quebec. While I was there, I married an Indian woman from the Cree tribe, putting me in the *envious* position of trading with her people for pelts, which I turned around and sold to Hudson Bay. I finally got tired of them trying to cheat me, so I worked my way west to Fort Nisqually to finish my contract obligation, hoping I might receive better treatment there. I didn't, and as soon as my contract was up, I told them I was done!"

Thomas knew exactly what Robert would say next.

"Hmm, Pierre, we might be able to do some business together.

We're manufacturing products to ship to San Francisco and other ports. You saw where we are located. Come and see us in a couple of days. Now, meet my brother, Thomas."

After the introduction, Pierre's dogs started whining and barking. He patted them on the head. "Be patient, *mes amis.*"

Thomas admired the dogs. "Pierre, I've never seen that breed of dog. What kind are they?"

"They're Karelian bear dogs. I had them brought over from Finland. They do their job well, and they're good companions. Right now they're letting me know I haven't given them their reward. Once I dress the bear, I give them the bear's liver. They adore it. I best get back to the task at hand. My dogs will only get louder until I do. I'll see you in two days' time. I hope your shoulder injury isn't severe, Thomas." He left and seemed to melt into the woods.

Finally, Benjamin returned with the doctor. The doctor proceeded to the wagon to inspect Thomas's shoulder.

"Hello, Thomas, I'm Doctor Ames." It was obvious to him Thomas had dislocated his shoulder. He carefully slid Thomas into a prone position. "Now, Thomas, I'm going to move your shoulder back into position. Be prepared, it's going to hurt."

Thomas winced in pain. Because of Benjamin's description of the injury, the doctor had come prepared with a sling to immobilize Thomas's shoulder.

"Thomas, it's important that you start moving your arm when it's not too painful. If you don't, the joints will stiffen up. I won't need to go with you at this time, but I'll stop by in two or three days to see how you're doing."

"Thank you, doctor. I'm concerned. Will I be able to hunt with my rifle again?"

"Yes, Thomas, over time."

***

Peter arrived back at the settlement in the workboat as planned. Several hours had passed, and there was no sign of Thomas, Robert or Benjamin. Peter and the rest of the group were worried.

"It's going to be nightfall soon," said Peter, "We'd better start looking for them."

He asked Christopher and Matthew to accompany him. "We'll start walking in the direction from which they should be coming. Matthew, fetch some lanterns and lucifers. We may need them."

They had barely begun the search when they heard the horses' hooves and the groaning wagon moving slowly toward them.

"There they are," exclaimed Christopher.

Peter yelled out, "What happened? We were about to search for you."

"We ran into a problem, or I should say a problem ran into us," said Robert. "It's a bit of a story, and Thomas is injured. Benjamin could use some help taking care of the wagon and livestock while I get Thomas out of this wagon and into the bunkhouse. He can walk, but his shoulder is hurt. After I get Thomas settled, I'll fill you in."

* * *

Two days later while Robert was working on the exterior of the business building, he heard Britta barking, signaling someone was approaching. It was the mountain man and his Indian wife. Pierre introduced her. She was carrying a leather pouch and a wooden bowl, and in her broken English, asked to see Thomas. Robert took them to the bunkhouse where Thomas was lying on a cot.

"*Bonjour, mon ami.* How is your shoulder feeling? Please meet my wife, Red Feather. I told her about your shoulder injury, and she insisted on bringing you her special tincture."

"*Bonjour* to you both. A pleasure to meet you, Red Feather. To answer your question, Pierre, my shoulder is plenty tender and aches constantly. It's hard to get comfortable on this darn cot."

Red Feather turned to Robert and instructed him to heat up some water in the kettle. Once the water was hot, she told Robert to bring a mug and the kettle to her. She sprinkled a handful of dried roots into the mug and poured in the steaming water. After the concoction had steeped long enough, she gave it to Thomas.

"Drink," she said. Her tea tincture was made from the roots of a tall stalk topped with small umbrella-shaped flowers called Valerian that grew near the water.

Pierre said, "Red Feather says it'll relax the muscles around your shoulder, Thomas, and help you sleep."

She emptied the rest of the herbs into the wooden bowl, which would be enough to make tea for several days.

Thomas thanked her as he drank the tea.

Robert pulled Pierre aside. "Come, let's sit at the table over there. We can talk a little business while your wife takes care of Thomas."

Red Feather gently massaged Thomas's shoulder while slowly moving his arm up and down. Thomas grimaced at first but began to feel some relief.

As she continued to work on his shoulder, Thomas studied her. Red Feather looked different than the local Flathead Indians he had seen thus far. She had an oval face with high cheekbones, a straight angular nose, full lips, and dark, penetrating almond eyes. Her ebony hair hung in braids tied with leather strips, and a beaded headband circled her head across the top of her dark eyebrows. She was a handsome woman. He wondered what her life was like as Pierre's wife. She was mysterious and exuded great inner strength and wisdom.

When she finished, Pierre said, "We will be back tomorrow, Thomas. Red Feather believes she has a duty to take care of you until your shoulder is healed. She believes I brought harm to you, and she must make up for it."

Thomas was impressed with her dedication and integrity. He turned to Red Feather, "Thank you, Red Feather." She nodded and motioned to Pierre she was ready to leave.

Thomas called out to Robert as he was following Pierre and Red Feather out, "When Red Feather comes back, I'd like her to meet Maggie, Rachel, and Annie. They might become friends and enjoy the female companionship."

"Brilliant, Thomas."

Chapter 30

May 1855
Teekalet

*T*he settlers had become a family. The little settlement along the Hood Canal was beginning to feel like home. They worked together and played together. Sometimes, on a Saturday night, they gathered around the campfire and told stories or sang. Often Benjamin played his violin, and Matthew his harmonica. The lively music put some of them in the mood to dance, and those who weren't dancing were tapping their foot or bobbing their head to the tune. Maggie, Rachel, and Annie took turns dancing with the men. Once in awhile, the loggers joined the gathering. Peter took advantage of the opportunity to hold Rachel in his arms. He asked her to dance as often as he dared. He was slowly developing a rapport with her. It wasn't a secret of how much he cared for Rachel.

The homesteaders waited patiently as the loggers cleared one parcel at a time. The loggers began their workday by 6:00 a.m. and continued until dark. There was an art to their work. Two axmen stood on each side of a tree to carve a notch in the direction they wanted it to fall. Then they used a long saw with one man on each side sawing in a rhythm, until they yelled "timber!" and the tree fell. As the giant tree fell, anyone nearby could hear it groan and crack, and when it hit the ground, they felt the thump radiate beneath their feet. Once the tree was down, a two-man crew sawed off the limbs and then used the crosscut saw to cut the tree into sixteen-foot lengths.

When the loggers finally depleted the timber close to the shoreline, they moved inland. They still needed to get the logs into the canal, so they created a skid road with a team of oxen pulling the logs down to the water. When there were enough logs banded together, the men towed the logs to the mill.

Removing the stumps was one of their biggest challenges. The task required endless hours of digging, chopping, and uprooting. Once the stumps were uprooted, they used oxen to pull them out. Finally, when a parcel was cleared, it was ready for the mill's construction crew to build the long-awaited house.

Since the stumps were such a time-consuming task, the settlers didn't bother to remove the stumps in the areas selected for their crops. The large trees, which could be as large as eight feet in diameter, were by nature spaced wide apart. They simply planted their crops between the stumps and used the same method when planting their orchards.

The architect and builder had acquired pattern books of the traditional home styles they knew the settlers desired. The Greek Revival style was the most current design. The appeal of this design was driven by more than just the design itself. It was a reminder of the spirit of the ancient Greeks' fight for independence from Turkey. The War of 1812 and the Battle of Independence with Great Britain hadn't been that long ago for the Americans and both were still fresh in their minds.

Since the waterway was the most efficient means of travel to and from Teekalet, the settlers built a large raft to use as an alternate method of travel. In some situations, the raft proved more efficient than the boat, such as transporting livestock. On one trip, they transported pigs and open-framed crates holding chickens.

The bakery business was in full production. The two cows were indispensable to the business. The women created cream, buttermilk and butter from the cows' milk. Soon there were more chickens, which provided the eggs needed for baking. They were no longer dependent on buying such items from the general store in Teekalet.

Through Matthew and Christopher's friendship with the local

Indians, the community developed a friendship with them as well and learned about the benefits of the Indian way.

The Indians taught them the importance of rotating crops, and about planting the *three sisters* together, which consisted of corn, beans, and squash. The corn provided support for the beans, while the beans provided nitrogen for the corn, and the large squash leaves shaded the soil. The shaded soil prevented weeds and discouraged pests. The settlers also planted potatoes, turnips, carrots, wheat, and oats.

The men learned to improve their skills in fishing, and how to hunt and trap. Robert learned additional techniques for making clothing from the hides, and Thomas learned how to make moccasin boots.

Red Feather visited often and taught the women to forage from nature, and which plant roots were edible, which were poisonous, and which were useful for medicinal purposes. They also learned where to find nuts and berries.

Annie and Red Feather became fast friends. When Red Feather had come to work on Thomas's shoulder, Annie was ever present watching and learning while Red Feather worked her magic.

Red Feather enjoyed Annie's company. She taught Annie about medicinal herbs and the art of massage. She was honored to be sharing her knowledge and skills with this inquisitive white girl.

While Thomas recuperated, he watched Red Feather and Annie working together with the herbs, and it took him back to fond memories of his daughters' penchant for using herbs. He wished they were here, too, forming a friendship with Red Feather and Annie. He thought, *What a fine group they would make foraging in the woods together.* Oh, how he missed his family. It wouldn't be much longer. September wasn't far off. He'd have to be patient.

Annie no longer pondered marriage. She became focused on the practice of nursing. When Dr. Ames had come to tend to Thomas's shoulder, she observed him intently.

With so many loggers working on the homesteaders' land, Dr. Ames found himself traveling to the Bennett settlement on a regular basis. There were many accidents, some minimal, and some serious. Annie rushed to their aid while Benjamin rode to Teekalet to summon the doctor. Annie didn't possess the skills to treat the loggers, but she knew how to make them more comfortable. The loggers began to call her their *Guardian Angel*. Once Dr. Ames arrived, she shadowed him, always watching and taking notes.

Dr. Ames was acutely aware of her devotion, and on one of his visits, said, "Annie, you have a talent for nursing. You've been a real help to me. Have you ever thought about becoming a nurse?"

"Oh yes, Dr. Ames. Red Feather has taught me so much about healing. I just know I'm meant to become a nurse."

He contemplated for a moment. This young lady could be a great help to him. Ever since his nurse had married and moved away, he desperately needed help.

"Annie, would you like to work for me in Teekalet? You can start as my assistant. You will be able to watch and learn, and I'll teach you as much as you can handle."

"I would love to work for you, Dr. Ames, but where would I stay? I have no money to pay for any rent."

"You can stay at our home, of course. My wife and I have plenty of room since our children have left the nest."

"Oh, that sounds wonderful, Dr. Ames, but I wouldn't be able to come immediately. My mother and Maggie are so busy with the bakery business, they need my help right now. I can't abandon them."

"That is quite commendable, Annie. You just let me know when you're ready. I'll try to get by until you can come. Right now, my wife has been pitching in." He chuckled, "Through the years she's learned a few things."

***

Thomas was on the road to recovery from his shoulder injury, and he was convinced Red Feather deserved most of the credit. He was pleased with his suggestion of introducing her to Maggie, Rachel, and Annie. Just as he had foreseen, they had bonded.

Finally, Thomas was able to get back to work. Together, the brothers produced a large number of products to sell, but not without help. Billy had become acquainted with some of the Chinese families who had come to Teekalet for employment at the mill. The absence of his own family haunted him. They were gone forever, but at least he could help those who were there. With his assistance, the Bennett brothers hired several Chinese boys. They proved to be excellent workers.

The bakery business was at a pell-mell pace. With the demand from the loggers still working the land and the increased demand coming from the mill cookhouse and the mill's general store, Maggie and Rachel also needed extra help. Billy came to their rescue and helped them hire a few of the Chinese girls living in Teekalet.

With the girls working on a regular basis, Annie dared to hope that she might be available to join Dr. Ames in the foreseeable future.

Matthew enjoyed his new freedom to explore other ways to be useful. He earned enough money to purchase a rifle. Christopher had also saved enough money to purchase a rifle. Peter taught them how to shoot, and the Indians taught them how to hunt. Now they could contribute to their family community. They also helped Peter plow the land, plant the crops, and build fences. He had become fond of them both.

Peter felt protective over Daniel Bly's family. He thought about Matthew. *He's a young man now, it's time for him to start thinking about his future.*

One day he said, "Matthew, have you thought about claiming your own land? You're nineteen, old enough to qualify, and there's still a parcel available next to mine. You have until December, but you should claim your land right away to take advantage of using the loggers who are still here clearing our land. By trading some of your timber with the mill, they will clear your land and build your house. I'll help you put in some crops. You're single now, but I am sure you will find some sweet lass to marry one day. With your property and house, not to mention your good looks, I have no doubt you would be considered a good catch. Think about it."

Matthew's mind raced. He had been confused about what direction he should take for his future and now he knew. He was excited.

"I don't have to think about it, Peter. I'm taking your advice. I like the idea of owning land and having my own house. No more living in the bunkhouse! And my mother and Annie can live with me. Yes, I will do it!"

Peter was silent for a moment. He felt a jolt.

He answered politely. "Yes, I am sure it would make your mother happy."

Rachel was always on his mind. He had tried to keep his feelings for her at bay, but now they were ever present. *I want Rachel to be my wife and live with me in **my** house.* He reassured himself that Daniel would be happy if he knew someone other than a stranger would be taking care of his beloved wife. He knew she cared for him, but did she think of him only as a friend? He was waiting for the courage and the right moment to ask her to marry him.

"Annie wouldn't be there long, Matthew. Someone is bound to come along and snatch her up. She's such a pretty little thing, and she has become a good cook."

"Maybe, maybe not. Red Feather has had quite an influence on Annie. She is talking about becoming a nurse. I happen to know she plans on asking you to escort her to Teekalet, so she can work for Dr. Ames as his assistant. She has already talked to him, but she knows she'll have to wait until mother and Maggie get caught up with the bakery demands. She doesn't want to abandon them. So, I guess it'll be just mother and me."

"If you take a wife, your mother might feel intrusive."

"Nah, I'll just build a house big enough for all of us."

"Well, my young man, you never know what the future holds for us."

Peter had also taken Benjamin under his wing. Benjamin was working hard to have a home waiting for Mary and the babe upon their arrival. He never stopped thinking about them.

Peter liked Benjamin. He was such a kind soul and always had a smile on his face, but Peter could see the sadness in his eyes. He felt sorry for Benjamin being separated from his bride so soon after their marriage. *He's probably a father by now, but he's forced to wait for what must seem like an eternity to meet his child for the first time.*

Benjamin's parcel of land was adjacent to Peter's on the opposite side. He and Benjamin teamed up to plant crops on both parcels. They planned to grow enough produce to sell to the general store, and to any neighboring communities along the canal. They also built a smokehouse for smoking and drying meat and fish to sell along with their produce. Eventually, they hoped the apple orchard they had planted would bear an ample supply of apples to sell as well.

Chapter 31

May 1855

San Francisco/Teekalet

It was early May when Philip and his crew boarded the *Tahoma* for another venture trip to San Francisco. The mill had kept Philip continuously busy delivering and selling lumber and related products to San Francisco, the Hawaiian Islands, South America, and Australia. On his return trips, he brought back needed supplies for the mill and his family community. If his destination was San Francisco, he carried outgoing mail. San Francisco was a principal port for sending and receiving mail. Sending mail to San Francisco with Philip proved to be the best method since mail service in Puget Sound was slow and unreliable. If and when the mail finally arrived, it was delivered to the port towns by canoe, but not on any particular schedule.

As Philip navigated through the Golden Gate harbor, he noticed a ship he hadn't seen before and decided to take a closer look. He brought his ship in tight to the wharf a short distance from the anchored vessel, *Vesta*. He gave Samuel the usual instructions and disembarked.

The wharf was a swirl of activity with people coming and going to and from the ships. Philip strolled past the *Vesta*. He observed a large group of men milling about the ship. They were wearing felt hats trimmed with red ribbons, and they carried side arms. *I wonder who they are?* He was curious, so he mingled among the throngs of people on the wharf until he found someone he thought would know something. He recognized a local captain he had seen many times.

Philip approached him, introduced himself, and inquired about the men on the *Vesta*.

The captain took a draw from his cigarillo and tapped the ashes. "Glad to know you, Captain Bennett. Yes, I do know who they are. They're going to the place from where I've just returned. I couldn't leave fast enough!"

"Where was that?"

"Nicaragua!"

An overwhelming feeling of uneasiness swept over Philip. *That's the direction Thomas's family is traveling.* "What's happening in Nicaragua?"

"It's becoming a dangerous place, for two reasons. There are rumblings of civil war between the Democrats and the Legitimists. The men on the *Vesta* are mercenaries looking for adventure and fame. Their leader is William Walker. He was an editor of a small newspaper here in Frisco, that is until the Liberals offered him adventure and profit he couldn't resist. He rounded up fifty-eight men for the mission—the men you saw. They call themselves the *Falange*. There is going to be some fierce fighting. I'm sure there will be quite a few natives who will want to join them when they get there."

Philip made a quick calculation. Walker and his men would land in Nicaragua in a month's time. "Do you expect it to be a few skirmishes or all-out war?"

"Oh, war is brewing for sure. There are a few bloodthirsty leaders who have no intention of losing."

"You mentioned there were two reasons?"

"Cholera! Just broke out! It will spread from one town to the next. The natives seem to be the most susceptible. People such as myself and my crew didn't get affected. Can't tell you why."

Philip abruptly ended the conversation and thanked the captain for the information. He had heard enough. He felt a sense of panic. *Jane and the children could end up in the middle of the war zone and possibly a cholera epidemic, and it would be my fault.*

He needed to post a letter immediately to Jane warning her about Nicaragua. She must postpone their trip in September. He figured the message would reach her in plenty of time. He would keep a close eye on the Nicaragua situation, and let her know when it was safe to leave. *I can't warn William. He's already out to sea working his way from the*

Hawaiian Islands toward New York. I'll instruct Jane to leave a message for him at the port office when he arrives. Like Philip, Captain Davis's standard procedure was to promptly check for messages at the port office of his destination.

He dashed to the post office building.

"Good morning, Hank. I have an urgent letter I need to post. Can you set me up to write it?"

"Morning, Captain Bennett. You can use my desk. You'll find everything you need there. While you're doing that, I'll check to see if there's any mail here for you."

"Thank you, Hank. You're efficient as usual."

Philip wrote the letter and sealed the envelope. "Hank, it's urgent that this letter goes out on the next mail ship for delivery to New York City. It will need to be forwarded to Delhi to Jane Bennett. I entrust this into your capable hands."

"I'll take care of it, Captain. I'm expecting a ship next month. Your letter should arrive there by mid-July. And I do have some mail for you."

"Thanks, Hank. I'll check in for an update on my next trip."

Philip breathed a sigh of relief. *The letter should get to Jane in plenty of time. I'm not looking forward to telling Thomas about this. At least we averted a disaster, and his family will be safe.*

Now that the letter would be on its way to Jane on the next ship, he could put his mind at ease and continued on with business. By the time he finished his transactions, it was too late in the day to head out of the harbor. He planned to spend the night on the ship and depart at first light. For the first time in a long time, his evening was free. Maggie was no longer in Frisco to visit, and he was very happy about *that* change. He thought about his old friend, Jeffrey Dawes. *I think I'll visit Jeffrey in this unexpected window of time. For some reason, he's on my mind.*

Philip had met Jeffrey in an unconventional way, many years prior while on his first jaunt to San Francisco. As the cabby drove Philip to the boarding house where Jeffrey resided, he reflected back to that perilous day when they met.

He still remembered the confusion he felt when he lost his way to his hotel. He had taken a wrong turn and ended up in a rough neighborhood. Two men accosted him, intending to shanghai him. Philip put up a good fight, but they had the best of him. Jeffrey happened to be a block away, heard the commotion, and ran to investigate. He was a tall, heavily-built man, about forty years of age, and never went anywhere without his knife tucked into the sheaf on his belt. Suddenly, the odds were evened out, and the two attackers fled. From that event, they formed a bond and a lasting friendship.

When the driver stopped in front of the boarding house, Philip asked him to wait while he checked to see if Jeffrey was in. He paid the driver since he assumed he would be staying. It was evening time, and he expected to find Jeffrey there. After Philip queried the desk clerk, he learned his friend was indeed in his room, so he signaled the driver to leave.

Philip tapped on the door. Not expecting company, Jeffrey queried who was there before opening the door. When he learned it was his old friend, he thrust the door open and greeted Philip with a bear hug.

"Philip! I didn't know you were in town. I haven't seen you in ages, but I'm happy to see you now. Come in, come in. Brandy?"

Philip smiled and nodded. As they clinked glasses, he brought Jeffrey up to date.

"And now you know why I haven't been stopping by lately. The mill has me going pell-mell, but I had a little extra time on this trip, and I had a nagging feeling to see you." Then he told Jeffrey about his brother's family and the Nicaragua situation.

"I'm glad you told me about that, Philip. I'm leaving for New York City on the same ship. I believe we will be going through Nicaragua before the heavy fighting breaks out. If you like, I'll follow up with Thomas's wife to make sure she received the letter. At least, if she didn't receive it for some reason, I can tell her in person about your warning."

"Once again, dear old friend, you're looking out for me. I wish I had known you wanted to leave Frisco, I would have twisted your arm to join me in Teekalet."

"That probably wouldn't have worked, Philip. I have friends back east who have offered me an investment opportunity in New York City. I've saved a few coins over the years, so I told the fellas I would throw in with them. Loading and unloading ship cargo is getting pretty tiresome. I figured it was time to make a change."

"I'm going to miss you, Jeffrey. Make sure to get your address to me. I'll connect with you whenever I come to New York City."

The two finished their brandy. Jeffrey looked at his empty glass.

"Well, Philip, we can either finish off this bottle, or you can join me for a light supper. Do you have time before you head back to your ship?"

"I would like that. Just like old times."

* * *

It was mid-May when Philip returned to Teekalet from his Frisco trip, and he arrived bearing letters for Benjamin and Thomas. He decided to give them time to read their letters before breaking the bad news. He found Benjamin first.

"Welcome back, Captain Bennett."

"Benjamin, I insist you call me Philip. After all, you are family, and speaking of family, I have a letter for you from Mary."

"Thank the Lord. I hope it's news about the babe. It should have been born by now. Not knowing anything has been driving me to distraction." He ripped open the envelope.

Delhi, New York
March 16th, 1855

My dearest husband. We have a beautiful daughter. She was born on March 13. The midwife described her as a towhead, and she has a sweet rosebud mouth. I think she has your nose, Benjamin. I named her Mollie like we agreed if we had a girl. It just wasn't God's will for us to have a son right now, but I promise I'll give you a son one day.

I wish you could hold her in your strong arms, but you will as soon as we are together again. I miss you so much, my darling.

Your loving wife,

Mary Spencer

While Benjamin read his letter, Philip looked for Thomas and found him at the Bennett Bros. building working with Robert.

Robert looked up from his work, "I see our brother has returned!"

Thomas set his tool down and smiled. "Welcome back, Philip!"

He noticed the letter in Philip's hand and smiled. "I see you have a letter for me?"

"Yes, from Jane." He watched Thomas open his letter and savor every word.

Thomas looked up at his brothers. "Well, Jane and I are grandparents! We have a granddaughter. Jane says she's beautiful! I'm actually a grandfather. The idea of it didn't seem real until this moment. It's going to be a happy day when we're all together again."

"Congratulations, grandpa," said Robert.

Philip smiled, but his eyes seemed distant. "Yes, congratulations, Thomas."

Thomas noticed there was something different about his brother. "Philip, are you feeling all right? You seem quiet."

"I wish I *did* feel better. I have some bad news."

Then at that moment, Benjamin burst through the door of the building. "I'm a father! I have a beautiful daughter. I can't wait to see her and watch her sleep in the cradle I made. Oh, how I long to see Mary holding our babe, and how I long to hold them both!"

The room was quiet. Thomas said, "That's wonderful, Benjamin. I just read Jane's letter with the news. I'm very proud to be Mollie's grandfather." He glanced sideways toward Philip. "Philip seems to have some news for us."

Philip didn't enjoy putting a damper on the happy moment. "Let's sit down. I found out something disturbing while I was in San Francisco." He proceeded to tell them about Nicaragua and about the letter he sent to Jane.

Thomas was stunned. "I don't know what to say, Philip. I thought Jane and I would be together in a few months. It's what's been keeping me going all this time. I miss them so much. Now, who knows when we'll be together again." He paused and looked down at the letter still in his hand. "I don't like it, but I realize you made the right decision, Philip. At least they will be safe."

Philip was anxious to say something positive. "If it helps to put your minds at ease, when I visited my old friend, Jeffrey, I learned he is going to be on the ship that will be carrying the letter. He offered to follow up with Jane to make sure she received the warning, and if not, tell her himself."

Benjamin was crestfallen. "I miss Mary so, and my daughter won't even know me by the time I see her. Mary will be devastated."

Robert put his hand on Philip's shoulder. "I can see how this has affected you, but you made the best decision under the circumstances."

There was a somber expression on Philip's face as he answered. "I'm grateful for your understanding. All of you. Now, I want to see Maggie. She won't like the news. She was looking forward to meeting everyone and getting married. Anyone want to join me for a shot of whiskey later tonight?"

Chapter 32

June 1855

San Francisco

*T*he weeks slid by quickly. It was late June, time for Philip to head back to San Francisco on another venture trip. When he arrived, he promptly disembarked from the *Tahoma* and checked in with Hank at the post office. He prayed the letter was on its way to Jane.

"Your letter is on the mail ship, Captain Bennett. The ship came and left here about a week ago."

"That is good news, Hank. Thank you." *What a relief!*

"Oh, a fella by the name of Dawes left you a letter before he boarded the ship. Said he was an old friend of yours."

Philip raised an eyebrow in surprise. "Thanks, Hank."

He tucked the letter into his waistcoat to read as soon as he had a free moment. The letter from his friend put him in a jovial mood. He looked forward to seeing what Jeffrey had to say. After he finished his business meetings, he sat down in a local coffeehouse and treated himself to a cup of coffee while he read Jeffrey's letter.

San Francisco, California
April 20ᵗʰ, 1855

Dear old friend,

I cannot tell you how much I enjoyed your visit. As you said, it was like old times.

I started thinking about your comment on wanting to twist my arm to join you at Teekalet. I am changing my plans. I won't be moving to New York after all. I'll just be visiting for awhile. I have decided to turn down the investment offer. I sense it could be chancy. When I return, I would like to join your settlement if I could hitch a ride on your ship when we both happen to be in Frisco at the same time. It will be interesting seeing you in action as a captain. As soon as I get back, I will leave a message for you with the man at the post office letting you know I have returned. I believe his name is Hank.

Until we meet again.

Your sincere friend,

Jeffrey Dawes

Philip smiled as he folded the letter. *Dear Jeffrey. I knew there was a reason I had to see him.*

Philip finished his remaining business tasks and steamed back to Teekalet. As always, after disembarking, he reported to the mill owners about the results of his trip.

One of the owners said, "You're doing an excellent job Captain Bennett. On your next trip, we would like you to go to the

Hawaiian Islands and then on to San Francisco. You'll be leaving in one week.

As Philip left the office, he thought about Maggie. *She's not going to like hearing I will be leaving again so soon. It looks like I'll be gone most of July and part of August. At least I can assure Thomas and Benjamin that the letter is on its way to Jane and Mary. The family will be safe.*

Chapter 33

*P*hilip extended his telescope. The beautiful Hawaiian Islands were straight ahead. As his ship approached, he had in mind to view the scene through Maggie's eyes. Once he and Maggie were married, he would surprise her, and whisk her away for a honeymoon to these islands. He just didn't know when that would be now with the arrival of Thomas's family delayed. They had planned to marry when the entire family was together.

As the ship approached the islands, Philip marveled at the snow-covered mountaintop rising above the thick fog on the island of Maui, then powerful waterfalls plunging down the mountainside turning ravines into rushing streams. The shoreline was bordered with waving palms, and beyond, lush foliage and green fields.

After Philip finished delivering the lumber orders to the buyers in Honolulu, he hired a boatman to take him to the largest island, Hawaii. He hadn't explored that island yet and was curious if it should be the location for his and Maggie's honeymoon. It was a peaceful ride. A feeling of tranquility swept over him. He thought, *I need this.* A cool wind refreshed him as it filled the sails, pushing the small boat over the rolling waves. The boatman sailed the boat to a dock in the quiet harbor where Philip disembarked. He continued his exploration on foot.

The island was extraordinarily beautiful. He saw undulating

hills, lush valleys, and numerous waterfalls. The paths were shaded with tall palms and rustling plantains. He passed by groves of coffee trees and fields of sugar cane. The trail took him past the natives' rush huts, and the more substantial wooden or stone houses, which belonged to foreigners.

He visited a small village and bought some fruit at one of the stands. While there, he met a pleasant man in a merchant's shop. Philip learned the man was also a captain. His name was Captain Maurice Durand. He was from France but now lived on the island. While on a business trip there, he had met an attractive Hawaiian woman and married her. She was the daughter of an influential native, and when they married, he came into control of a large tract of land where he raised cattle and grew sugar cane and coffee trees.

"If you have a couple of days, Captain Bennett, I would like to invite you to my plantation. You mentioned a bakery business at your settlement. When you see my sugar cane fields, you will know what I am thinking."

"I wholeheartedly accept your invitation, Captain Durand. You have piqued my interest!"

"I am pleased. My carriage is nearby, and do call me Maurice."

"Only if you call me Philip, kind sir."

As they entered the plantation, Philip marveled at the groves of coffee trees—there were thousands, some at least twenty feet tall.

"You'll have to come back in the spring, Philip. The trees are covered in the most fragrant white flowers."

Further out toward the rolling hills, Philip saw several herds of cattle. "Are those all yours, Maurice?"

"Yes, I also have horses. Do you ride?"

"I'm afraid not. Since the age of twelve, I've spent most of my time on the high seas."

Next, they passed massive fields of sugar cane.

"Tomorrow, Philip, I'm going to show you how we process sugar cane. You'll find it most interesting."

"I can see we are going to be doing business together, Maurice." *Maggie is going to love this idea. And why not coffee too? Rachel will like that.*

Finally, they arrived at Maurice's residence. It was a large, but not overly massive, English-styled house. When they entered, a servant stood ready to assist. The interior was striking. It evoked a sense of refinement and elegance.

Maurice called out to his wife. "We are very informal here, Philip."

Promptly, a lovely Hawaiian lady entered the room. "Philip, this is my wife, Leilani. Leilani, meet Captain Philip Bennett. He is from the Washington Territory. He's going to stay with us for a couple of days."

"I am pleased to meet you, Leilani. Your home is lovely."

"It is a pleasure to meet you, Captain. You must be thirsty after your ride. If you will excuse me, I will see about getting some refreshments."

"Your wife is quite beautiful, Maurice. You have made a good life here."

"Thank you, Philip. She is beautiful. I like being surrounded with beauty. We are happy here, there is no doubt about it. Oh, to let you know, my wife is quite shy so don't be offended if she doesn't come around much. She doesn't believe in being included in conversations between men. I like it that way, though," he winked.

After they finished their drinks, Maurice said, "Alana will show you to your room where you can freshen up for supper. I will look forward to seeing you at eight o'clock." He rang a brass bell sitting on a carved teak wood table.

A young Hawaiian woman appeared, "Yes sir?"

"Alana, please take Captain Bennett to one of the guest suites."

"Very good, sir."

Philip thanked Maurice and followed her.

The next day, Maurice gave Philip a tour of the plantation.

"Philip," said Maurice, "Are you ready to see how sugar cane is turned into syrup and sugar?"

"Lead the way." Philip was impressed. The two men ended the day by shaking hands on a deal for sugar, syrup, and coffee.

* * *

With his business transactions complete, it was time to leave the beautiful Hawaiian Islands. It had been a successful and uplifting trip. Philip navigated the *Tahoma* toward San Francisco. If all went well with the weather, he figured he would arrive in Frisco in about fifteen days. He was exhilarated about the deal he had made with Captain Durand. *I can't wait to tell Maggie.* Things were looking up. He steamed toward San Francisco with lifted spirits.

The foggy Golden Gate harbor had become a regular stop for Philip. It was the 25ᵗʰ of August. He eased the ship up to the wharf and Samuel dropped anchor. This trip would be a quick one. Philip anticipated finishing business by the end of the day and be ready to steam back to Teekalet the following morning.

As usual, after Philip finished his transactions, he went to the post office to check for any mail.

"Afternoon, Hank. Any mail for us?"

"Two letters for you, Captain Bennett. I'll get them. Uh, Captain? Did you hear about the ship that sank?"

"What ship, Hank?"

"It's bad, Captain. People died. And unfortunately, it was the ship that carried your letter."

Hank picked up a newspaper from his desk and handed it to Philip. He left him to read it while he retrieved the letters. The story was on the front page.

San Francisco Herald, 18 August 1855

HEART-WRENCHING DISASTER

The steamship MARIANA sunk in a hurricane off Cape Hatteras, North Carolina on July 15.

Nearly all her 300 passengers and crew along with valuable cargo, thousands of $20 Double Eagle gold coins recently produced at the San Francisco Mint, and mailbags went down with her to the ocean floor.

Because of the heroics of the men, some of the women and children were rescued. None of the men survived.

Philip stared at the paper. His hands trembled. His stomach churned. He thought he might heave. Hank returned with the letters. As he handed them to Philip, he saw the color had drained from his face.

Philip stared at Hank, "Jeffrey—gone? My dear friend was on that ship. And the letter. Gone." *Jane's letter is at the bottom of the ocean. She won't know about the dangers lying ahead. How do I tell Thomas and Benjamin?* He gripped the paper.

He asked in a somber voice, "Do you have an extra copy, Hank?"

"Go ahead and take it, Captain. I have one at home. This is big news. Even the banks in New York City have been affected. They've been counting on regular deliveries of gold since the Gold Rush. Of course, you can't put a price on all those lost souls. I am very sorry about your friend, Captain Bennett. And your letter of course."

"Thank you, Hank. I must take my leave now. I will see you on my next trip." He walked out slowly, grief-stricken.

With heavy heart and burden, Philip left San Francisco behind and returned to Teekalet the following morning.

Chapter 34

September 10, 1855

Teekalet

*T*he Teekalet bay was straight ahead. As the *Tahoma* crept through the harbor, Philip's mind was wracked with worry about how his news would affect Thomas and Benjamin. Would Thomas blame him for luring them to this untamed country? He longed for Maggie's arms to hold him and to hear her comforting words about the loss of his friend.

Philip was close to the anchor point, and his mind jolted back to the task at hand. He guided the ship to the wharf and jumped off, leaving Samuel in charge to unload supplies while he reported to the mill owners. The owners were glad to see him back so soon and told him they would have another shipment ready for San Francisco later that month. "I'll be ready," said Philip.

Philip assumed by their relaxed manner and no mention of the ship disaster, they hadn't heard the news.

He handed the newspaper to them. "I am afraid I have brought more than supplies from Frisco. I have some devastating news."

They were stunned as they read the article. "Terrible! Such a terrible loss of life, and *all* that gold! Gold is on everyone's mind these days," they added, "and because of the gold rush at Fort Colville, we've lost several of our workers. They're crossing over the Cascades to mine for gold!"

"Hopefully, it won't last as long as the California gold rush," said Philip. He wasn't in the mood for conversation. He tipped his hat and said goodbye.

After leaving the office, Philip boarded the mill's small workboat made available to him for traveling between Teekalet and his settlement. He welcomed the strong breeze, and hoisted the sail, letting the boat drift down the canal. He was too exhausted, mentally and physically, to use the paddles. And, he wanted to think. The sound of the waves lapping against the hull of the boat quieted his unsettled mind. He was deep in thought about how he would present the bad news. He concluded that he would buffer the news with the belief there is a strong possibility Thomas's family will arrive safely to San Francisco. *Yes, I will remind them that Jane is a smart, level-headed woman, and she is strong. Their sons are grown men now and will most assuredly look after their womenfolk. Yes, we must resolve not to dwell on something that may not happen but pray for the Lord's protection. We should all continue our plans with that resolve.*

When he reached the Bennett wharf, Britta charged toward him. He hopped off and tied the boat next to their own workboat and bent down to let Britta lick his face. Her unconditional love comforted him.

Britta's excitable barking alerted Robert of Philip's return.

Robert called out to Thomas, "By the sound of Britta's bark, I would say Philip has arrived. Shall we check to see if he needs help carrying anything?"

"Yes, I'm anxious to see if he has any news, and I'm hoping for a letter from Jane. She must have received Philip's letter by now. I'm figuring if Philip has a letter from her, their letters probably crossed."

Thomas and Robert walked to the wharf. Philip was in the process of grabbing his duffel bag out of the boat and saw them coming. He slung the bag over his shoulder and walked toward them, his face grim, with the newspaper folded under his arm. They sensed something was wrong and waited for him to speak.

"I'm afraid I have some bad news." He unfolded the newspaper and showed them the headlines. Then he read the story. The news was shocking and heartbreaking.

Thomas was the first to speak. "What does this mean, Philip?"

He feared the answer he was about to receive. "Was this the ship your friend was on?"

"Yes, Jeffrey, is gone," answered Philip, his voice full of sadness. "He had even left me a letter telling me he had decided to join us here in Teekalet."

Robert placed his hand on Philip's shoulder. "We're very sorry about your friend."

"I would have enjoyed meeting him," said Thomas in a sympathetic voice. "Are you all right? You look pretty rough."

Philip shook his head. "You know what else was on that ship, don't you, Thomas?"

"I presume your letter of warning to Jane, and it's at the bottom of the damn ocean?"

He nodded and clenched his jaw. "I thought I had everything under control. There is just nothing left that I can do. I am so sorry. I do believe in my heart they will come through this. You have a strong family, Thomas. Jane is resilient, and she is smart. Your sons are grown men now, and I know they will look after their womenfolk. All we can do now is pray for the Lord to watch over them."

Initially, Thomas was angry, but after listening to Philip and looking at his melancholy face, he could see the toll this was taking on him. He knew, if anything else could be done, Philip would have done it. It was obvious his brother had already suffered his own personal loss. He empathized with his pain.

He finally agreed with him. "You're right, Philip. My family is strong, and Jonathan and Jeremy will indeed be protective. I raised them to face any challenge square in the face."

Philip added, "I think we should persevere with our plans having faith our family will be with us in two or three months' time. We must not dwell on something that may not happen."

"We need to tell Benjamin," said Robert.

Thomas felt he should be the one to tell Benjamin. "I'll do it. I saw him working on his land earlier this morning, making it ready for Mary and their babe. This latest news will hit him hard."

Thomas gave Philip a supportive hug and walked away with his head low to find Benjamin.

* * *

When Philip walked through the door of the bakery building, Maggie took one look at him and knew something was wrong. She went to him and embraced him.

"Tell me everything," she said.

Then she told Rachel she would be back in a little while. She took Philip's hand and led him to a quiet area under a shade tree. She gestured toward the bench. "Sit," she said.

After he told her the bad news, he said, "It's not the best timing, but I do have some good news from my Hawaiian trip. I wouldn't mind the distraction by telling you about it. I haven't shared it with anyone else yet."

He continued and told her about his experience on the big island of Hawaii and the deal he had made with Captain Durand.

"I am happy about the idea of having our own sugar and coffee," she said. "Rachel will be thrilled."

The bad news overshadowed the good news, and Philip just wanted them to sit awhile in each other's arms. He had been numb about his friend's death, and now the reality of Jeffrey's fate descended upon him. As he quietly grieved, Maggie remained by his side. Words weren't spoken, they weren't necessary. Maggie was there for him, and Philip could feel her unshakeable love for him. It was a love he had never known until he met her, and he realized what had been missing in his life.

* * *

Later that night Robert invited Philip to come to their building and share a bottle of whiskey with him and Thomas.

"We need something to lift our spirits, and we have something else we need to talk about," he said.

"Lead the way," said Philip.

They sat around the table and Thomas filled their glasses.

Robert began. "Philip, our friend Pierre Mallet paid us a visit during your absence. He informed us he'll be gone for awhile. Evidently, ever since gold was discovered in the Fort Colville area this past spring, people have swarmed in like they did in California. A few of our neighboring settlers planned to go and needed a guide, so Pierre is leading them through the Nisqually Pass and the trail through Yakima Country.

Philip asked, "Isn't that Indian country?"

"It sure is," said Thomas, "and I foresee trouble."

Philip added, "While I was talking with the mill owners, they mentioned the gold rush at Fort Colville. They've been losing workers on a regular basis to go mine for gold. They're probably some of the same men following Pierre."

Chapter 35

A man wearing a coonskin hat mounted on a paint stallion rode into the settlement. Robert was the first to see him.

"Pierre, welcome! I'm not used to seeing you on horseback."

Thomas heard Pierre's voice and joined in. "Greetings, Pierre. You look exhausted. Can we offer you some coffee or a meal?"

"Not for me, *mes amis*," he patted his horse on the neck, "but Jacques could use some water. I have not come for pleasure, but with a warning."

Some of the Bennett settlers were within earshot and quickly gathered around to listen.

Robert turned to Matthew who was now holding the reins of Pierre's horse, "Matthew would you bring a bucket of water?"

Pierre dismounted to give his horse a much-needed break, and nodded at Matthew, "Merci."

Pierre's usual grin was noticeably absent as he spoke. "There is Indian trouble ahead, *mes amis*! The Yakimas killed several miners for trespassing on their land. I was their guide and witnessed the attack. I barely escaped. Several men were scalped alive, I'll never forget their cries. I couldn't help them, but I was able to lead a few of the miners out to safety. We split up to warn the settlers on this side of the mountain. The mountain range is all that separates us from Yakima Country. If they go through the pass before the heavy snow, they will easily cross to this side, and they will show no mercy, *mes amis.*"

The Bennett group stood in silence as they listened to Pierre's warning. Then the silence turned into nervous chatter. While Pierre was talking, one of the men who had come to listen stood out to him. He stared at him for a moment. He hadn't met any of the other men at the settlement other than Robert and Thomas, so why did this man seem familiar to him?

It was time to leave, so he pushed the mystery to the back of his mind. He would have to think about the man later.

"I must not tarry any longer," he said. "Au revoir." Pierre remounted his horse and signaled it into a trot and left the settlement.

He continued his mission to warn the settlers, but the man's face continued to plague him.

* * *

Pierre completed his mission and returned to his cabin in the woods where Red Feather waited. When he arrived, she was sitting on the porch making a pair of moccasins for her special friend, Annie. He sat next to her and told her about the Indian attacks in Yakima and of his fear that she may be in danger.

"Red Feather, if I am called up to serve, I want you to stay at the Bennett settlement. You will be safer there. There is a large blockhouse nearby in Teekalet for refuge. Perhaps you can stay with Annie and her mother? I couldn't bear it if you were here alone."

"I promise I will stay with Annie, my husband."

Pierre went inside and helped himself to the coffee Red Feather always kept ready on the stove. He would be lost without her. When he married her in Montreal, his intent was more for business with her tribe rather than companionship. She had been married before, but her husband divorced her when he discovered she couldn't conceive. She was one of three wives. Pierre had no intention of having children, so it was a perfect arrangement for him, but gradually, Red Feather captured his heart.

Pierre thought again about the man at the Bennett settlement. Who *was* he? It was driving him insane.

Suddenly, a moment of enlightenment. He jumped up from

his chair, nearly spilling his coffee, and dashed to the cupboard where he kept stacks of paperwork. He shuffled through the papers while cursing himself for saving so much paperwork. Then Pierre saw it—a wanted poster with a reward offered by the Hudson Bay Company with a sketch of a man's face resembling the man he saw at the settlement. Granted, the man wore a beard, but there was no mistaking the scar above his left eye. The man was wanted dead or alive for murder in Montreal. Pierre had torn the poster off a building while he was there.

It wouldn't be difficult to turn him in since the Hudson Bay Company had a heavy presence at Fort Nisqually, an easy distance to travel. *I could sure use that money.* He thought about what he should do next and decided to wait until he knew if there would be an Indian uprising. If they were attacked, they would need every man who could shoot. For now, he would keep the poster safe under his mattress.

* * *

Not long after Pierre's warning, the Bennett brothers heard rumors the Horse Indians on the eastern side of the mountain were planning an attack on the settlers in Puget Sound, and were seeking the support of the Canoe Indians. The Canoe Indians and the Puget Sound settlers had been co-existing on a friendly basis.

It was suspected the British had a hand in stirring them up, and the Hudson Bay Company was considered to be an arm of British power. The British discouraged settlers from coming to the Territory, and the Hudson Bay Company made it known the settlers were not to fur trade with the Indians.

The Company agents were suspected of providing Hudson Bay muskets, balls, and powder in trade with the Indians. Many of the employees took Indian wives, putting them in a favorable position with the Indians.

The Indians were upset because of prior treaties with the United States government, and the British took advantage of the situation. The Indians had relinquished six million acres for the compensation of $200,000 along with the promise the settlers wouldn't trespass on their remaining land, but when gold was discovered in Colville, the promise was broken. The miners ignored the ruling and trespassed anyway.

Many miners were killed, and in response, the sub-agent stationed at the Dalles was sent to the area to investigate. When he was killed, the government retaliated by sending troops into the Yakima Valley. The war had begun. As the troops flooded in, the Yakima Indians united with the Walla Walla and Cayuse tribes.

The Governor of the Washington Territory was working on treaties in the Blackfoot Country when he received word the tribes in the upper Columbia country and the Oregon tribes down to the Dalles had banded together and broke out into open warfare. Governor Stevens returned in haste and proceeded in person to address the hostilities on the eastern side of the mountain. He called for several companies of volunteers to join with the small force of regular soldiers and the volunteer company of Oregon.

The Nisqually tribe on the western side of the mountain was agitated because of the proposed Medicine Creek Treaty with the Territorial Governor requiring them to cede the lush land they felt had always belonged to them. They were to be relocated to a rocky landscape where it would be difficult to plant crops, and not having access to the river, meant no fishing, which was their livelihood. Their leader Leschi refused, stating they couldn't live on the proposed land. He was furious and thrust his fist into the air. "There will be war!"

The treaties had become necessary to validate the Donation Land Act being offered to the settlers. Settlers poured in, including the Bennett party.

After news of the Indian uprisings, the acting Governor issued a proclamation and called for enrollment of two companies—one in Vancouver, and one in Olympia.

When they heard about the proclamation, the men at the Bennett settlement figured it was only a matter of time before they were called up for service.

Thomas's first thought was of his family. *If they make it through the Nicaragua civil war, will they land in the middle of an Indian war here? No! I cannot let that happen!* He called for a meeting with Robert, Philip, and Benjamin.

Thomas was in a state of panic. "Philip, like you, I want to believe my family will arrive safely to San Francisco. Am I correct they would arrive next month? If that is true, I must send a letter to Jane warning her about the Indian war here and tell her to remain in San Francisco until the danger has passed. Benjamin, you may want to send your own letter to Mary."

Philip agreed, "Good plan, Thomas. I'm going to San Francisco any day now. I will leave your letters at the hotel where I have your family registered. The letters will be waiting for them when they arrive.

"I might add, I will be going to San Francisco for more than mill business. I have spoken to the Governor and volunteered to use my ship to transport supplies and munitions here from Frisco if the need arises. You can be assured, Thomas and Benjamin, I will check on our loved ones every time I'm in Frisco."

Chapter 36

October 3, 1855

San Francisco

$\mathcal{S}$an Francisco was dead ahead. The usual grey and white clouds hung over the harbor, and hundreds of ship masts poked through banks of fog. Philip guided the *California II* into the familiar harbor and brought her next to the wharf to unload and load the cargo. Samuel called out, "Drop anchor!"

After finalizing the business transactions for the mill, Philip checked at the post office for mail.

"Yes, I do have some mail for you, Captain Bennett," said Hank.

There were two letters, one for Thomas and one for Benjamin, postmarked 31 August 1855.

"Thanks, Hank." *These would have been their final letters before leaving New York City. They will mean a lot to Thomas and Benjamin.*

Philip was deep in thought about Thomas's family. They would be well into the journey. By now, they would have transferred from Captain Davis's ship to a smaller steamer. Philip figured they had to be crossing through Nicaragua, which usually would take about a week. *They could be in the middle of the war zone right now. And what about the cholera? If only I could know how they are. There's just nothing left that I can do except to deliver these letters.*

Philip hailed a cab to take him to the Elliott Hotel. When he arrived, he walked through the promenade entrance to the front desk and asked for the manager.

"I am the manager, sir. My name is Gilbert Conyers. What can I do for you?"

"If I may introduce myself, I'm Captain Philip Bennett. I have pre-registered my family members to stay here under the name of Jane Bennett."

"Yes, I have seen the name on our register. I believe they are due in later this month, aren't they?"

"You are indeed correct, Mr. Conyers. May I ask you to give them this parcel the moment they check in?"

"That won't be a problem, Captain Bennett. I will take care of it personally."

"Splendid, thank you, sir." He tilted his hat. "Good day." *Whew! That's done! I only pray they arrive safely.*

Philip had one letter left to deliver. He hailed a cab to take him to the residence of his friend, Captain Davis. He knew the captain would still be at sea, so he planned to leave the letter with the captain's wife, Victoria. As he stepped from the cab, he asked the driver to wait.

Victoria was just coming down the staircase when she heard Bridget answer the front door. She recognized Captain Bennett's voice and went straight to the foyer to greet him.

"Captain Bennett, what brings you here? I am sure you must know my husband is not back yet."

"Good day, Victoria. Yes, I knew I wouldn't find him here. I have come to leave a letter for him."

"Please, do come in. We'll sit in the library."

"Thank you," he said as he removed his hat and followed Victoria to the library.

"May I offer you a refreshment, Captain?"

"That's very kind of you, but no thank you, Victoria. I won't be staying long."

Then he shared his concern about Thomas's family traveling through a war zone in Nicaragua. As if that wasn't enough, he told her about the threat of an Indian uprising in Puget Sound.

"We were worried about them arriving in the middle of an Indian war so when they check in at the Elliot Hotel, they will find a message from me telling them to remain in San Francisco until it is safe to continue on to Puget Sound. My brothers and I, along with the other men, expect to be called to serve at any time. Would you and William be so kind to check on them from time to time?" He handed her the letter. "This letter will save you from having to repeat the whole story to William."

"Of course, Captain Bennett. I shall give William the letter as soon as he arrives. I am sure he will be alarmed to hear about the war in Nicaragua. We will pray for their safe arrival and be happy to look after the Bennett family while they are here."

"Thank you, Victoria. They should arrive toward the end of this month. I expect to be making trips to Frisco often in the near future so I will be checking on them as well. Please give William my regards. It has been a pleasure seeing you again, Victoria. You are most gracious and with that, I shall take my leave now."

Philip had one task remaining and asked the driver to take him to 418 and 420 Market Street. He stood before a building with a sign that read *GUNS* in giant letters across the top of the three-story building. Philip knew the owner, A. J. Plate, an importer and dealer in guns, rifles, and pistols.

Philip had met Adolph in 1850 on one of his trips to San Francisco. He had been looking for a gun dealer to buy a sidearm, and someone told him to check with the man down by the waterfront selling guns from a tent.

Like Philip and his brothers, the vendor had come to America for a better life. Adolphus Joseph Plate had come to New York from Prussia in 1830 where he set up as a cabinet and furniture maker. Shortly after 1849, he heard about the California gold rush and traveled via Panama to San Francisco.

Panning for gold didn't turn out to be as successful as he had hoped, but he accumulated enough of a stake to start a business. Adolph's business flourished, and by 1855, he no longer sold from a tent. He was able to buy his own building. Selling firearms and ammunition had made his fortune.

Philip swung the door open and entered a room with walls covered by rifles and firearms. "Good day to you, Adolph. I have to say this is quite an improvement from the tent. I'm impressed."

Adolph came around the counter and greeted Philip with a firm handshake.

"Well, Captain Bennett, it's been over a year since I've seen you. I can guess why you're here. I've heard rumors about an Indian uprising in your part of the country."

"So the rumors have come this far? It seems we may be in for a battle. I want to arm our womenfolk with rifles. Show me what you recommend, Adolph."

While Adolph brought down a few selections from the walls, Philip leaned on the glass case serving as a counter. Inside the case, he saw several handguns and derringer pistols. He had wanted to bring a gift back to Maggie, and it struck him that her gift should be a derringer pistol.

"Adolph, if you don't mind, I would like to look at some of these derringers." As he surveyed the selection, he narrowed the choice down to one. "I'll take this pearl handled derringer, Adolph. This will fit well in Maggie's hand. Wrap it up and three of those rifles. On second thought, add in five more rifles. I'll need ammunition too."

Philip roamed around the gun store while he waited. He scanned the room. In a far corner, he noticed what looked like a cannon mounted on a two-wheeled carriage. He walked over to get a closer look. It *was* a cannon. He stroked the cool bronze surface, and upon closer examination, saw the engraved words, *Le Achille*.

Philip motioned for Adolph's attention. "Adolph, tell me about this cannon. I didn't know you sold cannons."

"Well, I hadn't *planned* on selling cannons. A few months ago, while I was on the wharf waiting for a shipment to be unloaded, I saw it come off a ship, which had just come into the harbor from France. I inquired and bought it on the spot. It's a Dutch bronze 6-pounder field gun that was used by Napoleon's army. It was part of a captured set by the Duke of Wellington from Napoleon's forces at Waterloo in 1815. I learned it was made in 1813 in the Hague. I have the ammo, fuses, and gunpowder to go along with it."

"Make me a deal, Adolph, and I will need it loaded onto my ship by the end of the day. I'll be leaving the harbor tomorrow morning."

* * *

October 20, 1855

Teekalet

During the voyage home, Philip mentally listed his accomplishments. His business transactions for the mill had been successful, as usual. He had left the letters at the hotel for Jane and Mary, hand-delivered a letter to Captain Davis, and was happily bringing back mail for Thomas and Benjamin. He had not only purchased rifles to arm the women but also bought five additional rifles to have on hand. Then there was the unexpected weapon he was bringing to their settlement—the cannon.

Before his departure to Frisco, he had told Peter about his plan to return with rifles for the women and asked him if he would teach Maggie, Rachel, and Annie to shoot. Peter had agreed it was a good idea, and by the time he was done training them, they would be able to hit a moving target. He had already taught Matthew and Christopher.

Philip looked forward to giving Maggie her gift. The beautiful pearl-handled derringer would fit in her hand perfectly, and it would be easy for her to keep close by. He didn't like leaving Maggie if there was war, but he was duty-bound to do his part.

The *California II* steamed slowly into the harbor. Philip sounded the whistle. The vessel glided past the Indian village at Point Julia on the opposite shore where several sets of eyes stared in awe. The ship slid next to the mill's wharf, and the crew tied the lines. The cannon sat conspicuously on the bow of the ship, causing quite a commotion. Normally, Philip would have checked in at the mill office while the cargo was unloaded, but the owners and managers had rushed to the wharf to see what was causing so much excitement.

"My Lord," said one of the mill owners. "What a weapon! If word gets out about this cannon, our community might not get attacked. Take a gander at our Indian friends across the way. Their eyes are glued on it! Word is bound to get around."

"We may end up owing you our lives, Captain Bennett," said another mill owner.

Philip answered, "Let us pray we won't have to use it. I plan to test it when we get it situated, so don't panic when you hear a loud sound." He looked toward the ship to see if the cargo was unloaded. "Well, gentlemen, I see the cargo is unloaded. I believe we are finished for now. If you don't mind, I shall take my leave." He reboarded the *California II* and continued down the canal.

When the settlement was in sight, he noticed something new on the horizon. It appeared to be a large two-level log blockhouse. Finally, he reached the Bennett wharf. He blew the whistle and brought the ship tight to the side.

Philip jumped onto the wharf while Samuel and the crew tied the lines. Then they unloaded the cannon, the boxes of ammo, gunpowder and fuses, and the guns. When they finished, Samuel and the crew reboarded the ship and released the lines. Philip waved as Samuel took the *California II* back to the mill's wharf where she would remain until the next trip.

Robert and Thomas heard the whistle and rushed to greet Philip. Peter and Benjamin followed close behind.

"Welcome back, Philip," said Robert as he looked at the wharf. "Looks like you brought back an arsenal. And a cannon?"

"Your timing couldn't be more perfect," said Thomas while gazing at the cannon.

"I thought as much," said Philip. He pointed at the cannon, "What do you think of our cannon?"

They were spellbound at the sight of the bronze beast sitting so prominently on the wharf.

Staring in open-mouthed wonder, Benjamin exclaimed, "I've never seen a cannon up close!"

Philip pointed at the blockhouse. "I see we have a blockhouse." He pondered for a moment. "I wonder what it would take to get this cannon on top?"

Peter had an idea. "Maybe we can use our oxen to hoist it up?"

Robert patted the cannon. "If we're going to try it, we'd better do it soon, and learn how to use it. Two days ago, we heard that Lieutenant Taylor and his men returned from the other side of the mountain. They witnessed three to four thousand Indians on the warpath.

"We're ordered to leave any day to build several blockhouses throughout the Sound, and the loggers have the same orders. The blockhouses go up fast, so we shouldn't be gone long. Billy, Christopher, and Matthew will stay here, and they know how to shoot."

Thomas thought about his family. "Philip, I know I don't have to ask, but please set my mind at ease. Are the letters in safe hands?"

Benjamin interjected. "That was on my mind too."

"Yes, I wrapped them as a parcel and handed it directly to the manager of the hotel, and he assured me he would personally give it to them the moment they register. I also delivered a letter to Captain Davis and his wife informing them of the change of plans. I asked them to look after your family. And now, I am pleased to tell you I have letters from Jane and Mary for you."

Philip reached into his waistcoat pocket and handed a letter to each of them.

"Since they have begun their voyage by now, I am sure, knowing it would take two months for their mail to get to Frisco, these would be the final letters they would have posted before leaving."

While Philip described his trip to Peter and Robert, Benjamin stepped away and sat on the wharf to read his letter. Thomas hadn't moved and was already deeply immersed in Jane's letter.

Delhi, New York

July 15, 1855

My dearest husband,

I can now count days instead of months until we are reunited. I long for the sound of your voice and to feel your arms about me. We all miss you so much.

The children and I have been gradually packing and making decisions about what to leave behind. For me, leaving my parents and sister behind and saying goodbye to them is going to be the most heartbreaking thing I will ever do. As the time to depart draws near,

I've hardly been able to look them in the eye, for fear I will break down. We have all been putting on a brave front, but I know it won't last.

Jonathan and Jeremy are excited about traveling on the ship. I know Jonathan will besiege Captain Davis with at least a hundred questions. Elizabeth is looking forward to writing in the journal you gave her, and Emily is taking every dress she owns. Mary, of course, is being the wonderful mother she was meant to be. Little Mollie is bringing so much joy into our lives. I never realized being a grandmother would be so much fun. You are going to love being a grandfather.

I must close now, my darling, so that I may post this letter in time. This will be the last letter I will write before we leave. I pray it will reach you, otherwise you may worry if you haven't heard from me.

Your loving wife,

Jane Bennett

Jane's letter meant everything to Thomas. He was sure it was the same for Benjamin. He folded the letter and tucked it inside his shirt close to his heart. *She won't be as happy about my letter telling her to stay in San Francisco, and that I will surely be called up soon to serve in the Indian War. I am sorry, my love.*

He looked over at Philip and Robert standing next to the weapons, and asked, "Philip, what are your plans for the rifles? I see eight."

"Three of the rifles are for Maggie, Rachel, and Annie. Peter is going to teach them to shoot."

Peter picked up three rifles along with some ammo. "I'll start tomorrow."

Philip continued, "I figured we might need some extra rifles.

Now, I see we can use them to arm the blockhouse. If we get caught off guard and have to run there, we'll be prepared to defend ourselves."

Philip gazed at the blockhouse. "Peter, if we can get the cannon up to the top of the blockhouse, we're going to need access to it, and from the inside only."

Peter had also been looking at the blockhouse. "I was thinking the same thing. We'll make a trap door with an opening in the ceiling and build a ladder to climb up to it."

"We'll start on it tomorrow before we get called away," said Robert as he eyed the rifles, then turned to Thomas, "For the moment, let's get these rifles and ammo loaded into the blockhouse."

"Yes, said Thomas, "and we should also bring in some provisions along with a keg of water."

"We might as well bring in some blankets and straw," replied Robert. "I hope we're not caught in there long enough to need them."

As he bent to pick up a small package from the wharf, Philip said, "We'll gather here tomorrow morning then. It should be a most productive day. Now, if you will all excuse me. I need to see Maggie. I have something to give her."

Philip found Maggie in the bakery building. He grabbed her hand and took her to their refuge under the shade tree. They sat down next to each other, and Philip put his arm around her bringing her close to him.

Maggie thought *He looks so serious, and what is the mysterious package he has on his lap? A gift for me, perhaps?* "Philip, you look so serious." She pointed at the package, "Is that something for me?"

"Yes, my darling. Not the typical gift a man would give his fiancée, but it seemed appropriate during these uncertain times." He handed the package to her.

She quickly opened it to find the pearl-handled derringer. "Oh, Philip, it's beautiful." She gripped it. "It fits my hand so well. I haven't held a gun or rifle since my days with Father. Peter told me about your plan to provide rifles for us. Does this mean I need to worry?"

In the recess of his mind, he dreaded the thought of having to tell her to shoot herself if they were overrun and he wasn't there to protect her. It sent a chill down his spine to think of her being scalped alive. Her beautiful red wavy hair would be considered a prize to hang on an Indian warrior's pole.

"I hope not. As you know, we are about to be called away to build several blockhouses, and later, I expect I will be bringing back supplies and munitions from Frisco. That means I won't be here to protect you. Follow me to the wharf. I want to show you what I found while I was shopping for our guns. It might make you feel better."

When Maggie saw the cannon, she walked up to it and stroked the cold metal. "This is incredible, Philip."

"Word will get out about this, especially after we test it. Let us hope it will discourage any attacks. We won't be easy pickings with this."

* * *

The settlers spent the next two days preparing to defend themselves.

Inside the blockhouse, the hinged trap door and ladder had been constructed and was ready for use. Sunlight gleamed through the chest-high cross-shaped gun holes on the walls. Robert and Thomas loaded the rifles and strategically placed them next to the holes.

Then they loaded their fortress with the necessities and comforts they would need. It certainly felt like a place of refuge.

Finally, they hoisted the cannon and the two-wheeled carriage to the hefty log roof of the blockhouse. Philip rotated the formidable weapon in the direction of the canal. "Are we ready to test it?"

They loaded the cannon.

Philip called out. "Step back and cover your ears."

When he lit the fuse, a thunderous boom followed. Britta howled and ran in the opposite direction. Everyone had turned out to witness the spectacle. They watched in awe as the shot penetrated the surface of the water creating an explosion of spray.

The entire population of Teekalet heard the boom. Windows rattled, dogs barked, and birds squawked. The sound continued, bouncing off the water and echoing through the hills. The Indians at Point Julia scurried about, shading their eyes as they looked toward the origin of the sound.

One of the mill owners said, "Well, I'd say Captain Bennett just tested his cannon."

* * *

After two days of teaching the women to shoot with the rifles, Peter concluded that Maggie and Annie were ready to target practice on their own.

Maggie and Annie had a head start. Maggie used a rifle as a young girl, and Annie had enlisted her brother's help when they heard the rumors about a possible uprising.

Rachel had not been exposed to any kind of gun her entire life, so it took longer for her to feel comfortable handling a weapon. She didn't feel confident without Peter by her side. As he helped her hold the rifle, his arm around her waist, he wondered if she could feel his love for her emanating from his touch. He dreaded the day he would have to leave her alone. He knew the men would be called up soon.

* * *

It had been less than a week since they had prepared their own blockhouse when the men were called to help build blockhouses throughout Puget Sound. Upon reporting, they learned there was more to the project than anticipated. They had no idea how long they would be away from their settlement. This worried them. Philip learned he wouldn't be involved in the building project. As he expected, the Governor had other plans for him and his ship.

They were mustered and sworn in as a regular company of volunteers. These men were a mix of army and marine veterans, farmers, and new settlers such as the Bennett group.

Their task began by opening an old overgrown military wagon road, which led across the mountains over the Naches Pass. This road was the only known route across the mountains, and because of winter storms, blown-down trees blocked it in several places. By opening this road, and building a line of blockhouses and fortifications, gaining access to the mountainous country would be possible. This would potentially force the Indians out of their hiding places, drive them east across the mountains, and if the war on the eastern side of the mountains continued, communication with the Sound would be possible.

As they progressed on the road, they stopped and built a blockhouse at selected points. Not far behind them, drivers of ox-teams drawing heavily loaded wagons of supplies followed. While the volunteers continued ahead, they camped in the cold drenching rain without fire, shelter or cooked food.

"I never knew there could be so much rain," said Benjamin. "I am soaked."

When some of the volunteers asked why they couldn't warm up by a campfire, they were asked if they wanted to become an easy target for the Indians hiding in the woods waiting to pick them off with an arrow or a bullet.

One night they camped near a steep hill. The captain placed three men on guard a short distance up the hill. At daybreak, they heard gunshots in the vicinity of the guards. Staying undercover, they rushed to the guards, calling out to them. There was no answer. When they reached the guards, they found them shot dead. The volunteers now understood what they were up against.

As Robert stared at the murdered men, he said, "And to think I was going to volunteer."

"Yeah, until I stopped you," said Thomas. "We don't need heroics. Let's just stay alive. We have people to protect back at the settlement, and I want to see my family whenever this godforsaken conflict is over."

Peter frowned, and said, "I'm worried about our people. *Rachel.* We have no way of knowing if they are all right. At least everyone is armed, and the mill whistle will warn them if enemy canoes are spotted entering the bay."

"Philip is probably back at the settlement by now," said Thomas. "He's on standby to go to Frisco for more weapons and supplies. I hope he ends up in Frisco when my family arrives. Then we will know if they made it through Nicaragua. It's all I think about."

* * *

A few days later, a company of replacements arrived to relieve the Teekalet volunteers freeing them to return to their homes.

When the Bennett group arrived back at the settlement, their fears were quieted to find there hadn't been an attack. Philip was there, still on standby for both the mill and the Governor.

The men had experienced their first taste of the Indian uprising. They saw death firsthand, and to see blockhouses lining up the entire way to the mountain pass confirmed the severity of what was about to happen. Everyone was pensive and uneasy.

As the day waned, the three Bennett brothers walked along the canal and lingered. They looked up at the bronze object of destruction perched on top of the blockhouse. As the red sun took its last breath and sank into the horizon, it cast a lurid glow onto the cannon, and except for the sound of lapping water along the shore, there was an eerie silence. Still gazing at the monstrous weapon, none of them could avoid the question burdening their mind, *Will we have to use the cannon?*

A Note From Lilly

Thank you for reading *Intrepid Journey: An Untamed Frontier,* Book One of the Bennett Family Saga. I hope you enjoyed meeting the Bennett family. If you liked the book, I would be grateful if you could take a moment and leave a review on the book's Amazon page.

The Bennett Family Saga continues in Book Two of the series, to be published in the near future. If you would like to learn when it is available, feel free to visit my website at *www.lillyrobbinsbrock.com,* where you may subscribe to be notified. While you are there, check out my blog.

Make sure to visit me on my Facebook page at *www.facebook.com/ lillyrobbinsbrock,* where you are welcome to interact and find tidbits of interest surrounding the book project. I look forward to sharing my next novel with you.

Lilly

Acknowledgements

Each time I begin a book project, my family faithfully supports me and tolerates my obsessive personality while I am in writing mode. They deserve a heartfelt thank you. My husband, Phil, read and edited at least three drafts. His male perspective and creativity was invaluable. My daughter, Alecia, was extremely helpful on my original draft as the story evolved. It was always an exciting moment when she came up with an idea for a particular character. My sister, June, has always been supportive and a great proofreader. She's been a cheerleader on every project.

I also want to thank my editor, Tracy Cartwright of Editing by Cartwright. I appreciate her editing skills. It was a pleasure working with her.

And finally, a huge thank you goes to my other daughter, Vivi Anne. She continues to work by my side utilizing her skills and education to format the book as well as to design and create the book cover.

I feel very fortunate to have such a wonderful group of people surrounding me.

About The Author

Lilly Robbins Brock was born in Olympia, Washington where her pioneer family homesteaded in the late 1800s. She loves history and one of her passions has been researching her family tree. Learning about the past lives of her hometown inspired Lilly to write *Intrepid Journey: An Untamed Frontier*, Book One of her historical fiction series. She is presently working on Book Two to continue the Bennett family saga.

Lilly has also written three nonfiction memoir/biographies to honor three members of the Greatest Generation who served our country during World War II. The first book, *Wooden Boats & Iron Men*, is about a PT sailor and his love for PT boats. The second book, *Ever A Soldier*, tells the story of a soldier who saw action on the European front. The third book, *Victory On The Home Front*, is about a Rosie the Riveter and her husband who was a fighting Seabee.

In her professional career, Lilly has been a legal secretary, teacher, and for the past thirty-five years, an interior designer. She and her husband are now retired. They live in a quiet country setting on the shores of the Columbia River in Cathlamet, Washington, which has become the perfect place to pursue her lifelong desire to write stories, and where she wrote her first book, *Food Gift Recipes from Nature's Bounty.*

Made in the USA
Coppell, TX
05 December 2020